ONE DEADLY NEEDLE

A AGATHA ROYALE MYSTERY
BOOK 3

ELLA ANDREW

BACKSPACE PRESS

First paperback edition March 2024

Backspace Press

Houston, Texas

Cover design by MIBLART

ISBN 979-8-9859898-6-1 (paperback)

ISBN 979-8-9859898-5-4 (ebook)

Printed in the United States of America

1

THE MANUSCRIPT

The rhythmic clacking of keys filled the quiet kitchen as Agatha Royale typed furiously on her vintage Royal KMM typewriter. She paused, fingers hovering over the keys, and rubbed her tired eyes, trying to shake off the exhaustion of staying up all night to finish her manuscript. The dim light above the kitchen table cast a warm glow on the cluttered surface, scattered with coffee mugs, ink smudges, and a few crumpled pages. Agatha yawned, stretching her arms wide, and shook her head as if to clear it. She flexed her wrists, took a deep breath, and resumed typing, the comforting sound of the typewriter keys once again breaking the early morning stillness.

She glanced from the page on the typewriter to Mike, her miniature schnauzer, who was lying comfortably on a plush dog bed under the table. Agatha pushed her light brown bangs away from her forehead, tucking a wayward strand of her long, wavy hair behind her ear. Her hazel eyes, framed by the hint of crow's feet that spoke of her 39 years, sparkled with a mix of excitement and fatigue. This mystery novel represented a fresh start after the dual blows of divorce and losing her librarian position had brought her to Bristol Lake and the unlikely new chapter of bookstore ownership.

The quaint town hadn't been her first choice—or even her tenth—but she was gradually finding her place among its eccentric residents and charming streets.

"Can you believe it, Mike? One more paragraph and I'll finish the first draft of my book," she exclaimed, her voice blending enthusiasm and weariness, mirroring the mix of excitement and fatigue on her face.

Mike wagged his tail, lifted his head, and gave her a sleepy, encouraging look before settling back down with a contented sigh.

Agatha smiled at her loyal companion, then returned to the rhythmic clacking of the typewriter keys. The scent of freshly brewed coffee, now cold and forgotten on the table beside her, filled the kitchen. The first light of dawn began to creep through the window, painting the room with a soft, golden hue.

About an hour later, she finally typed "The End." Agatha leaned back in her chair, a wide smile spreading across her face. She carefully pulled the paper off the type-writer and placed it face down on the neatly stacked pages on the table. She flipped through the manuscript, feeling the weight of her hard work in her hands, and smiled proudly at her accomplishment.

After organizing the pages into a folder, Agatha stood up and stretched, feeling a sense of fulfillment wash over her. She padded into the living room, her sock-clad feet silent on the hardwood floor. Approaching the antique side-board that had been her grandmother's, she pulled open the middle drawer.

"In you go," she whispered, gently placing the folder inside. "Safe and sound until revision time."

She closed the drawer with a soft thud and patted the polished wood affectionately. Returning to the kitchen, Agatha glanced at Mike, who was now snoring softly. She decided it was time for both of them to get some well-deserved rest. Switching off the kitchen light, she left the room in a gentle twilight and headed to her bedroom, feeling happy and accomplished.

Agatha paused in the hallway, running her fingers along the worn spine of her mother's copy of "And Then There Were None" on the bookshelf. How many times had she read Christie's masterpiece as a girl, dreaming that one day she might create mysteries of her own? Now her first manuscript was complete, a tangible symbol of a dream she'd nearly abandoned after her divorce. "We did it, didn't we?" she whispered to the empty hallway, to the ghost of her younger self who had scribbled stories in lined note-books. The house creaked in response, a familiar sound that had become comforting in the months since she'd moved to Bristol Lake. This old house with its quirky corners and temperamental plumbing wasn't what she'd imagined for herself at thirty-nine, but standing here in the soft glow of the hall light, manuscript completed and tucked away safely, it felt remarkably like home.

Stifling a yawn, Agatha continued toward her bedroom, mentally planning which reading nook in town she'd visit tomorrow. The bench by the lake was lovely in the morning light, perfect for diving into the new mystery novel Emma had recommended—something about missing artwork and mistaken identities. No sleuthing, no murder, no typewriter. Just Agatha Royale, bookstore owner, enjoying a peaceful morning with a cup of coffee and someone else's mystery for a change.

~

Later that morning, Agatha shuffled into the kitchen, still in her robe, her hair piled in a lopsided bun that defied gravity. Mike sat near his food bowl with a look of betrayal that said, 'how dare you sleep through breakfast'.

"Hold your horses, sir," she mumbled, scooping his kibble into the bowl. "The literary life is exhausting."

As Mike crunched happily, Agatha poured herself coffee, reheated it in the microwave—twice—and scanned the sticky notes taped to her fridge. One caught her eye: *Don't forget to smile today!* She smiled.

She stood in the kitchen for a moment, sipping her coffee and staring out the window at the quiet backyard. The air still had a bite of morning chill, and the idea of curling up in her bookstore with a cinnamon scone suddenly sounded perfect.

~

An hour later Agatha walked into One Deadly Chapter Books and Brew, her mystery bookstore cafe nestled in the heart of Bristol Lake. The smell of freshly brewed coffee mingled with the scent of books, creating a warm and inviting atmosphere.

Celeste Martin, her young employee, was already busy arranging a new display of mystery novels. The 21-year-old's thick, long brown hair was neatly braided, and her large tortoiseshell glasses slipped down her nose as she concentrated on her task.

"Morning, Celeste," Agatha greeted, her voice cheerful despite her tiredness.

"Good morning, Agatha!" Celeste replied, glancing up with a smile. "You look like you had a late night."

"I did. But it was worth it—I finished writing my book!" Agatha beamed, her eyes sparkling with pride. "The first draft is finally complete!"

"That's fantastic news! Congratulations!" Celeste exclaimed. "You should celebrate."

Agatha nodded. "I plan to. But first, I need to visit Aunt Edna. She moved to Bristol Lake about a month ago, and I've been so wrapped up in finishing the book that I haven't had a chance to see her new place yet."

She sighed, a mix of excitement and guilt crossing her face. "She's been settling into Green Acres Assisted Living, and I promised I'd visit her this Sunday. I can't wait to tell her about the book – she's always been my biggest supporter."

Just then, the espresso machine sputtered violently behind the counter. Agatha rolled her eyes. "Again?" she muttered, grabbing a dish towel. She flipped the switch and gave it a scolding look. The sputtering stopped.

Celeste watched her with amusement. "You should name it. You spend more time fixing it than I do shelving books."

"Maybe I will," Agatha said, wiping her hands. "What do you think of Agatha the Second?"

"Too confusing," Celeste said. "How about Frothington?"

Agatha grinned. "Frothington it is. Long may it steam."

~

As the morning progressed, the bell above the door chimed, announcing the arrival of Lorraine Dubois, the town's self-appointed gossip queen. She breezed in, her silver-streaked auburn hair bouncing with each step, a vibrant scarf adding a splash of color to her ensemble.

"Bonjour, Agatha! I heard you finished your book. That's merveilleux!" Lorraine exclaimed, her eyes sparkling with curiosity. Her French accent, a remnant from a concussion she'd suffered years ago in New Orleans, added a unique charm to her enthusiastic personality.

Agatha couldn't help but smile at Lorraine's exuberance. "News travels fast in Bristol Lake, doesn't it?" she said, shaking her head in amusement.

"Oh, ma chère, you have no idea," Lorraine replied with a conspiratorial wink. She leaned in, lowering her voice dramatically. "Now, tell me all about this book of yours. I simply must know every detail!"

Agatha chuckled, shaking her head in amusement. "Well, Lorraine, it's a cozy mystery set in a small coastal town. There's a bookstore owner who gets tangled up in solving a local murder. But I'm afraid that's all I can say for now – I don't want to spoil the surprise."

She paused, then added with a smile, "How about I let you be one of the first to read it once it's published? I'd love to hear your thoughts."

"Oh là là, to be one of the first to read it? C'est merveilleux! I can't wait to dive into your mystery." She leaned in closer, lowering her voice conspiratorially. "You know, I've been volunteering at Green Acres lately. If you need any inspiration for quirky characters or mysterious happenings, ma chère, I've got stories that would make your hair curl!"

Agatha chuckled, her eyes crinkling with amusement.

"Oh, Lorraine, I can always count on you for the inside scoop. I'm sure volunteering at Green Acres keeps you on your toes.

Just then, the bell above the door chimed, and a familiar redhead poked her head in. Emma Fletcher, Agatha's neighbor and closest friend, burst into the shop with a wide grin on her freckled face.

"Agatha!" Emma exclaimed, her green eyes sparkling behind her tortoiseshell glasses. "I got your message about finishing the manuscript. Congratulations!" She rushed over to give Agatha a warm hug, a white bakery box clutched in her hand.

"Thanks, Emma," Agatha said, returning the hug with genuine warmth. She stepped back, her hazel eyes twinkling with pride. "I finally finished it. And get this—it's fully typewritten. No digital version."

Emma's eyes widened, a mix of admiration and concern crossing her freckled face. She set the bakery box on the counter, the aroma of cinnamon and butter escaping as she lifted the lid. "Agatha, that's incredible, but... what if you lose it? You should really make a copy."

Agatha chuckled, shaking her head. "I'll take good care of it, don't worry." She gestured to the shelves of mystery novels surrounding them. "Besides, there's something special about a typewritten manuscript. It feels more authentic, especially for a mystery writer."

Emma nodded, understanding in her eyes, but she wasn't quite convinced. "I get it, but still—"

"After losing an entire hard drive full of great ideas a few years back when my computer died, I'm terrified of it happening again," Agatha interrupted, a shadow briefly crossing her face. She ran her fingers along the spine of a nearby book. "No, this way is safer. And it connects me to all these great authors who came before us."

Emma laughed, reaching for a scone. "Well, when you put it that way, it does sound rather perfect for Bristol Lake's resident mystery author. Just promise me you'll keep it in a fireproof safe or something, okay?"

"Ah, mon Dieu, Agatha," Lorraine chimed in. "You are brave! But Emma's right. You should be careful." Lorraine took a sip of her tea before continuing. "Speaking of which, I met your Aunt Edna at Green Acres. Quelle femme fascinante! We bonded over our love for mystery novels, and when I mentioned your bookstore, her eyes lit up. She suggested starting a weekly book club at Green Acres, and I thought it was a brilliant idea!"

Celeste looked puzzled. "What did she say?" she asked, turning to Lorraine.

Lorraine smiled and translated. "I said, 'What a fascinating woman!' Her eyes twinkled with excitement. "Aunt Edna said she'll speak to you when you visit. With your new book coming out soon, it would be the perfect debut selection. Qu'en penses-tu, Agatha?"

Agatha's face broke into a wide smile, though she let out an awkward chuckle. "A book club does sound delightful, but I may not be able to have my novel ready in time." She gave Lorraine an apologetic look. "It's still in the very first draft stages. I'm afraid you're getting a bit ahead of yourself there."

Lorraine blinked in surprise. "Oh? I thought for sure you were close to publishing."

"Not quite yet, I'm afraid," Agatha replied. "But once I've revised it into publishable shape, I'd be honored to have it be the book club's selection both here and at Green Acres." She clasped her hands excitedly. "I'm just so glad to hear Aunt Edna is settling in well and making friends already. Leave it to her to hit the ground running."

The friends continued to chat for a while, catching up on the latest happenings and discussing their upcoming book club meeting. As the morning wore on, Lorraine and Emma eventually had to bid Agatha farewell, as they both had errands to run and tasks to attend to. Agatha hugged them warmly, thanking them for stopping by and promising to keep them updated on her book's progress.

Later that day, as Agatha prepared to close up the bookstore, she decided to make a quick stop at Eliza's Bakery and Patisserie on her way home. She thought it would be nice to pick up some scones for her visit with Aunt Edna the following day. Aunt Edna had been raving about trying these famous scones ever since Agatha first mentioned them in her letters. "You simply must bring me some of these magical scones you keep writing about," Aunt Edna had insisted during their last phone call. "If they're half as delicious as you describe, I'll be in heaven!"

As Agatha pushed open the door to Eliza's Bakery and Patisserie, a wave of warmth and the intoxicating aroma of freshly baked goods enveloped her. The shop buzzed with activity, customers chattering as they pointed at the array of tempting treats lining the display cases. Behind the counter, Agatha spotted Eliza Martin, her friend and the bakery's owner, deftly boxing up a towering cake.

Weaving through the crowd, Agatha made her way to the counter, a smile spreading across her face. She was eager to catch up with Eliza and, more importantly, to select the perfect scones for her upcoming visit with Aunt Edna. The thought of sharing tea and Eliza's famous pastries with her aunt at Green Acres brought a warmth to Agatha's chest, a moment of simple joy in her busy day.

"Eliza, these scones look amazing," Agatha said, her eyes roaming over the display case filled with golden, buttery pastries.

"Thanks, Agatha. They're fresh out of the oven. How's everything at the bookstore?" Eliza asked.

"Wonderful." Agatha paused and smiled. "Guess what?"

Eliza raised her eyebrows. "What?"

"I just finished writing my manuscript," Agatha replied.

Eliza's eyes widened with delight. "It's about time! Congratulations! That's fantastic news."

"Thanks, Eliza," Agatha said, her face lighting up. "It's been quite the journey."

Eliza nodded, reaching for a box. "I bet it has. Here, take a dozen scones on the house. Give my best to Aunt Edna."

"Thanks, Eliza. She'll love these," Agatha said, gratefully accepting the box of scones. "I'll be sure to let her know they're from you."

With the manuscript safely tucked away and a box of scones in hand, Agatha felt a deep sense of contentment. She was excited to share her achievements with her aunt. As she stepped out of the bakery, her phone rang, the familiar tone of Aunt Edna's number lighting up the screen.

"Agatha, dear," Aunt Edna's voice crackled with excitement. "Can you come by tomorrow? There's something I need to tell you."

"I was already planning on visiting you tomorrow, so I'll be there bright and early with some scones Eliza is sending to you," Agatha explained.

"That's perfect, my dear." Aunt Edna was silent for a moment on the other side of the line.

"Aunt Edna? Are you there?" Agatha listened to some mumbled noises on the other side.

"I'm here, dear. See you tom—"

The line dropped.

She must be having phone problems, Agatha pondered. *I'll see her in the morning.*

As she walked home, Agatha's mind buzzed with questions. What could be so important that Aunt Edna wouldn't reveal over the phone? The sun was beginning to set, casting a golden glow over the quiet streets of the small town. Mike trotted happily beside her, stopping from time to time to sniff an interesting scent.

Agatha looked down at Mike. "What do you think, boy? What could Aunt Edna have that's so important?" Mike wagged his tail in response, his bright eyes gleaming with curiosity.

They passed the familiar shops, with their colorful awnings and neatly trimmed window boxes. The aroma of freshly baked bread wafted from the bakery, and Agatha couldn't help but smile, thinking of the scones in her bag.

As Agatha strolled with Mike, she noticed the old Victorian house that had stood empty since her arrival in town looked different. As she passed, she saw the lights on in what was supposedly a study. The blinds were open, revealing an elderly lady with a head full of silver hair, playing the piano and singing along. She looked like she was having the time of her life.

Agatha mused aloud to Mike, "Interesting. Looks like someone moved in. I'm shocked Lorraine didn't mention someone new in town. She seems to know everything around here." She shook her head with a smile. "The town gossip will catch up," she said. "I'm sure Lorraine will have something to say about it tomorrow, even if she doesn't know yet."

And with that, she and Mike continued merrily on their

walk toward home. When they reached her home, Agatha unlocked the front door and stepped inside. The scent of lavender greeted her, and she set the box of scones on the kitchen counter.

Mike trotted in after her, heading straight for his water bowl.

Agatha couldn't shake the feeling of anticipation. Whatever Aunt Edna had to tell her; it must be significant. She poured herself a cup of tea and sank onto her favorite spot on the couch, her mind racing with possibilities.

Mike jumped onto the couch beside her, resting his head on her lap. Agatha gently stroked his fur, feeling a sense of calm wash over her. "I know you're curious about what Aunt Edna needs to tell us. We'll find out tomorrow, Mike," she murmured.

Agatha glanced down at her loyal companion. "I'm so glad I got you certified as an emotional support dog. I knew Aunt Edna would want you to visit her at Green Acres, and I didn't want any issues with that. You're going to make her so happy." Mike's tail wagged as if he understood, and Agatha smiled.

2

AUNT EDNA

Agatha arrived at Green Acres Assisted Living, walking up the neatly trimmed pathway to the front entrance. Mike trotted happily beside her, his tail wagging in excitement. The sun shone brightly, and birds chirped, creating a serene atmosphere that matched the facility's polished exterior.

As Agatha stepped into the lobby, her eyebrows rose in surprise. She had expected an upscale look for a high-end facility like Green Acres, but the interior resembled a tired nursing home instead. The décor was dated, with worn carpets and faded wallpaper giving the space an institutional feel. A faint smell of disinfectant hung in the air. Agatha frowned, wondering if Aunt Edna had noticed this disparity.

Scanning the room, Agatha spotted a young woman with dark brown hair and eyes heading her way, a practiced smile on her face.

"Welcome to Green Acres," the young woman said, her voice cheerful despite the lackluster surroundings. "I'm Lindsay, the receptionist. How can I help you today?"

Agatha smiled. "Hi, I'm here to see my aunt, Edna Ashton. She moved in recently."

"Oh, Ms. Ashton," Lindsay said, recognizing the name. "Isn't she the almost-famous Hollywood star?"

Agatha chuckled. "I guess so." She paused and glanced around the lobby before continuing. "She's expecting me this morning."

Lindsay glanced at Mike, who wagged his tail and looked up at her with friendly, expectant eyes. Despite his charming demeanor, Lindsay's brow furrowed as she said, "Well, ma'am, I don't think you can bring your dog in.

Mike tilted his head, as if confused by Lindsay's words, and gave a small, hopeful whine.

Agatha placed a reassuring hand on his head. "Actually, he's a certified emotional support dog," she explained, her voice calm but firm. "He's allowed to visit."

Lindsay nodded slowly, considering this. "Alright, I'll call her apartment and let her know you're here." She walked behind the desk and picked up the phone, dialing Edna's number. After a moment, she spoke into the receiver. "Ms. Ashton, your niece Agatha is here to see you... Yes, with her dog, Mike... Okay, I'll let her know." Lindsay hung up and smiled at Agatha. "She'll be right down."

A few moments later, Edna Ashton appeared from around the corner, her entrance as grand as if she were stepping onto a Hollywood stage. Despite her age, she glided down the hallway with a grace that hinted at her glamorous past. Her silver hair, styled in soft waves, framed her face and drew attention to her bright, expressive eyes. She wore a vibrant, floral blouse that complemented her lively personality, paired with well-tailored pants and comfortable yet stylish shoes.

As Edna spotted Agatha, her eyes sparkled with mischief and joy. "Agatha, darling!" Edna called out, her voice still carrying the theatrical flair that had captivated audiences during her acting days. She opened her arms wide, enveloping her niece in a warm, loving hug that filled the room with its affection.

"Hi, Aunt Edna," Agatha said, returning the hug with equal warmth. She held up a small basket. "I brought you some scones from Eliza's Bakery. She thought you'd like to taste it."

Edna's eyes lit up at the mention of the scones. "Eliza's famous scones? Oh, you shouldn't have! That's so kind of her," she exclaimed, her voice filled with genuine appreciation. "Come, let's sit in the lounge and catch up. I've got so much to tell you."

Edna's gaze then fell upon Mike, who sat obediently by Agatha's side. Her face brightened even more. "And there's my favorite little gentleman! Hello, Mike," she cooed, bending down to give Mike a gentle pat on the head.

Mike's tail wagged enthusiastically, clearly happy to see a familiar face.

"Come, let's sit in the lounge and catch up. I've got so much to tell you." With a gentle tug on Agatha's arm, Edna led the way, her steps confident and full of energy that belied her years.

As they settled into a corner of the lounge, sinking into the comfortable armchairs, Edna reached for a scone and took a bite, savoring the taste. "Mmm, just as delicious as you described," she said, closing her eyes for a moment to fully appreciate the flavors. Opening her eyes again, she fixed her gaze on Agatha. "I'm so glad you're visiting, my dear. How have you been?"

Agatha smiled, feeling the warmth and love in her aunt's presence. "I've been busy, but good. The bookstore is doing well, and I finally finished my book. It's my first one, and I'm really proud of it."

Edna beamed. "That's wonderful, Agatha! I can't wait to read it. You've always had such a gift with words."

Agatha felt a sense of contentment wash over her as she began to share more about her life. "The bookstore has been bustling. We've had a few events that drew in quite a crowd, and it's been great seeing the community come together. Also, Mike has become a bit of a local celebrity. The customers adore him."

Edna laughed softly. "Of course they do. He's a charmer."

Agatha continued, "And the book—I'm really excited about it. It's a cozy mystery set in a small town, with a bit of romance thrown in. I think readers will love it."

Edna's eyes sparkled with excitement. "I have no doubt they will. You've worked so hard, and it shows."

Agatha couldn't help but feel a sense of contentment. Aunt Edna's vibrant spirit and genuine interest in her life were a welcome respite from the solitude of her writing. "Thank you, Aunt Edna. Your support means the world to me."

Edna reached over and squeezed Agatha's hand. "Always, my dear. Now, tell me more about these bookstore events. Any interesting stories?"

As Agatha shared more details, the warmth of their conversation filled the room, making the day even brighter.

Agatha sat down and took a deep breath. "Aunt Edna, you mentioned on the phone that you had something important to tell me?"

Aunt Edna looked puzzled. "Did I? I'm afraid I can't remember. My memory isn't what it used to be."

Just then, Beatrice Belafonte approached them. She had aged gracefully, with silver hair styled in a sleek bob and a posture that still hinted at her Hollywood days. Her sharp blue eyes scanned the room, taking everything in with a critical air. Beatrice wasn't the most pleasant person in the world, known for her rude remarks followed by quick apologies. "Don't worry, Edna. We all forget things sometimes," she said, her voice carrying a tone that was both reassuring and slightly condescending.

Agatha sensed a flicker of tension between Aunt Edna and Beatrice. "It's strange, though. Are you sure you don't remember calling me?"

Aunt Edna shook her head, genuinely confused. "No, dear. I don't remember."

Before Agatha could ask more, the Green Acres director, Mr. Roger Collins, walked by with Nurse Amanda. They were deep in conversation but paused to greet Agatha.

"Good morning, Miss Royale," Mr. Collins said politely. "How is everything?"

"Good morning. Everything is fine, thank you," Agatha replied, surprised by their friendly demeanor.

As they moved on, Agatha turned to Aunt Edna, her voice low. "That's odd. Mr. Collins and Nurse Amanda are usually so moody. I've never seen them this pleasant before."

Aunt Edna chuckled softly, shaking her head. "Oh, don't let their act fool you, dear. They're not exactly the warmest people I've ever met. I suppose they can turn on the charm when they need to, though."

Agatha nodded thoughtfully, filing away this information for later. After a moment, Aunt Edna leaned closer to

Agatha. "Did I ever tell you that Beatrice and I knew each other from our days in Los Angeles?"

Agatha's eyes widened. "Really? You never mentioned that."

"Yes," Aunt Edna continued, "we both tried to make it in Hollywood. Those were interesting times."

"Some of us made it a little further in Hollywood than others," Beatrice said with a faint, almost smug smile.

Edna's eyes narrowed, a flicker of something unspoken passing through them, but she kept her composure. "Yes, Beatrice, we all have our paths."

"We have many stories from those days, but some are best left in the past." Beatrice smiled faintly.

Sensing the tension, Agatha quickly shifted the conversation. "Aunt Edna, Lorraine mentioned something about your idea for a book club here at Green Acres. How about we start a branch of my mystery book club?"

Edna's face brightened at the suggestion. "Oh, Agatha, that's a wonderful idea! I've been wanting something engaging to do here, and I think the residents would love it."

Beatrice's smile softened, though a hint of reservation remained. "A book club could be interesting. It would certainly add some culture to this place."

Mildred Hickman, a sweet-talking former con artist, had been lingering nearby, her ears perked. "You can bring the books to sell here," she chimed in, her eyes glinting with opportunity. Without missing a beat, Mildred glided into the community room, her whispers spreading like wildfire. Within minutes, curious residents flocked around Agatha, Aunt Edna, and Beatrice, their excited murmurs filling the air with a palpable buzz of anticipation.

As the residents buzzed with excitement, Mr. Collins

and Nurse Amanda returned, overhearing the conversation. "A book club?" Mr. Collins said, sounding uncertain.

"We'll need to discuss this," Nurse Amanda added, her brow creasing.

Mike, who was standing next to Agatha, growled quietly as he stared at Nurse Amanda.

Amanda's face contorted into a scowl when she looked at Mike. "I'm sorry, Miss Royale, but this place prohibits dogs. Make sure he stays outside." She gestured towards Mike as she spoke.

Agatha stood her ground. "Mike is a certified emotional support dog, Nurse Amanda. He's allowed to be with me."

"I see," Amanda said, her voice dripping with barely concealed disdain. Her eyes narrowed, and her lips pressed into a thin, disapproving line.

Agatha glanced down at Mike, noticing his restless behavior. "Looks like someone needs a potty break," she said with a gentle smile. Turning to aunt Edna, she added, "I'll be right back. Just going to take Mike outside for a quick walk."

Mike wagged his tail, happy to stretch his legs. As Agatha led him outside, she noticed Amanda speaking harshly to Beatrice. "You should know better than to sit here all day doing nothing."

Beatrice's face reddened, but instead of being sad, she snapped at Aunt Edna. "This is your fault, Edna. You should have taken care of things when you had the chance."

Aunt Edna looked hurt. "I did what I could, Beatrice. It's not fair to blame me."

Agatha watched the exchange with growing curiosity. What was going on between them? Her mind drifted back to the phone call the previous night. What did Aunt Edna want to tell me? It can't be that important if she forgot it.

Mr. Collins interrupted Agatha's thoughts as he approached. "Miss Royale, most of the residents want to have your stupid book club...

"Excuse me?" Agatha interrupted.

"I mean, your mystery book club," Mr. Collins muttered.

"That's great news," Agatha replied, smiling. "I'll stop by tomorrow to discuss the book for our first meeting. I'll bring some books to sell."

Mr. Collins frowned and cleared his throat. "Well, remember Green Acres will take a percentage of anything you sell for charity."

Agatha looked taken aback and hesitated before responding, "Okay... we can discuss it tomorrow."

Mr. Collins nodded and walked away.

As Agatha watched Mr. Collins reach Nurse Amanda, and they walked back to their offices, the residents continued to discuss the book club. Agatha's mind was elsewhere, filled with questions and a growing sense of unease.

Outside, the fresh air helped Agatha clear her head. She walked slowly along the pathway beside the flower beds, letting Mike sniff every tuft of grass.

"Something's not right here," she murmured. Mike paused, ears perked, as if in agreement.

She glanced back toward the building's windows. Nurse Amanda's voice, sharp and scolding, echoed faintly from inside. Agatha frowned.

"It's not just Aunt Edna's memory," she said quietly. "It's the whole place. Something feels... off."

Mike gave a short bark, then resumed sniffing around a fire hydrant.

Agatha pulled out her phone, opened the notes app, and typed:

> *Book club at Green Acres – great idea.
> Staff seems too polished.
> Edna forgot phone call.
> Beatrice = tension.
> Ask Lorraine if she's heard gossip?*

She saved the note, tucked her phone away, and scratched Mike behind the ears. "Good boy. Let's see what else we can sniff out tomorrow."

3

BOOK CLUB AT GREEN ACRES

The next morning Agatha met with Emma and Lorraine at the bookstore before heading to Green Acres. She would usually walk to the bookstore but today she drove Eleanor, her 1962 Ford Falcon as she had to transport several books to sell to the mystery book club members at Green Acres.

Emma arrived first, her footsteps echoing on the hard-wood floor as she entered the bookstore. The bell above the door chimed cheerfully, announcing her presence. Lorraine followed shortly after, a warm smile on her face as she spotted Emma browsing the new arrivals section.

Celeste was already busy at work when they arrived. She moved gracefully behind the counter, preparing a fresh pot of coffee and arranging the delectable pastries that would tempt customers throughout the day. The aroma of freshly brewed coffee mingled with the scent of new books, creating an inviting atmosphere.

Shortly after Emma and Lorraine's arrival, the bell above the door jangled once more. Agatha stepped into the bookstore, her eyes sparkling with anticipation. She waved to Celeste, who looked up from her tasks and greeted her with a friendly smile.

"Well, if it isn't our favorite mystery author!" Celeste called out, setting a box down on the table. "Emma and Lorraine are already here waiting for you."

Agatha paced towards the back of the bookstore, where Lorraine and Emma were engrossed in a lively discussion about the book of the week. The bookstore was filled with the scent of freshly brewed coffee and the soft murmur of their voices.

"Good morning, ladies," Agatha greeted. Both women looked up, curiosity piqued by her tone. "You won't believe what happened at Green Acres yesterday."

Lorraine, with her usual playful demeanor, raised an eyebrow. "Ooh là là, do tell! Did someone find where Mrs. Johnson hid her dinner plate last night?"

Agatha chuckled, shaking her head. "She hid her dinner plate? Why?"

"Mon Dieu, no one knows, but she keeps hiding her plates full of food and they're all on pins and needles, afraid of rats. The last time I was there, it was a literal treasure hunt looking for the plate." Lorraine burst into laughter, her giggles filling the room. Her infectious laughter had everyone around her eager to join in, showcasing her vibrant and funny nature.

"Not quite, but it was eventful. Aunt Edna called me the night before and said she had something important to tell me, but when I got there, she couldn't remember calling me at all."

"That's strange," Celeste said, leaning forward with concern. "Do you think she's alright?"

"I hope so," Agatha replied. "But that's not all. There was some tension between Aunt Edna and another resident,

Beatrice Belafonte. They used to know each other from their Hollywood days, but there are definitely some unresolved issues there."

Lorraine nodded sympathetically. "Sounds like a soap opera in the making. Très dramatique!"

"Exactly," Agatha said with a sigh. "But on a brighter note, Aunt Edna and I were discussing an idea that Lorraine had mentioned - starting a mystery book club at Green Acres. When I brought it up to the residents, they loved it. They're all very excited about the idea."

"A book club at Green Acres? That sounds wonderful! I'd love to help out," Emma said enthusiastically.

"Really?" Agatha's face brightened. "There's a lot to organize, and having some extra hands would be fantastic."

"Count me in too," Lorraine added, grinning. "It sounds like a great way to spend time with the residents and share our love for mysteries."

Celeste, busy stacking books behind the counter, chimed in. "I'll hold down the fort here at the bookstore so you all can focus on the book club. Just let me know if you need anything."

"Thanks, Celeste," Agatha expressed gratefully. "I really appreciate it."

～

Agatha fussed with the stack of books in her arms, rearranging them for the third time as Emma watched with amusement.

"They're just seniors, not literary critics," Emma teased, adjusting her tortoiseshell glasses. "Why so nervous?"

"I want to make a good impression," Agatha admitted, setting down the pile to smooth a wrinkle from her blouse.

"These people have been reading mysteries longer than I've been alive."

"And yet, none of them solve real ones like you do," Emma reminded her with a gentle nudge.

Agatha rolled her eyes. "That's hardly a marketable skill set. 'Local bookseller: decent at choosing inventory, excellent at stumbling across dead bodies.'"

Lorraine breezed in from the café area, balancing three mugs of steaming coffee. "Pre-book club fortification!" she announced. "With a splash of that vanilla syrup you like, Agatha."

As they sipped their coffee, Agatha found herself mentally rehearsing her book recommendations. Before opening the store, her only public speaking had been at library events—always with prepared notes and usually to audiences of children who were easily impressed by puppet voices.

"What if they hate my selections?" Agatha asked, voicing the worry that had kept her awake. "Some of them have been reading Agatha Christie since before Christie finished writing them."

"Impossible," Lorraine declared with a dismissive wave. "Anyone who doesn't appreciate your literary taste is simply uncultured. Besides," she added with a wink, "I've packed extra scones as a backup plan. Food bribes work wonders with book clubs, trust me."

"Oh, and remember to tell them about that new mystery series from the British author," Emma suggested. "The one with the vicar who solves crimes between Sunday services."

"Good call," Agatha nodded, grateful for the reminder. Despite her name, she'd never had Agatha Christie's confidence. Ironic that her parents had named her for the Queen of Mystery, never imagining she'd one day run a mystery bookstore. They'd hoped for a professor, not a shopkeeper with ink-stained fingers and a penchant for fictional murders.

Together, they loaded the box of books into Eleanor. The car's trunk was soon filled with novels, ready to be shared with the eager members of the new mystery book club at Green Acres.

As they drove to the assisted living facility, Lorraine wrinkled her nose and said with a grin, "Mon Dieu, I hope people won't get intoxicated with those books soaked in gasoline because your trunk literally smells like a gas tank!"

Agatha laughed, shaking her head. "Don't worry, it's just Eleanor being quirky. This old girl has her gas pump in the trunk, believe it or not. Sometimes it leaves a bit of a smell, but the books will be fine." She patted the car's fender affectionately. "It's all part of her charm, even if it means airing out the trunk now and then."

Emma rolled down her window with a chuckle. "I still can't believe you drive this thing."

Agatha grinned as she turned onto the winding road leading to Green Acres. "She's not just a car. She's the only constant I brought from my old life."

Lorraine leaned forward from the back seat. "Mon Dieu, it smells like a 1960s gas station in here, but it does have character."

Agatha tapped the dashboard affectionately. "Eleanor's like me—vintage, maybe a little temperamental, but reliable when it counts."

～

Upon arrival, several residents who had already gathered in

the community room greeted them, their faces lighting up at the sight of the books.

"Hello, everyone!" Agatha called out cheerfully. "We brought some wonderful mystery novels for you to choose from for our first meeting."

The residents buzzed with excitement as they gathered around, eager to see the selection of books. Aunt Edna, seated near the front, beamed with pride at her niece's initiative.

Lorraine and Emma quickly set to work, arranging the books on a table while Agatha spoke with Mr. Collins about the logistics of the book club meetings.

"We'll need to figure out a regular schedule that works for everyone," Agatha explained. "And maybe we can have themed meetings or invite guest speakers."

Mr. Collins nodded. "That sounds like a great idea, Miss Royale. We'll do our best to support you. Just remember, any sales from the book club should include a small percentage donated to Green Acres' charity fund. It's important to give back to the community, after all."

Nurse Amanda, however, was less enthusiastic. She approached Agatha with a stern expression. "This book club better not interfere with the residents' routines or cause any disruptions," she snapped.

Agatha maintained her composure. "We'll make sure it fits into their schedules without affecting their routines."

Nurse Amanda huffed and walked away, leaving Agatha to wonder what had soured her mood.

As the residents picked out their books and settled into their seats, Agatha felt a wave of satisfaction wash over her.

"Alright, everyone," Agatha said, clapping her hands to get their attention. "Welcome to the first meeting of the Green Acres Mystery Book Club. Today, we'll be discussing which book to choose for our first read. We have a wonderful selection here, so let's talk about which one intrigues us the most."

The room filled with animated conversations as the residents discussed their preferences and interests. Lorraine and Emma facilitated the discussion, jotting down notes and trying to guide the group towards a consensus.

"I think we should start with a classic," suggested Harold, his voice carrying an air of authority. "Something by Agatha Christie, perhaps."

"Agatha Christie is so predictable," Beatrice scoffed. "I'd prefer something more modern. How about a Louise Penny novel?"

"I agree with Harold," said Mrs. Whitaker, adjusting her glasses. "There's nothing like a good old-fashioned mystery."

"But we've all read Agatha Christie a hundred times," Lorraine interjected playfully. "Let's try something new. What about 'The No. 1 Ladies' Detective Agency' by Alexander McCall Smith? It's charming and different."

"Charming?" Mr. Edwards snorted. "We need something with real suspense. How about a thriller by Harlan Coben?"

Nurse Amanda, passing by, couldn't resist chiming in. "This is never going to work if you all keep bickering. Why not just draw a name from a hat and get it over with?"

Ignoring Amanda's rudeness, Mrs. Johnson raised her voice. "We should consider something from a lesser-known author. Give the underdogs a chance!"

Lorraine laughed. "Underdogs or not, we need to pick a book sometime today, folks!"

Aunt Edna, who had been quietly listening, finally spoke up. "Why don't we compromise? We can start with a classic and then move on to a more contemporary author. That way, everyone gets a little of what they want."

Beatrice rolled her eyes and said with a condescending smile, "Oh, Edna, always the diplomat. But maybe we should leave the decisions to those of us who actually keep up with current literature."

Agatha sensed the tension between Aunt Edna and Beatrice, her eyes flickering briefly over their uneasy faces. She took a breath, her smile unwavering as she continued with the meeting.

"That sounds reasonable," Harold conceded. "In that case, my vote is for 'The Mysterious Affair at Styles' by Agatha Christie to start us off."

Beatrice sighed dramatically but nodded. "Fine, but the next book has to be something more modern."

The group murmured in agreement, and Lorraine clapped her hands together. "Great! 'The Mysterious Affair at Styles' it is.

We'll start reading this week and meet again to discuss it. In the meantime, enjoy your reading and feel free to share your thoughts and theories as you go along."

The book club meeting was in full swing, the ladies of Green Acres Assisted Living gathered in the community room, discussing their latest read. The room was filled with the hum of animated conversations, the scent of freshly brewed coffee, and the occasional rustle of turning pages. Agatha sat beside Aunt Edna, who was wearing her favorite lavender perfume, the same one she had worn for years.

"Edna, you smell lovely tonight," Mrs. Johnson said with a warm smile, leaning in to catch a better whiff of the floral scent. "What is that perfume? It's so elegant."

Aunt Edna beamed, pleased with the compliment. "Oh,

it's just a little something I've been wearing for years. Lavender and a hint of vanilla."

Mrs. White, who was seated across the table, nodded in agreement. "Yes, it's absolutely delightful. Very classic."

As the conversation continued, Beatrice, who was seated next to Aunt Edna, began to fidget uncomfortably. Her nose twitched, and she quickly pulled a handkerchief from her bag. "Excuse me," she muttered, her voice muffled by the cloth.

Beatrice's eyes watered as she gave a dramatic sneeze. "Ah-choo!" She dabbed at her nose, glaring at Aunt Edna. "Edna, your perfume is just too strong. I can't breathe sitting next to you all evening."

The room fell silent for a moment, the sudden outburst catching everyone off guard. Agatha exchanged a puzzled glance with Aunt Edna, who looked taken aback by Beatrice's reaction.

"I'm so sorry, Beatrice," Aunt Edna said, her voice soft and apologetic. "I didn't realize it was bothering you."

Beatrice continued to sniffle; her irritation was evident. "Well, it is. Maybe next time you could go a little lighter on it."

Mrs. Johnson tried to smooth over the awkward moment. "Perhaps it's just a bit too much for some people. But really, Edna, I think it smells wonderful."

As the conversation gradually shifted back to the book discussion, Agatha noticed a fleeting, triumphant glint in Beatrice's eyes as she glanced at Aunt Edna. It was a look of victory, not the reaction of someone genuinely bothered by a scent.

Agatha's mind raced. Beatrice had done it on purpose, she realized. The sneezing fit, the dramatic complaint – it was all an act to belittle Aunt Edna, to embarrass her in front of the others.

She reached over and gave her aunt's hand a reassuring squeeze. "Don't worry about it, Aunt Edna. Some people just have sensitive noses," she said, loud enough for Beatrice to hear.

The tension in the room slowly dissipated as the residents turned their attention back to the upcoming book selection. Excited chatter filled the air, with suggestions and opinions being tossed around like confetti.

Agatha scanned the room, a smile of satisfaction on her face as she watched the residents excitedly discuss the upcoming book club meeting. Her smile faltered when she noticed Beatrice and Harold were missing from the group. Suddenly, she caught sight of Aunt Edna, who wore a worried expression and was glancing around nervously. Before Agatha could approach her, Aunt Edna abruptly stood up and hurried out of the room, moving with surprising speed for someone her age.

Just as Agatha was about to follow Aunt Edna, Lindsey approached her with an eager smile.

"Agatha! I've got great news," Lindsey said, her eyes sparkling with enthusiasm. "Mr. Collins approved my request to join the book club. I'm over the moon!"

She held up a copy of the book she'd just purchased from Emma. "I've been dying to join your Mystery and Scones Tuesdays at the bookstore for ages, but my shift always got in the way. This is perfect timing."

Agatha couldn't help but smile at Lindsey's excitement, even as her mind raced with thoughts of Aunt Edna's sudden departure. "That's wonderful, Lindsey," Agatha replied, returning her smile. "We're thrilled to have you join us."

As Agatha and Lindsey chatted about their favorite mystery novels and their expectations for the book club, Agatha found her thoughts wandering back to Aunt Edna's peculiar behavior. Just as she was about to excuse herself to check on her aunt, a loud crash echoed from the back room, followed by raised voices and the clatter of objects being tossed about.

The lively chatter in the room came to an abrupt halt, replaced by a stunned silence. Agatha's eyebrows shot up as she exchanged a worried look with Lindsey.

"Oh dear," Agatha said, her voice a mix of concern and curiosity. "I'd better investigate this little disturbance."

Lindsey's earlier excitement morphed into a look of apprehension. "I'll tag along if you don't mind. Sounds like quite the ruckus back there."

The pair hurried towards the source of the commotion, their pace quickening with each step. As they drew closer, Agatha could distinguish the unmistakable voices of Aunt Edna and Beatrice engaged in a heated exchange.

What in the world has gotten into those two? Agatha wondered, her mind conjuring up all sorts of scenarios.

Reaching the door, she paused for a moment, took a deep breath, and with a slight nod to Lindsey, pushed it open.

The scene that greeted her was chaotic. Furniture was overturned, and papers were scattered across the floor. Aunt Edna stood with her fists clenched, her face red with anger, while Beatrice pointed an accusing finger at her, her expression equally furious.

"You had no right!" Aunt Edna shouted, her voice shaking with emotion.

"No right?" Beatrice retorted, her voice booming. "I did what needed to be done!"

Agatha stepped into the room; her presence momentarily unnoticed by the feuding pair. "What's going on here?" she demanded, her voice cutting through the tension like a knife.

4

THE FEUD

Both Aunt Edna and Beatrice turned to look at Agatha, their faces a mix of surprise and defiance. Agatha could see Harold standing nearby, looking uncomfortable and avoiding eye contact.

"Agatha," Aunt Edna began, her voice trembling.

Beatrice Interrupted her. "I have something to say," she announced, her voice dripping with condescension. She turned to Agatha. "You think you're so clever, organizing this book club. But it's clear to everyone here that you're just like your aunt—jealous and envious."

Gasps erupted around the room. Agatha felt her cheeks flush with a mix of embarrassment and anger. "What are you talking about, Beatrice?"

Beatrice sneered. "Your dear Aunt Edna has always been jealous of me. She's never accepted that I've always been the better woman."

"That's not true!" Aunt Edna shouted, her face flushing red with fury. She clenched her fists at her sides, trembling with indignation. "You've always been the envious one, Beatrice. You never accepted that I won the knitting competition at the Modesto fair and square. And that's why you stole my fiancé, Harold!"

The room fell silent. All eyes turned to Harold, who stood in the corner, looking horrified and uncomfortable. Murmurs of shock rippled through the group as the revelation sank in.

Beatrice's eyes flashed with anger. "He chose me, Edna. You never accepted that. You've been bitter ever since, trying to undermine me at every turn."

Tears welled up in Aunt Edna's eyes. "I loved him, Beatrice. And you took him from me out of spite."

Agatha stepped forward, trying to comfort her aunt. "Aunt Edna, please, let's not do this here."

But Beatrice wasn't done. She smirked. "Oh, really? And what exactly are you going to do, Edna? Knit me to death? You can't deal with the fact that you lost Harold when we were younger because he chose me, and now he chose me again."

Aunt Edna's face turned a deeper shade of red. "He didn't choose you... you stole him! And if he had chosen you, why did he marry Gemma?"

The residents gasped again, their eyes darting between the two women. Beatrice's smirk faltered for a moment. "He made a mistake with Gemma, but he always loved me. And you know it."

Aunt Edna's hands shook with rage. "You've ruined everything for me, and I won't let you get away with it any longer."

Beatrice laughed coldly. "And you've always been delusional. Face it, Edna, you're nothing but a bitter old woman who can't let go of the past."

Beatrice's eyes narrowed dangerously. "Oh, Edna," she sneered, "you've always been jealous of what Harold and I have."

Aunt Edna's face flushed with indignation. Her voice quivered with emotion as she retorted, "Jealous? Ha! You've got it all wrong, Beatrice. If I can't have Harold, then neither can you. Mark my words, I'll make you regret ever getting involved with him. I'll turn your perfect little world upside down!"

A shocked silence fell over the room. Agatha looked around at the stunned faces of the residents, realizing the gravity of Aunt Edna's threat. She gently led her aunt away from the group, trying to calm her down.

"Let's take a walk, Aunt Edna," Agatha whispered. "You need to cool off."

As they left the room, the residents began whispering amongst themselves, casting suspicious glances at Beatrice and Harold.

Agatha stared in surprise as Aunt Edna's features transformed from sad and distraught to inexplicably happy and content. The shift was so sudden that it left Agatha momentarily speechless.

"Are you okay, Aunt Edna?" Agatha asked, her voice tinged with concern.

"Of course I am okay, dear. Why do you ask?" Aunt Edna replied, her eyes twinkling with an unsettling cheerfulness.

"Because of the fight with Beatrice and all," Agatha stated, trying to understand the sudden change.

"Fight?" Aunt Edna's brow furrowed in confusion. "I don't know what you're talking about, dear."

Agatha stared at her aunt in silence, her face puzzled. "Okay, Aunt Edna, never mind," she said, deciding not to press the issue further.

Before Edna had a chance to say anything, Agatha heard Mr. Collins shouting her name from across the room.

"Ms. Royale! Ms. Royale! Stop where you are!"

Agatha stopped in her tracks, trying to understand what the commotion was about. "What's the matter, Mr. Collins?" she asked, her heart pounding.

Mr. Collins approached, his face red with anger and frustration. "I need you to leave now. Your visit is causing problems for the residents."

"What do you mean? I've had nothing to do with this," Agatha protested, her eyes wide with confusion.

"I'm not sure about that," Mr. Collins replied, his tone accusatory. "We've had enough for today. Please take your books and your friends, and leave."

Agatha's mind raced as she tried to process his words. "But—" she started, but Mr. Collins cut her off.

"Don't forget to leave my cut of the sales," he added, his voice lowering as he cleared his throat. "I mean, the donation to Green Acres."

Agatha's mouth fell open in shock. She glanced at Aunt Edna, who seemed completely unperturbed by the entire exchange. "Mr. Collins, I think there's been a misunderstanding," Agatha began, but it was clear he was not interested in hearing her out.

"No misunderstandings, Ms. Royale. We need to maintain order here, and right now, your presence is disrupting that."

Agatha felt a mix of anger and helplessness. She looked around the room, noticing the whispers and glances from the other residents. They were clearly unsettled by the morning's events.

"Fine," Agatha said, her voice steely. "I'll gather my things and go. But this isn't over, Mr. Collins."

She turned to leave, feeling the weight of the morning's chaos pressing down on her. Lorraine and Emma, hurried over, their faces etched with concern.

"What happened?" Lorraine asked, glancing between Agatha and Mr. Collins.

"We're being asked to leave," Agatha explained, frustration evident in her tone. "Apparently, we've caused too much trouble for one day."

Emma looked shocked. "But we didn't do anything wrong!"

"Tell that to Mr. Collins," Agatha replied, gesturing towards the director who was now talking sternly to another staff member.

As Agatha and Emma gathered their books and prepared to leave, a cloud of unease settled over them. Agatha's mind whirled with the morning's events: Aunt Edna's uncharacteristic outburst, the heated argument with Beatrice, and now Mr. Collins's sudden dismissal.

"Emma," Agatha whispered, her brow furrowed, "doesn't this all seem a bit odd to you? Aunt Edna's mood swings, this blow-up with Beatrice, and now we're being asked to leave..."

Emma nodded, her eyes reflecting Agatha's concern. "You're right. It's like pieces of a puzzle that don't quite fit together."

Agatha sighed, clutching her bag of books closer. "I can't shake the feeling that there's more going on here than meets the eye. These things can't all be happening by chance."

As they walked towards the exit, Agatha turned to take one last look at her aunt, who was now calmly chatting with another resident as if nothing had happened. A chill ran down Agatha's spine.

"Let's go," she said to Lorraine and Emma. "We'll figure this out, but not here."

They exited Green Acres, the whispers and curious stares of the residents following them out. As they stepped into the brisk afternoon air, Agatha's mind raced with unanswered questions.

"Agatha," Emma said softly, "what really happened back there? What triggered that outburst?"

Agatha shrugged, her thoughts jumbled. "I don't know, but something doesn't feel right. Aunt Edna's behavior, Beatrice's accusations, Mr. Collins's reaction—it's all too strange."

Lorraine glanced back at the facility, her brow furrowed. "Do you think your aunt is hiding something?"

"I think there's more to this than we understand," Agatha replied. "And I'm going to find out what it is."

Just as they reached the car, Agatha's phone buzzed. She glanced at the screen and saw an unknown number. Frowning, she answered. "Hello?"

"Ms. Royale," a hushed voice said. "You don't know me, but I have information about your aunt and what happened today. Meet me at the old park bench by the lake tomorrow at 7 PM. Come alone."

The line went dead before Agatha could respond. She stared at her phone, a mix of curiosity and dread settling over her.

"Who was that?" Emma asked, noticing Agatha's expression.

Agatha blinked, still processing the unexpected call. "I'm not sure. Someone said they have information about Aunt Edna and what happened today. They want to meet at the old park bench by the lake tomorrow at 7 PM. Alone."

Emma's eyes widened. "An anonymous phone call?

That's kind of frightening. Maybe you should tell the police."

Agatha shook her head. "Tell the police what? That my aunt is having memory problems, and someone wants to talk about it with me? I don't think they'd take me seriously."

Lorraine, trying to lighten the mood, gave a playful smirk. "Just another typical day, huh? First, a knitting feud, now a secret rendezvous. I knew we should have brought more scones. C'est la vie!"

Agatha chuckled despite herself. "You're right, Lorraine. We'll need all the scones we can get for this one."

"Maybe you need to talk to Aunt Edna's doctor. They have a medical provider at this facility, right?" Emma asked, concern etched on her face.

"They do. I saw him when I was volunteering last week... Dr. Gregory Hartman, I think," Lorraine added.

"That's a great idea," Agatha responded thoughtfully. "I'll do that tomorrow."

Emma asked Agatha, intrigued, "Aren't you even a little curious about who called you about Aunt Edna? You seem so nonchalant about it."

Agatha shrugged, her expression thoughtful. "I am very curious. Just not sure I want to go meet some unknown crazy person at the park."

Lorraine's eyes twinkled mischievously as she raised an eyebrow. "Oh là là, Agatha! Are you starring in your very own mystery novel now? This is how all the best cozy mysteries begin!" She let out a theatrical gasp. "Just promise me you won't end up as the next book club selection, ma chérie!"

Agatha chuckled, shaking her head. "Thanks for the reassurance, Lorraine. I'll make sure to be extra cautious."

⁓

The next morning, Agatha met with Dr. Gregory Hartman, the facility's medical provider, to discuss Aunt Edna's recent behavior.

As she entered the building, Lindsey greeted her at the reception desk. "Good morning, Ms. Royale. What brings you in today?"

"Good morning, Lindsey. I called last evening for a meeting with Dr. Hartman this morning," Agatha replied, forcing a smile.

Lindsey looked surprised but nodded. "Dr. Hartman's office is just down the hall on the left. I hope everything is okay."

"Thank you, Lindsey. I'm just checking on Aunt Edna," Agatha reassured her.

Agatha followed the directions, her steps echoing in the quiet corridor. She knocked on the door marked "Dr. Gregory Hartman" and waited.

"Come in," a voice called from inside.

Agatha entered the office, finding Dr. Hartman seated behind a large mahogany desk. He was a tall man with salt-and-pepper hair, meticulously combed back, and he wore a pair of thin-rimmed glasses that gave him a scholarly appearance. His office was neat and orderly, with framed medical certificates adorning the walls and a faint scent of antiseptic lingering in the air.

"Ms. Royale, please have a seat," Dr. Hartman said, gesturing to the chair opposite him.

"Thank you for seeing me on such short notice," Agatha began as she sat down. "I wanted to talk to you about my Aunt Edna. She's been acting strangely, and I'm worried about her memory."

Dr. Hartman leaned back in his chair, folding his hands in his lap. "I understand your concern. What specific changes have you noticed?"

"She seems to have forgotten some recent events, and her mood swings have been quite sudden. Yesterday, she didn't even remember a significant argument she had with another resident," Agatha explained, watching his reaction closely.

Dr. Hartman nodded slowly, his expression carefully neutral. "Memory issues can be quite common in elderly patients, Ms. Royale. There could be various reasons for the changes you've noticed."

Agatha leaned forward, concern etched on her face. "But she was perfectly fine just a few days ago before she moved here. Could something about the move be causing this?"

Dr. Hartman adjusted his glasses, his eyes not quite meeting hers. "It's difficult to say without a thorough examination. Changes in environment can sometimes affect a person's behavior."

"Is there a way to check what's causing these changes?" Agatha pressed.

"There are various assessments we can perform," Dr. Hartman began, just as the door opened and Nurse Amanda entered the room. She walked over to Dr. Hartman and whispered something in his ear. His demeanor suddenly changed.

Dr. Hartman cleared his throat and straightened up, his expression becoming more guarded. "I'm afraid I can't discuss your aunt's health issues without her explicit consent, Ms. Royale. It's a matter of patient confidentiality."

Agatha sensed that something was off. "I understand,

but as her closest relative, I'm really worried. Can't you at least give me some general advice?"

Dr. Hartman shook his head, standing up to signal the end of the conversation. "I'm sorry, Ms. Royale, but I must adhere to the privacy regulations. I assure you, we are monitoring her closely and will inform you of any significant changes."

Agatha rose from her chair, feeling a mix of disappointment and suspicion. "Thank you, Dr. Hartman. I appreciate your time."

As she left his office, Agatha couldn't shake the feeling that Dr. Hartman was hiding something. Nurse Amanda's sudden appearance and his abrupt dismissal only heightened her concern. "I guess I'm headed to the park at 7 p.m. tonight," she muttered to herself, determined to get some answers about Aunt Edna's health.

5

TILDA MORRISON

The bookstore was comfortably busy that morning. Sunlight poured through the windows, warming the polished wooden floors and illuminating the rows of mystery novels. Mike lounged by the 'Staff Picks' display, a red bandana tied around his neck, attracting more customer attention than any sign ever had.

Agatha was restocking the Agatha Christie shelf when Mr. Wilkes shuffled up, holding a hardback copy of *The Body in the Library*.

"Is this the one where the vicar's daughter is the killer?" he asked.

Agatha smiled. "Nice try, but no spoilers allowed. You'll have to read it."

He chuckled. "I keep hoping one of these days you'll slip up."

Lorraine breezed in from the back, holding a cup of cinnamon tea. "Agatha, darling, we sold out of the last two copies of your aunt's favorite mystery. We might need to order more."

Emma poked her head out from the café corner. "Also, someone just asked if Mike could sign a paw-print on their book receipt."

Agatha laughed. "Did you let him?"

"Of course. I dipped his paw in non-toxic ink. He's practically co-author now."

The bell above the door jingled again as a group of teens wandered in. Agatha watched them scatter toward the graphic novels and paperbacks. For a moment, she let the calm of the store settle her nerves — just enough to carry her through the mysterious meeting at the lake.

～

"Are you really going to the park to meet this person?" Emma asked, her eyebrows knitting together in concern. "This is insane. You have no idea who called you."

Agatha nodded, a determined look in her eyes. "I am. I mean... I hope we are." She smiled, locking eyes with Emma.

Emma sighed, shaking her head. "Of course we are. That's what friends are for, right?" She laughed lightly, though worry still edged her voice.

Agatha's smile widened. "I was wondering if it would be better for you to observe the encounter from a distance. That way, if you notice anything strange or suspicious, you can intervene or call for help." She paused, considering her next words carefully. "After all, the person did insist that I come alone."

Emma pursed her lips, thinking it over. "Sure, but I thought we agreed on no more stakeouts after the episode at the boulangerie."

"Just this one time!" Agatha pleaded, a hopeful smile on her face.

Emma shook her head and finally smiled back. "Alright, I'll be at your house around 6:30."

Agatha bit her lip, then leaned in closer to Emma. "You know, I can't help but worry about Aunt Edna," she confided, her voice low. "Ever since she moved to Green Acres, she's been as forgetful as a goldfish. It's not like her at all." She shook her head, a wry smile playing on her lips. "And don't get me started on Dr. Hartman and Nurse Amanda. Those two are acting fishier than the harbor on market day. I can't help but wonder what's really going on in that place."

Emma's eyes sparkled with excitement. "Oh, Agatha, this is just like in those mystery novels we love! Count me in!"

"I knew you'd be up for a little sleuthing," Agatha grinned. Then, lowering her voice dramatically, she added, "Maybe we should arrive separately. You know, to throw off any potential shadowy figures."

Emma stifled a giggle. "Ooh, very cloak-and-dagger! I love it. I'll be the mysterious lady on the park bench, nose deep in a book."

Agatha couldn't help but chuckle. "Perfect! Just don't get so engrossed that you forget to keep an eye out for me."

"As if I could miss my partner in crime-solving," Emma winked. "Just be careful, okay? And remember, I'll be your backup if any nefarious characters appear."

"Got it," Agatha nodded, feeling a mix of nervousness and excitement. "See you at the park, Agent Emma."

~

Agatha sat on the bench, her fingers nervously fidgeting with the strap of her purse as she waited for the mysterious caller to arrive. The voice on the phone had been robotic, making it impossible to discern whether it belonged to a man or a woman. As she scanned the area, her eyes fell upon a slender figure approaching, dressed in a gray sweater with a hoody concealing their face.

The figure took a seat next to Agatha, and a soft voice emerged from beneath the hoody. "Agatha?" the figure asked, a hint of uncertainty in their tone.

Agatha turned to face the stranger, her heart racing with anticipation. "Yes, are you the person who called me?" she inquired, trying to keep her voice steady.

The figure nodded, glancing around cautiously before pulling the hoody back to reveal a young woman's face. "Yes, I called you because I have concerns about your aunt and Beatrice." She paused, her eyes darting around once more before continuing. "My name is Tilda... Tilda Morrison."

Agatha studied Tilda's face, a flicker of recognition sparking in her mind. "Wait... I think I saw you at Green Acres yesterday. Didn't I?" she asked, her brow furrowed in concentration.

Tilda looked around again, her body language tense and guarded. "Yes, I work there. Well, kind of... I work for Beatrice," she admitted, her voice barely above a whisper.

Agatha's eyes widened in surprise. "That makes sense, and why did you want to meet?" she asked, leaning in closer to Tilda, her curiosity piqued.

Tilda took a deep breath before beginning her story. "Well, you see... I used to work for Beatrice for years as her assistant, and I moved here when she did to be closer to her," she explained, her fingers twisting nervously in her lap.

Agatha's eyebrows shot up in surprise. "You were Beatrice's assistant?" she asked, leaning in. "That's news to me. Can you tell me more about it?" she encouraged, her curiosity piqued by this unexpected revelation.

Tilda nodded, a wry smile tugging at the corners of her mouth. "Yes, I was, but when she moved to this godforsaken town, she let me go." She made air quotes with her fingers. "Well, she then rehired me part-time with the condition that I agreed to move here with her. To make ends meet, I also took a job at Green Acres as a general assistant. You'd be surprised how much you learn about a place when you're responsible for a bit of everything."

Agatha listened attentively, her eyes locked on Tilda's face, absorbing every word.

Tilda leaned in, her voice dropping to a whisper. "I called you because something fishy is going on. You see, Beatrice and Edna have always been frenemies - you know, friends with a dash of rivalry. When your Aunt Edna started raving about this quaint, mysterious town, Beatrice couldn't resist the allure."

She paused, making air quotes. "They claimed they wanted 'something different' in their lives. But here's the kicker - they really moved here because of Harold."

Agatha leaned forward, her eyes narrowing as she processed this new piece of information. "Harold? What's his involvement with Bristol Lake?" she asked, her voice tinged with a mix of curiosity and apprehension.

Tilda shifted in her seat; her hands clasped tightly in her lap. She took a deep breath before continuing, "Apparently, when Harold was young and romantically involved with Edna, they visited your father in Bristol Lake. Harold fell in love with the charm and allure of the small town, with its quaint shops, friendly residents, and picturesque surroundings."

Agatha nodded, understanding the appeal of her hometown. "Bristol Lake does have a certain magic to it," she acknowledged.

"Yes, and that's not all," Tilda continued. "When you reconnected with Edna, she told Harold all about everything you shared with her. The mysteries you've solved, the festivals the town holds, and how Bristol Lake has gained fame as a 'mystery town.' It seems that your stories and descriptions of the town's unique character really captured Harold's imagination."

Agatha's eyes widened as she realized the impact her words had on Harold. "I had no idea my stories would inspire him to move here," she said, a mix of surprise and curiosity in her voice.

Tilda smiled softly. "Harold was drawn to the idea of starting a new adventure in his life, surrounded by the charm and intrigue of Bristol Lake. He wanted to be a part of the community, to experience the festivals and maybe even witness a real-life mystery unfolding."

Agatha chuckled, shaking her head. "Well, he certainly picked the right place for mysteries and adventures."

Tilda nodded, her expression turning thoughtful. "It's true. But what's interesting is that both Edna and Beatrice decided to move here shortly after Harold did. Neither of them admitted it, but it seems they both had an interest in him."

Agatha nodded; her brow furrowed in thought. "This certainly adds context to their argument yesterday. It seems Harold is at the center of their conflict."

Tilda sighed, shaking her head. "That fight was something else, wasn't it? I've never seen them so openly hostile before. It's like all their old rivalries and resentments just bubbled over."

Agatha leaned in, lowering her voice. "What I don't understand is why they're all acting so strangely now. There's more to this than just an old love triangle, isn't there?"

Tilda leaned in, her voice dropping to a whisper. "There's more to it, Agatha. Their odd behavior started after Dr. Hartman began treating them. It's like they became different people overnight."

Agatha's eyebrows knitted together. "Dr. Hartman? The physician at Green Acres? What kind of treatment is he providing?"

Tilda shrugged, frustration evident in her gesture. "That's just it - I don't know. But ever since they started seeing him, Beatrice and your aunt have been acting... well, not like themselves. It's unsettling."

Agatha nodded slowly, her mind racing. "So we have an old rivalry, a shared interest in Harold, and now this mysterious treatment. There's a connection here somewhere, but I can't quite put my finger on it."

Tilda leaned in closer to Agatha, her voice dropping to a barely audible whisper. "Agatha, I need you to promise me something," she said urgently, her eyes darting around to ensure no one was within earshot. "Please, don't tell anyone that I told you any of this. If Beatrice or Dr. Hartman found out, I don't know what they might do."

Agatha squeezed Tilda's hand reassuringly. "Your secret is safe with me, I promise."

Tilda's shoulders relaxed visibly. "Thank you. I knew I could trust you," she said with a grateful smile. "Just be careful, okay? Something's not right here, and I don't want you getting caught up in it."

Agatha nodded, her jaw set with determination. "I'll be careful, Tilda. And I promise, I will get to the bottom of what's going on here," she said, her voice filled with a quiet strength.

After Tilda left, Emma waited for a while to make sure she was gone before joining Agatha on the bench. Agatha, her face etched with concern, turned to Emma and recounted everything Tilda had told her, her voice barely above a whisper.

Emma listened intently, her brow furrowed in concentration. "That's interesting, Agatha, but what could they possibly be doing to your aunt and Beatrice that would cause them to argue and, worse... cause your aunt to lose her memory?" she asked, her voice tinged with a mix of curiosity and apprehension.

Agatha shook her head, her eyes distant as she pondered the question. "I'm really not sure. I'll have to spend more time at Green Acres and do some investigation," she said, her voice filled with determination.

Emma tilted her head, a thoughtful expression on her face. "Hmmm, don't you think it's time to contact Detective Dawson?" she suggested, her eyes searching Agatha's face for a reaction.

Agatha hesitated for a moment before responding, "Not yet. I need something concrete to tell him."

~

Later that afternoon, the three women found themselves at Dotty's Diner, Bristol Lake's favorite spot for a cup of too-strong coffee and the town's best cherry pie.

Lorraine slid into the booth with theatrical flair. "After that mess, I need pie and answers. But mostly pie."

Emma set her purse down and grabbed a menu. "You order the pie every time. Why even look?"

"To keep the illusion alive," Lorraine said, lifting her chin.

Agatha sipped her coffee and watched a pair of older ladies at the counter whispering and glancing over at them. One of them—the ever-nosy Mrs. Cartwright—leaned toward the waitress and said a bit too loudly, "That's the one from the book club at Green Acres. The wannabe writer."

Agatha sighed, setting down her cup. "News travels faster than Mike chasing a squirrel."

Just then, their waitress, Trina, appeared with a pad in hand and a conspiratorial grin. "So... what'll it be, ladies? And do I get to hear the juicy details about the nursing home drama?"

"No drama," Agatha said. "Just book club politics."

"Oh sure," Trina replied, scribbling. "That's what they all say. Three slices of cherry, right?"

"You know us too well," Lorraine said, then leaned over to Agatha. "Do you think Edna's memory lapse was real, or just convenient?"

Agatha hesitated. "I'm not sure. That's what's bothering me."

Mike gave a soft woof under the table, earning a few smiles from nearby diners. Trina returned with their plates and bent to scratch his head. "You be good, mystery pup."

As they dug into their slices, the warmth of the diner, the buzz of conversation, and the normalcy of dessert wrapped around them like a comfort blanket. Agatha felt a little steadier—but only a little.

There were too many questions still unanswered.

~

The next morning, Agatha picked up a box of pastries from Eliza's Bakery before heading to Green Acres. As she approached the assisted living facility with Mike trotting beside her, a sense of unease settled in her stomach. The cheerful exterior of well-manicured lawns and blooming flower beds seemed at odds with her growing suspicions about what was really going on inside.

Taking a deep breath, Agatha pushed open the heavy glass doors and stepped into the lobby. The familiar scent of disinfectant and faint echoes of residents' chatter greeted her. She nodded a quick hello to Lindsey at the reception desk before making her way down the hallway towards the dining room, the box of pastries clutched tightly in her hands.

As Agatha entered the dining room, Mildred's voice rang out above the usual breakfast chatter.

"Has anyone seen Edna?" Mildred called, her tone more curious than concerned. "She's usually the first one here, snagging all the good muffins."

Agatha couldn't help but smile at Mildred's typical dramatic flair. She watched as the spirited woman made her way to Mrs. Johnson's table.

"How about you, dear? Seen our early bird?" Mildred asked, leaning in conspiratorially.

Mrs. Johnson shook her head, looking a bit bewildered. "Not since she beat me at gin rummy last night," she replied with a chuckle.

Mildred then turned to Beatrice, who was stirring her tea with more vigor than necessary. "Beatrice? Any Edna sightings?"

"Haven't seen her," Beatrice muttered, not looking up. "And I'm not exactly holding my breath for a reunion."

Agatha raised an eyebrow at Beatrice's grumpy response. Before she could ponder it further, Nurse Amanda breezed into the room, looking like she'd rather be anywhere else.

"Alright, Mildred," Amanda sighed, plastering on a smile that didn't quite reach her eyes. "How about you enjoy your breakfast, and I'll go check on our missing resident? Can't have her missing out on the daily crossword competition, can we?"

Amanda's shoes squeaked softly on the linoleum floor as she walked out. Mr. Collins approached Agatha, his weathered face etched with lines of concern. His gray eyes held a seriousness that commanded attention. He leaned in close, his voice low and gruff, almost conspiratorial.

"Ms. Royale, I need to tell you something. Your aunt, Edna, didn't sleep in her room last night. Please remind her about the facility's rules and why she needs to stay in her designated room overnight. We can't allow residents to wander unsupervised."

Mr. Collins' words made Agatha pause. His serious expression was at odds with the cheerful breakfast chatter around them. Agatha felt a flutter of concern in her chest as she noticed the slight furrow in his brow.

"Where did she sleep?" she asked, her voice gentle yet insistent, her eyes widening with surprise and a growing sense of unease.

Mr. Collins shrugged his shoulders, a look of confusion and helplessness etched across his weathered face. "I don't know, to be honest," he muttered, his voice barely audible, as if he were afraid to admit his own uncertainty. "Maybe you should ask her." His words trailed off, leaving a heavy silence in their wake.

Just as Agatha opened her mouth to press further, a sudden commotion shattered the tense atmosphere. Nurse Amanda burst into the dining room, her face ashen and her eyes wild with panic. "Mr. Collins, please hurry!" she cried out, her voice sharp and piercing, cutting through the murmurs of the gathered residents. "It's Edna!"

6

THE GOLD KNITTING NEEDLES

Mr. Collins and Nurse Amanda rushed down the hallway towards Aunt Edna's room, their haste palpable in the air. Agatha followed behind, with Mike trotting alongside her. The little dog seemed to sense the tension, his ears perked up and his eyes alert.

As they navigated the hallway, a buzz of activity among the residents caught Agatha's attention. Whispers and concerned glances followed them, heightening her unease. Some residents peeked out from their rooms, curiosity and worry etched on their faces as they watched the unusual commotion.

Mike's tail wagged as they approached Aunt Edna's room. Agatha frowned at the open door - her aunt always kept it firmly shut. Mr. Collins and Nurse Amanda exchanged worried glances before the administrator gently pushed the door wider.

"That's odd," Agatha murmured, peering around them into the room. The space was neat as a pin, bed unrumpled. The air felt still, as if no one had been there for hours.

Agatha turned to Mildred, who hovered in the doorway. "Any sign of her this morning?"

Mildred's brow furrowed. "Not a peep. First time in ages she's missed her morning crossword and coffee."

They asked around, but blank looks and shaken heads greeted them at every turn. As they passed the common room, Mildred suddenly grabbed Agatha's arm.

"Wait a minute," she said, eyes widening. "Harold's not in his usual spot either. He should be holding court with his war stories by now."

Agatha felt a little jolt in her chest. "Harold's room - we should check there!"

They hurried down the hallway, the smell of lemon cleaner sharp in their noses. At Harold's door, Agatha hesitated, her hand on the handle. It was ajar, just like Edna's had been.

"Ready?" she asked Mildred, who nodded grimly.

Agatha took a deep breath and pushed the door open. The sight that greeted them made her gasp.

Harold lay motionless on his bed, looking far too still. Agatha's heart raced as she stepped closer, hoping to see some sign of life.

"Oh dear," Mildred whispered, her voice shaky. "Should we call for help?"

Before Agatha could answer, she noticed something by the side of the bed. She moved closer, her eyes widening in shock.

There, on the floor, was Aunt Edna, looking as still as Harold. In her hand glinted something gold - one of her prized knitting needles. Agatha's stomach dropped as she noticed the needle wasn't its usual shiny self.

"Mildred," Agatha said, her voice surprisingly steady, "go get Nurse Amanda. Quickly, please."

As Mildred hurried off, Agatha knelt beside her aunt, her mind whirling. What on earth had happened here?

Agatha's eyes widened as she took in the scene before her. Harold lay motionless on the bed, and there, nestled against his chest like a macabre brooch, was the second gold needle from Aunt Edna's prized knitting set.

"Oh, good grief," Agatha muttered, her hand flying to her mouth. Her stomach did a somersault as she realized the gravity of the situation. Those needles, once the pride and joy of Aunt Edna's craft corner, now seemed to have taken on a sinister new role.

Agatha's gaze dropped to the floor, where Aunt Edna lay crumpled beside the bed. Her mind whirled with questions. What in the world had transpired between Aunt Edna and Harold? Had there been a heated argument over purls and knits gone horribly awry?

"Aunt Edna?" Agatha called out softly, kneeling beside her aunt's still form. She gave Edna's shoulder a gentle shake. "Aunt Edna, can you hear me? What happened here?"

Aunt Edna stirred slightly, mumbling something that sounded suspiciously like a knitting pattern. Agatha let out a sigh of relief at the sign of life, but her eyes couldn't help but dart to the blood-stained needle still clutched in her aunt's hand like a tiny, golden sword.

"Well," Agatha said to herself, trying to inject some levity into the dire situation, "I suppose this gives a whole new meaning to 'killer craft projects.' "She shook her head, knowing that unraveling this mystery would be far more complicated than any sweater Aunt Edna had ever knitted.

Just then, Lorraine, who had arrived to volunteer, burst into the room. Her jaw dropped as she absorbed the shocking tableau. "Mon Dieu!" she exclaimed, her French accent thickening with each word. "Agatha, darling, we need to get the police here before you wake her up! What if she opens her eyes and decides to kill us all?"

"I don't think she's going to hurt anyone, Lorraine," Agatha reassured her friend, though her voice wavered. "We need to find out what happened here. Can you go and call for help while I stay with Aunt Edna?"

Lorraine hesitated for a moment, her gaze darting between Agatha and the unconscious Edna. "Are you sure, mon ami? Will you be okay to be left alone with a potential murderer?"

Agatha shook her head, a small chuckle escaping her lips despite the seriousness of the situation. "Aunt Edna is not a murderer, Lorraine. I'll be fine. Please, just go and get help."

Lorraine nodded, her eyes still wide with shock. "Oui, of course. I'll fetch help faster than you can say 'croissant'!" With that, she turned and hurried out of the room, her heels clicking rapidly on the polished floor.

Agatha turned her attention back to Aunt Edna, gently shaking her shoulder once more. "Aunt Edna, please wake up," she pleaded, her voice soft but insistent. "We need to know what happened here."

Slowly, Aunt Edna's eyes fluttered open, confusion and fear clouding her gaze as she took in her surroundings. "Agatha?" she whispered, her voice hoarse and weak. "What... what's going on? Where am I?"

7

THE CRIME SCENE

few residents who'd gone to breakfast early and were back in their rooms emerged into the hall-way, drawn by the commotion. Their curious whispers created a soft buzz of speculation. "Oh my, what's all the fuss about?" Mrs. Johnson asked, her curlers still in place as she peeked out her door.

"I heard it's something to do with Harold's room," Mr. Patel replied, adjusting his robe. "Quite the to-do, isn't it?"

Agatha's mind was spinning faster than Aunt Edna's knitting needles on a good day. She wanted to believe her aunt wasn't involved in this, but the scene before her was like something out of one of her mystery novels - except this was all too real.

Detective Dawson and Sheriff Salinger entered the room, their faces as serious as judges at a pie-baking contest.

"Well now, what do we have here?" Detective Dawson asked, his gaze bouncing between Harold on the bed and Aunt Edna on the floor.

Agatha took a deep breath, trying to keep her voice

steady. "I found Aunt Edna unconscious next to the bed. She woke up confused and upset. She says she found Harold like this and didn't know what to do."

Sheriff Salinger's eyebrows knitted together as he looked at Edna. "Ma'am, can you explain the blood on your hands?"

Edna's voice was as soft as a kitten's purr. "I... I panicked when I saw him. I touched the needles without thinking."

The room grew quieter than the library on a Sunday morning. Agatha's heart ached to defend her aunt, but a tiny seed of doubt had taken root. What in the world had happened here?

Nurse Amanda bustled in with Mr. Collins, her eyes widening like saucers. "Hold your horses," she said, her voice cutting through the tension like a hot knife through butter. "Edna, aren't those the needles from your knitting competition? The ones you won against Beatrice?"

Nurse Amanda's gaze fixed on the needles, recognition dawning on her face. She remembered the pride in Edna's voice when she had recounted her victory over her rival, Beatrice. The needles had been a symbol of Edna's triumph, and now, they seemed to be at the center of a new mystery.

As if drawn by an invisible force, everyone's gaze shifted to the needle clutched in Edna's trembling hands. The color drained from her face, leaving her complexion as pale as the stark white walls of the room. "Yes," she hissed, her voice barely above a whisper. "These are the needles I won. I always keep them with me, like a talisman of my victory."

Nurse Amanda crossed her arms, her posture radiating disapproval. She fixed Edna with a stern look, her eyes narrowing as she spoke. "So, let me get this straight. You had a fight with Beatrice last night because of Harold, and now we find you standing over his body, holding the very needles you won when your beat Beatrice in a knitting competition. It doesn't look good, Edna. Not good at all."

Detective Dawson's eyes narrowed to mere slits, his suspicion palpable in the air. "Is this true?" he demanded, his voice low and gruff. "Did you have a fight with Beatrice?"

Edna nodded, her reluctance evident in the slow, hesitant movement of her head. "I... I can't recall if we did," she admitted, her voice trembling. Each word seemed to catch in her throat, as if the very act of speaking was a struggle. "But I swear, I would never hurt anyone. Never." Her eyes, wide and pleading, locked onto Agatha's, desperate for her niece to believe her. "I found him like this. I swear it on my life."

Nurse Amanda sighed, her expression a mix of concern and skepticism. She crossed her arms, her gaze shifting between Edna and the lifeless body of Harold. "There were some issues between her and Beatrice, especially concerning their feelings for Harold," she revealed, her voice low and conspiratorial. "Edna was very emotional about it, and it caused a lot of tension with Beatrice. It seemed like some kind of lover's quarrel, a rivalry that had been simmering beneath the surface for quite some time."

Agatha's heart sank at Nurse Amanda's words, a sickening feeling settling in the pit of her stomach. She couldn't believe what she was hearing, couldn't fathom the idea that her aunt might be capable of such a terrible act.

Nurse Amanda's next words hit Agatha like a punch to the gut. "Maybe she did it out of jealousy," the nurse suggested, her tone a mixture of pity and accusation. "It wouldn't be the first time that love has driven someone to do the unthinkable."

Agatha shook her head vehemently, refusing to accept the implication of Nurse Amanda's words. "No," she said firmly, her voice rising with each syllable. "My aunt is not a murderer. There has to be another explanation, something we're missing."

Detective Dawson nodded, his expression serious as he absorbed the information provided by Nurse Amanda. "Thank you, Nurse Amanda. Every bit of information helps," he said, his voice steady and professional. "Even the smallest detail could be crucial in piecing together what happened here."

Nurse Amanda, sensing an opportunity to further involve herself in the investigation, seized the moment. She stepped closer to the detective, her eyes wide with curiosity. "So, Detective," she began, her voice tinged with a hint of eagerness, "can you tell when this happened? Do you have any idea of the timeline?"

Detective Dawson exchanged a glance with Sheriff Salinger, a silent communication passing between them. He turned back to Nurse Amanda, his expression guarded. "Not yet," he replied, his words measured and cautious. "But from the looks of things, it was probably sometime overnight." He glanced down at the notes in his hand, the pages filled with scribbled observations and theories. "Forensics will tell us more later, once they've had a chance to analyze the scene and gather evidence."

Nurse Amanda's face twisted into a smirk, her eyes glinting with a mixture of satisfaction and accusation. She pointed a finger at Aunt Edna, who was still kneeling on the floor beside Harold's body, her face pale and stricken. "Guess who wasn't in her room all night?" Nurse Amanda asked, her voice dripping with sarcasm. "Her." She frowned, her gaze boring into Aunt Edna with an intensity that made Agatha's skin crawl.

Agatha felt a surge of anger and protectiveness rise within her at Nurse Amanda's words. She stepped forward, placing herself between her aunt and the accusing stares of the others in the room. "That doesn't prove anything," she said firmly, her voice steady despite the pounding of her heart. "Just because Aunt Edna wasn't in her room doesn't mean she had anything to do with this."

But even as she spoke the words, Agatha could feel the weight of suspicion settling over the room like a suffocating blanket. She looked around at the faces of the detective, the sheriff, and the nurse, and saw the same doubt and uncertainty reflected in their eyes.

Agatha felt another layer of confusion settle in, like a thick fog obscuring her path. The detective's words echoed in her mind: *Overnight? That means the window for someone else to have been involved is wider than I thought.* She knew she needed to piece together Beatrice's last hours, to uncover any clues that might help clear Edna's name.

With a critical eye, Agatha surveyed the scene before her. The room was eerily undisturbed, as if frozen in time. *Very interesting,* she thought, her brow furrowed in concentration. *Nobody around saw or heard anything unusual.* She paced around the room, her footsteps muffled by the plush carpet. Every object seemed to be in its perfect place, untouched by the violence that had occurred.

"Isn't it curious," Agatha pondered aloud, her voice cutting through the heavy silence, "that someone could stab another person with gold knitting needles, and yet there are no signs of a struggle?" She paused, her gaze shifting towards Detective Dawson and Sheriff Salinger, seeking their reaction.

Detective Dawson turned to her, his expression a mix of acknowledgment and caution. "That's a keen observation, Agatha, but we're still in the process of collecting evidence."

Sheriff Salinger, his voice firm and authoritative, interjected, "Miss Royale, I must insist that you leave the investigation to the police this time. Will you?" He motioned towards the door, his eyes brooking no argument.

Agatha's shoulders tensed, her hands balling into fists at her sides. "She's my aunt, Sheriff, and I'm not leaving her alone," she declared, her chin lifting in defiance. Her voice, though soft, carried a steely determination that filled the room.

"Fair enough," Sheriff Salinger conceded, his tone softening slightly.

Mr. Collins, the assisted living facility director, who had been silent until now, stepped forward. His voice boomed through the room, his words laced with urgency. "You need to move quickly, as we don't want a murderer living among our residents."

Detective Dawson nodded, carefully taking the needle from Edna's trembling hands. "We'll have these checked by forensics," he said, his voice steady and professional. "In the meantime, we need to gather as much information as possible from all of you."

Edna, her voice shaking like a leaf in the wind, added, "I... I panicked when I saw him like that. I pulled the needle out of Harold. I didn't mean to disturb anything; I just didn't know what to do." Her words were tinged with desperation, a plea for understanding.

Detective Dawson's expression softened, a glimmer of empathy in his eyes. "We'll take that into account, Edna," he reassured her. "But we need to follow all procedures to ensure we get to the truth."

He continued, his gaze sweeping across the room, "We'll need to review any security footage and interview everyone who might have seen or heard something unusual last night." Turning to Agatha, he added, "Agatha, can you stay close in case we need more information from you or Edna?"

"Of course," Agatha agreed without hesitation, determination hardening in her chest like a shield. She was going to get to the bottom of this, no matter what it took.

As they were talking, Beatrice appeared in the doorway, her face pale and eyes wide with shock. She let out a heart-wrenching cry, "Harold! No!" Tears streamed down her face as she rushed forward, her gaze fixed on Harold's lifeless body. "How could this happen?" Her grief quickly turned to anger as she spotted Aunt Edna. "You! You did this! I knew you were jealous of us, but I never thought you could do something like this!" she accused, her voice trembling with rage and sorrow.

Beatrice looked at Detective Dawson, her voice wavering. "Last night she said if she couldn't have him, nobody else would, Detective."

Detective Dawson exchanged a glance with Sheriff Salinger. The Sheriff called Dawson to the side, his voice low and urgent. Agatha strained to hear their whispered conversation, catching only fragments. "But she's an elderly and obviously confused lady," Dawson said, his voice louder than intended, a hint of disbelief coloring his words.

Sheriff Salinger shrugged his shoulders, his expression unreadable. The two men paced back towards the others, their footsteps heavy with the weight of their decision.

"I'm sorry to do this," Dawson said reluctantly, his eyes filled with regret, "but we'll have to take Aunt Edna to the station for interrogation."

8

THE ARREST

Agatha watched with a heavy heart as Aunt Edna was escorted into the police car. She hurried to her own car, determined not to let her aunt go through this alone. As she followed the police car to the station, her mind raced. She needed to call Emma. Once she arrived at the station and parked, she quickly dialed Emma's number. The phone rang twice before Emma picked up.

"Agatha, what's wrong?" Emma's voice was filled with concern.

"It's Aunt Edna. They took her to the station for interrogation," Agatha said, her voice trembling. "I need you here, Emma. I need your help."

"I'm on my way," Emma replied without hesitation. "Hang tight. I'll be there as soon as I can."

Agatha waited anxiously in the station lobby, her thoughts a whirlwind of worry and determination. Not long after, Emma rushed in, her face set with concern.

"Agatha, what happened? You look like you've seen a ghost."

Agatha sank into a chair, her hands trembling. "Emma, it's... it's awful. Harold's dead."

"What?" Emma gasped, sitting down next to her friend. "How?"

Agatha took a shaky breath. "They found him in his room this morning. And Emma... Aunt Edna was there too, unconscious on the floor next to him."

Emma's hand flew to her mouth. "Oh no. Is she okay?"

"Physically, yes, but..." Agatha's voice trailed off. She swallowed hard before continuing. "He was killed with gold-plated knitting needles. Aunt Edna's needles."

"You can't be serious," Emma whispered, her eyes wide with disbelief.

Agatha nodded grimly. "It gets worse. When they found her, she was holding them. The police... they think she's involved."

Emma shook her head vehemently. "That's ridiculous! Edna would never hurt anyone, let alone Harold. There has to be some mistake."

"I know," Agatha said, her eyes narrowing with determination. "That's why we need to figure out what really happened. And fast."

Emma gave Agatha's hand a reassuring squeeze. "So, where do we start?"

"Green Acres," Agatha replied, not missing a beat. "That's where we begin."

~

The bell above Eliza's Bakery door jingled as Agatha stepped inside. After the sterile chill of the county jail, the warmth and sweet aromas enveloped her like an old friend's embrace.

"Morning, Agatha," Eliza called from behind the counter, her hands dusted with flour. "The usual?"

"Please," Agatha nodded, sinking into a small table by the window. This had been her Wednesday ritual before Aunt Edna's arrest: thirty minutes of solitude with a cup of tea and one of Eliza's scones. Strange how quickly life could upend itself, transforming simple pleasures into stolen moments between crises.

Eliza set a steaming mug and a fresh scone on the table, then hesitated. "How's your aunt doing?" she asked quietly.

"Holding up," Agatha replied, surprised by the sudden tightness in her throat. "She's tougher than she looks."

"Must run in the family," Eliza said with a gentle smile before returning to her baking.

Agatha wrapped her hands around the warm mug, watching rain begin to speckle the window. She hadn't realized how exhausted she was until this moment of stillness. The morning newspaper lay folded on the table, but she couldn't bring herself to check the headlines. Instead, she closed her eyes and let the bakery's soothing symphony wash over her: the clatter of plates, quiet conversations, the oven timer's soft ding, and rain tapping against glass. For just a few minutes, she let the mystery wait.

The bell jingled again, pulling Agatha from her brief respite. Emma hurried in, shaking raindrops from her umbrella. Her cheeks were flushed from the brisk morning air, and her ever-present book bag hung heavily from one shoulder.

"Sorry I'm late," Emma said, sliding into the chair opposite Agatha. "Library meeting ran over. Sarah had opinions about the new catalog system." She rolled her eyes good-naturedly, then leaned forward, lowering her voice. "Any news on Aunt Edna?"

"Nothing new… she's trying to stay positive, but I can tell the walls are closing in on her." Agatha replied with a sigh.

Emma reached across the table and gave Agatha's hand a quick squeeze. "We'll figure this out. Between your stubbornness and my research skills, we make a pretty good detective team."

Eliza appeared with a to-go cup. "Your usual tea, Emma. Figured you might need it for the road."

"You're a lifesaver," Emma said, accepting the cup gratefully. She glanced at her watch. "We should probably head to Green Acres soon.

Agatha nodded, gathering her things.

〜

"As Agatha and Emma pulled into the parking lot of Green Acres Assisted Living, a quiet determination settled between them.

Agatha drummed her fingers on the steering wheel, her mind already racing with plans. "First things first," she said, turning to Emma. "We need to chat with the residents and staff. Someone must have seen or heard something."

Emma nodded, "good thinking. And we should try to get a look at that security footage, too."

They made their way into the building, Mike trotting obediently beside them. As they approached the front desk, Nurse Amanda and Mr. Collins came into view. Immediately, Mike's fur bristled and he let out a low growl.

Agatha and Emma exchanged a knowing glance. "Mike's at it again," Agatha murmured. "You know what that means."

Emma nodded grimly. "His instincts haven't failed us yet. We'd better keep a close eye on those two."

As they continued down the hallway, they spotted Lindsey, the receptionist, hunched over a stack of papers at her desk. Agatha's lips curved into a small smile. If anyone knew the comings and goings of Green Acres, it would be Lindsey.

"Ready to do some sleuthing?" Agatha whispered to Emma.

Emma grinned back. "Lead the way, detective."

"Lindsey," Agatha called softly, not wanting to startle her.

Lindsey looked up, her eyes widened in recognition when she saw them. "Oh, Agatha, Emma. How can I help you?" she asked, her voice friendly but carrying an undercurrent of nervousness.

Agatha took a deep breath, preparing herself. "Lindsey, I need to ask a big favor," she began, choosing her words carefully. "I know you're probably not supposed to, but we really need to see the security footage from last night."

Lindsey's eyes flickered with uncertainty. "I don't know, Agatha. That's usually something only the police can access. I could get into a lot of trouble for that."

Agatha nodded, understanding the gravity of her request. "I understand, Lindsey, and I wouldn't ask if it weren't important. But my aunt is in serious trouble. The police think she might be involved in Harold's death, and I need to prove her innocence."

Lindsey bit her lip, glancing around as if seeking reassurance. "I really shouldn't..."

Emma stepped forward, her voice gentle yet persuasive. "Lindsey, you know Edna. You know she couldn't have done this. We just need a chance to see if there's anything on the footage that might help us understand what happened."

Lindsey hesitated, her fingers tapping nervously on the desk.

Agatha could see the conflict in her eyes, the desire to help warring with the fear of breaking the rules. She pushed a little further. "Lindsey, please," Agatha said softly. "This is my aunt we're talking about. I just need a few minutes to see if there's anything that can help clear her name. I promise we won't cause any trouble."

Lindsey exhaled slowly, her shoulders slumping in resignation. "Okay," she said quietly. "But you have to be quick, and if anyone asks, you didn't get this from me."

Agatha's heart leaped with gratitude. "Thank you, Lindsey. You have no idea how much this means to us."

Lindsey nodded, leading them to the security office. She unlocked the door and quickly accessed the footage from the previous night. As the video played on the screen, Agatha and Emma leaned in, their eyes scanning every frame for any clue that might lead them to the truth.

The footage showed a quiet hallway at Green Acres, dimly lit by the night lights. At around midnight, they saw Aunt Edna entering Harold's room. Agatha's breath caught in her throat.

"Look, there she is," Emma whispered, her eyes wide.

They watched as Aunt Edna disappeared into Harold's room. Minutes ticked by, and then suddenly, the footage went blank.

"What happened?" Agatha asked, her voice tinged with frustration. "Why did it cut out?"

Lindsey frowned, tapping a few keys on the keyboard. "I don't know. There must have been a glitch or something."

The footage remained blank for several hours. Then, at

around 3 a.m., the video resumed. They saw Aunt Edna leaving Harold's room and heading towards the main entrance. She looked disoriented, as if she had just woken up from a deep sleep. She made her way to the couch near the entrance, laid down for about an hour, and then got up and went back to Harold's room.

Agatha's mind raced as she tried to piece together the fragmented images. "So, she went into Harold's room around midnight, and then... nothing until 3 a.m.," she murmured. "Why would she leave Harold's room, go sleep on the couch, and then go back to his room?"

Emma shook her head, her brow furrowed. "I don't know, but something's not right. We need to find out what happened during those missing hours."

Lindsey glanced at the door nervously. "I wish I could help more, but this is all we have. You should be careful, Agatha. If anyone finds out I showed you this..."

"As they stepped back into the reception area, they noticed Mike sprawled out on some pillows by the desk, fast asleep. His soft, rhythmic breathing was the only sound in the room. Agatha exchanged a glance with Emma before turning to Lindsey."

"Could you keep an eye on him for a while?" Agatha asked softly, not wanting to disturb the peaceful moment.

Lindsey nodded, her expression warm and understanding. "Of course, Agatha. I'll make sure he's comfortable."

Agatha placed a reassuring hand on Lindsey's arm. "Thank you, Lindsey. You've already helped more than you know." Lindsey's gentle smile was all the confirmation Agatha needed.

As they left the security office, they noticed Detective Dawson talking to Nurse Amanda in the hallway. They approached quietly, not wanting to interrupt but eager to hear any new information.

Detective Dawson's voice was calm but probing. "Nurse Amanda, when was the last time you saw or spoke to Harold?"

Nurse Amanda looked flustered but answered quickly. "It was last evening, around dinner time. He seemed a bit upset, but I didn't think much of it. He often got that way."

Dawson nodded, taking notes. "Did he mention anything specific that was bothering him?"

Amanda hesitated for a moment, then spoke. "Well, actually, he did mention a fight in between Edna and Beatrice. They were arguing about him again. He said Edna threatened him and Beatrice, she said he would regret ever getting involved with Beatrice."

Agatha's eyes widened in shock, and she felt Emma's hand tighten on her arm. That didn't sound like Aunt Edna at all. She knew Nurse Amanda was twisting the facts.

"Are you sure about that?" Dawson asked, his pen hovering over his notepad.

"Absolutely," Amanda replied, her voice firm. "I think Edna was really upset about the whole situation. It wouldn't surprise me if she did something in a fit of rage."

Agatha exchanged a glance with Emma. They both knew there was more to uncover. As they continued down the hallway, Agatha's mind buzzed with questions. So many pieces were still missing. "We need to find out what happened during those missing hours," Agatha said. "And why Aunt Edna went to sleep on the couch."

Emma nodded, her eyes sparkling with determination. "I think we should ask Mr. Collins about who was on shift that night. If someone was working, they might have seen or heard something that could help us fill in the blanks." She leaned forward, her voice lowering conspiratorially. "It's worth a shot, don't you think?"

Agatha's brows furrowed as she pondered the suggestion. She shifted uncomfortably in her seat, her hands fidgeting with the hem of her sweater. "Mr. Collins?" she asked, her tone hesitant. "I don't know, Emma. He's always in such a foul mood. The thought of approaching him makes me uneasy." She paused, chewing on her bottom lip as she searched for an alternative. Suddenly, her face lit up with an idea. "What about Mildred? She lives here, so she's bound to have some insider knowledge. Maybe she can point us in the right direction."

Emma's eyes widened, and she snapped her fingers in excitement. "That's brilliant, Agatha! Mildred could be a valuable source of information. We should definitely go and find her." She stood up, ready to embark on their new lead.

As they made their way towards the door, Agatha halted, a realization dawning on her. "Wait a minute," she said, turning to face Emma. "Isn't Lorraine volunteering here today? You know how she is—always in the loop, always privy to the latest gossip. Maybe we should ask her first. If anyone has the scoop on what's been going on around here, it's Lorraine."

Emma's face broke into a wide grin, and she clapped her hands together. "Oh my gosh, you're so right! I can't believe we didn't think of that sooner. Lorraine is like a walking, talking news bulletin. If there's anything to know, she'll know it." She linked her arm through Agatha's, her excitement palpable. "Let's go find her. With Lorraine on our side, we'll get to the bottom of this mystery in no time!"

Agatha smiled, feeding off Emma's enthusiasm. Together, they set off in search of Lorraine, their footsteps muffled by the worn carpeting that lined the hallways of

Green Acres. The assisted living facility had an air of faded elegance, with outdated artwork adorning the walls and the occasional flickering light fixture. The scent of industrial cleaner mingled with the faint aroma of yesterday's dinner, creating an unusual blend that seemed to permeate the air.

As they walked, Agatha couldn't help but notice the cracks in the paint and the scuffs on the baseboards. For a place that charged its residents a substantial fee, the level of upkeep seemed surprisingly lacking. Emma, too, had a puzzled expression on her face as she took in the surroundings.

"I thought Green Acres was supposed to be a top-notch facility," Emma remarked, her voice tinged with disappointment. "But looking at the state of things, it's hard to believe they're charging so much."

Agatha nodded in agreement. "It does seem a bit run-down, doesn't it? I wonder if the management is aware of these issues. Surely, they should be addressing them, given the prices they charge."

As they continued their search for Lorraine, they couldn't shake the feeling that something wasn't quite right at Green Acres. The assisted living facility had always been praised for its exceptional care and amenities, but the reality seemed to fall short of the glossy brochures and glowing testimonials.

Emma and Agatha exchanged a knowing look as laughter echoed from a room down the hall, followed by a familiar voice exclaiming, "Sacrebleu! These stains are putting up a fight, but they're no match for me!"

"The laundry room," they said in unison, quickening their pace."

As they approached the laundry room, the hum of aging washing machines and the rattle of dryers filled the air.

Pushing open the door, they were greeted by the sight of Lorraine, elbow-deep in a pile of linens, her face alight with determination.

"Ah, mes amies!" Lorraine exclaimed, her eyes twinkling despite the less-than-glamorous surroundings. "What brings you to this humble abode of cleanliness? Don't tell me you've come to admire my laundry skills."

Emma chuckled, shaking her head. "As impressive as your laundry prowess may be, Lorraine, we're actually here on a different mission. We were hoping you might be able to help us with something."

Lorraine raised an eyebrow, intrigued. "Ooh, a mission? Do tell! You know I'm always ready for a little excitement. Laundry can wait, but gossip waits for no one!"

Agatha stepped forward, lowering her voice. "We were wondering if you knew anything about the night of the incident with Harold. Did you happen to see or hear anything unusual?"

Lorraine's expression turned thoughtful. "Hmm, let me think. I was here that night, helping Mrs. Thompson with a stubborn wine stain on her favorite blouse. As for unusual things..." She paused dramatically, a mischievous glint in her eye. "Well, I did overhear a rather heated conversation between two residents. Something about a missing piece of jewelry, if I recall correctly."

Emma leaned in closer, her curiosity piqued. "A missing piece of jewelry? That sounds intriguing. Do you know who was involved in the conversation?"

Lorraine tapped her chin, feigning concentration. "Let's see... I believe it was Mrs. Sinclair and Mr. Delaney. They were quite agitated, exchanging accusations in hushed tones. But you didn't hear it from me, of course. I'm just an innocent bystander, n'est-ce pas?"

Agatha and Emma exchanged a glance, their initial excitement fading. While they appreciated Lorraine's willingness to share, they realized this information didn't seem directly related to their investigation.

"Thank you, Lorraine," Agatha said with a small smile. "We appreciate you telling us, but I don't think Mrs. Sinclair or Mr. Delaney are involved in what we're looking into."

Emma nodded in agreement. "Still, it's good to know what was happening that night. Every little bit helps paint the picture."

As they thanked Lorraine and prepared to leave, Lorraine called out after them, "Bonne chance, my darlings! And remember, if you need a partner in crime-solving, I'm just a laundry room away!"

Agatha sighed heavily, her shoulders slumping under the weight of discouragement. She leaned against the wall, feeling the rough texture of the outdated wallpaper beneath her fingers. The hallway seemed to stretch endlessly before her, mirroring the daunting task that lay ahead.

"I don't know how to proceed, Emma," Agatha confessed, her voice barely above a whisper. "We don't have a single clue to go on. It's like we're grasping at straws in the dark."

Emma opened her mouth to respond, but before she could speak, movement at the end of the hallway caught their attention. Tilda Morrison was approaching, her face etched with concern.

Tilda approached, a worried smile on her face. "Agatha, I heard about Harold. It's awful they're suspecting your Aunt Edna."

Agatha sighed. "Thanks, Tilda. We're doing our best to clear her name."

"Remember our chat about Edna's memory?" Tilda

lowered her voice. "I've been noticing some odd things about the medications here."

Emma perked up. "Oh? What kind of things?"

Tilda glanced around before continuing, "Well, usually the nurse would drop off Beatrice's medications and leave. I'd help Beatrice take them later. But a few days before Harold's death, things changed."

Agatha leaned in, her brow furrowed. "Changed how?"

"The nurse started giving Beatrice her medications directly," Tilda explained. "She wouldn't let me see them or help anymore. It was... odd."

"That does sound strange," Agatha mused. "Did you notice this happening with other residents too?"

Tilda nodded. "Yes, it wasn't just Beatrice. I saw similar changes with a few others."

Emma and Agatha exchanged worried glances. "We should definitely look into this," Agatha said, her detective instincts kicking in. "The timing is certainly suspicious."

"Especially given what happened to Harols," Emma added softly.

Tilda nodded. "There's more. Did you know Beatrice was paying over $10,000 a month to live here?"

Emma's eyes widened. "For this place? But it's so... worn down."

"Exactly," Tilda said. "They're even turning apartments into tiny rooms with kitchenettes in the bathrooms. It's like a fancy sardine can in here."

Agatha couldn't help but chuckle at the image. "Tilda, you're a wealth of information. We need to investigate this further."

Emma grinned. "Mystery solving time! Should we wear trench coats and carry magnifying glasses?"

Agatha playfully swatted her friend's arm. "Let's start

with the medication logs and financial records. No costumes required... yet."

As Tilda left, Agatha turned to Emma. "Ready to play detective?"

Emma struck a dramatic pose. "Elementary, my dear Agatha. Let's crack this case wide open!"

With a shared laugh, they set off down the hallway, ready to uncover the secrets of Green Acres – one clue at a time.

9

A BITTER PILL TO SWALLOW

The next morning, Agatha stood behind the counter, her fingers absently tracing the worn edges of a well-loved paperback. The comforting scent of books, creating a cozy atmosphere that enveloped the store like a warm hug.

Mike lay curled up in his bed behind the counter, his soft snores punctuating the gentle hum of the air conditioning. The store was ready for the day, the shelves meticulously organized, and the displays artfully arranged, awaiting the arrival of eager readers and curious browsers.

The tinkling of the bell above the door announced Eliza's arrival, drawing Agatha's attention away from the book in her hands. She looked up to see her friend bustling in, a tray of delectable pastries balanced in her hands. The aroma of freshly baked scones, croissants, and cinnamon rolls filled the air, adding to the cozy warmth that had settled over the bookstore.

"Morning, Agatha!" Eliza called out cheerfully as she maneuvered through the narrow aisles. She balanced a large box with practiced ease, the scent of fresh pastries wafting ahead of her. "Today's delivery is here! And guess what? I snuck in a few extra almond croissants – your favorite!"

Agatha managed a weak smile, her heart warmed by Eliza's cheerfulness even as the weight of her aunt's situation pressed down on her. The possibility that Aunt Edna might be involved in a crime felt like a heavy stone in her chest. "Thanks, Eliza," she said, her voice a mix of gratitude and worry. "Your pastries always know how to brighten even the darkest days."

Eliza set the tray down on the counter, her brow furrowing as she took in Agatha's somber expression. "Is everything alright?" she asked, concern etched into the lines of her face. "You look like you've seen a ghost."

Agatha sighed, the sound heavy and laden with worry. She gestured to the chair beside her, inviting Eliza to sit. "It's Aunt Edna," she began, her voice barely above a whisper. "Everything is such a mess."

Eliza leaned forward, concern etching her features. "What happened, Agatha?"

Agatha's fingers twisted together in her lap as she recounted the morning's events. "I found Harold's body this morning," she said, her voice catching. "Aunt Edna was there too, collapsed on the floor beside him. One of her gold knitting needles was... was in Harold's chest." She paused, swallowing hard. "The other needle was in Aunt Edna's hand."

Eliza's eyes widened, her hand flying to her mouth in shock. "Oh, Agatha," she breathed. "That's terrible! But surely they don't really believe Edna could do something like that?"

Agatha shook her head, uncertainty clouding her eyes. "I don't know what to think anymore, Eliza. Aunt Edna said she just found him like that and panicked. But the detectives... they took her to the police station for interrogation. They think she might be involved in Harold's death."

Eliza reached out, her hand warm and comforting as she placed it over Agatha's. "Agatha, listen to me," she said, her voice firm but gentle. "I may not have known Aunt Edna for long, but I know you. And if she's anything like her niece, she's not capable of murder." Eliza's eyes softened with understanding. "Remember when I was a suspect? There's always more to the story than meets the eye. We'll figure this out, just like we did before."

Agatha nodded, drawing strength from her friend's unwavering support. Her voice grew more determined as she spoke, "You're right, Eliza. That's why I need to find out what really happened. I can't just sit back while Aunt Edna's in trouble. I need to clear her name."

Eliza squeezed Agatha's hand, her eyes shining with determination. "And you will, Agatha. You're the smartest, most tenacious person I know. If anyone can get to the bottom of this, it's you."

Agatha managed a small smile, the knot in her chest loosening ever so slightly. "Thank you, Eliza. I don't know what I'd do without you."

Eliza grinned, the corners of her eyes crinkling with warmth. "Well, for starters, you'd be without your daily dose of almond croissants and scones," she teased, trying to lighten the mood.

Agatha chuckled, the sound a welcome respite from the heaviness that had settled over her. "You're right. I definitely can't solve a murder on an empty stomach."

Eliza stood up, brushing off her apron. "Speaking of which, I should get back to the bakery. The lunch rush will be starting soon, and I need to make sure everything is ready." She paused, her expression turning serious once more. "But Agatha, if there's anything I can do to help, anything at all, just say the word. I'm here for you, always."

Agatha stood up, pulling Eliza into a tight hug. "Thank you, Eliza," she whispered, her voice thick with emotion. "Knowing that you're in my corner means the world to me."

Eliza hugged her back, the embrace a silent promise of support and friendship. When they pulled apart, she gave Agatha a final, reassuring smile before heading towards the door. "Keep me updated, okay?" she called over her shoulder. "And don't forget to eat those croissants. They're no good to anyone if they go stale."

Agatha laughed, the sound a small victory against the darkness that threatened to engulf her. "I won't," she promised, waving as Eliza disappeared through the door.

As the bell chimed once more, signaling Eliza's departure, Agatha turned back to her computer,

In the quiet of the empty store, Agatha settled behind the counter, her laptop open before her. The screen glowed, casting a pale light across her features as she lost herself in thought. The medication issues Tilda had brought to light weighed heavily on her mind, a tangled web of questions and suspicions that demanded unraveling.

Agatha's fingers hovered over the keyboard, her eyes distant as she pondered her next move. A flicker of inspiration crossed her face, and she began to type, her fingers flying across the keys with purpose. Dr. Hartman's name appeared in the search bar, and Agatha held her breath as the results loaded, her heart pounding in her chest.

As Agatha stared at the screen, her heart raced, and a sense of dread settled in the pit of her stomach. The information about Dr. Hartman was damning, painting a picture of a man with a troubled past and questionable practices.

"Oh my god," Agatha muttered under her breath, her

eyes scanning the articles and reports. "How could they let someone like this work with vulnerable people?"

She leaned back in her chair, rubbing her temples as her mind whirled with the implications. The bookstore's cozy atmosphere seemed to fade away, replaced by a growing sense of unease. The once-comforting scent of books and pastries now felt stifling, as if the weight of the discovery was pressing down on her.

"I have to tell Emma," she thought, reaching for her phone with trembling fingers. "She needs to know what we're up against."

As if on cue, the bell above the door chimed, and Emma breezed in, her red curls bouncing with each step. "Morning, Agatha!" she called out cheerfully, her voice cutting through the heavy silence. "I brought you a latte from that new coffee shop down the street. Thought you might need a pick-me-up."

Agatha looked up, her expression grave. The sight of her friend's smiling face was a stark contrast to the turmoil brewing within her. "Emma, you need to see this," she said, her voice strained and urgent, gesturing to the screen.

Emma's brows furrowed as she set the coffee down on the counter and leaned in to read over Agatha's shoulder. Her eyes widened as she took in the information, her cheerful demeanor quickly replaced by a growing sense of horror. "Dr. Hartman? Isn't that the doctor at Green Acres?" she asked, her voice barely above a whisper.

Agatha nodded, her jaw clenched tight. "Look at his history, Emma. Malpractice suits, disciplinary actions, and complaints from patients and their families. It's a wonder he's still practicing medicine."

Emma's eyes widened as she scrolled through the information, her fingers gripping the edge of the desk so tightly that her knuckles turned white. "This is bad, Agatha. Really bad. We need to find out if he's been mistreating the residents at Green Acres."

"I know," Agatha agreed, her mind racing. "And I can't help but wonder if there's a connection between his questionable practices and the strange things happening at the facility."

Emma pulled up a chair, her expression determined. She leaned forward, her elbows resting on her knees as she met Agatha's gaze. "We need a plan, Agatha. We can't let him get away with this."

Agatha nodded, her resolve strengthening. She took a deep breath, the weight of responsibility settling on her shoulders. "You're right. We need to gather more evidence, talk to the residents and their families, and see if we can find a pattern."

As they huddled together, brainstorming their next moves, Agatha's mind wandered to Aunt Edna. She could almost see her aunt's familiar face, complete with those laugh lines that crinkled when she smiled. "Don't worry, Aunt Edna," Agatha thought, feeling a rush of affection. "We'll sort this out faster than you can say 'whodunit'."

Emma's voice snapped her back to reality. "Hey, Earth to Agatha! I think we should chat with Tilda again. She might have the scoop on any weird medication side effects the residents have been experiencing."

Agatha nodded, her fingers already dancing across her phone screen. "Great idea, Emma. I'll text her now. Oh, and we should definitely peek at those financial records too. I have a hunch there's a connection between those sky-high fees and the not-so-five-star care."

Agatha's fingers flew across her phone screen, composing a message to Tilda.

Agatha: Hey Tilda, quick question – do you have access to the medication room at Green Acres?

Agatha paused, looking discouraged as she stared at her phone screen. Suddenly, her phone vibrated, announcing she'd received a text message. Agatha sighed as she read the message.

Tilda: I don't have access to the medication room or medical records.

She took a deep breath, then her phone vibrated again with another message from Tilda:

Agatha: Hey Tilda, quick question -- do you have access to the medication room at Green Acres?

Agatha paused, looking discouraged as she stared at her phone screen. Suddenly, her phone vibrated, announcing she'd received a text message. Agatha sighed as she read the message.

Tilda: I don't have access to the medication room or medical records.

She took a deep breath, then her phone vibrated again with another message from Tilda:

Tilda: Only Nurse Amanda and the Nurse's Assistant, Dotty Pendleton have access. I know Dotty well and will talk to her. I didn't ask her myself because I didn't want to risk my job if anyone found out. I'll see if she's willing to meet with you about this instead.

"Yes!" Agatha exclaimed, smiling at Emma. "Tilda will talk to Dotty, the nurse assistant. As soon as I hear back from her, I'm paying Dotty a visit."

"Yes!" Agatha exclaimed, smiling at Emma. "Tilda will talk to Dotty, the nurse assistant. As soon as I hear back from her, I'm paying Dotty a visit."

10

PAJAMAS AND PREDICAMENTS

Tilda burst into Agatha's bookstore, her face alight with excitement. "Agatha, darling, I have fantastic news!" she exclaimed, her voice carrying through the quiet shop, disrupting the peaceful atmosphere.

Agatha looked up from the stack of books she was sorting, a bemused smile on her face. "What's got you so excited, Tilda?"

Tilda leaned against the counter, her eyes sparkling with mischief. "Dotty agreed to talk to you, but it has to be in secret. She's a bit paranoid, you know. Probably thinks the government is listening in on her conversations." She handed Agatha a piece of paper with an address scribbled on it in barely legible handwriting. "She lives in a trailer park in North Petunia Heights. Quite the charming place, if you don't mind the occasional stray cat and the smell of burnt rubber."

Celeste, who had been arranging a display of true crime books nearby, couldn't help but overhear. She pushed her glasses up her nose and leaned in, lowering her voice conspiratorially. "North Petunia Heights? Oh, Agatha, I've heard it can be dangerous there, especially after dark. It's like something out of these books," she said, tapping a nearby mystery novel. "Maybe it's not the best place for a solo adventure. Want some company? I've got pepper spray and a mean right hook!" She grinned, only half-joking.

Agatha raised an eyebrow, a hint of worry creeping into her expression. "Dangerous? In what way?"

Celeste shrugged, her eyes wide with a mix of excitement and apprehension. "Let's just say it's a neighborhood with a reputation. Lots of shady characters and suspicious activities. But don't worry, I know exactly where it is. I can give you directions."

Agatha nodded, grateful for Celeste's knowledge. She turned to Emma, who had been browsing the shelves nearby. "Emma, I could use your company on this little adventure. What do you say?"

Emma looked up, a grin spreading across her face. "Count me in, Agatha. I'm always up for a good mystery."

Armed with Celeste's directions and Emma by her side, Agatha set off towards North Petunia Heights. As they navigated the winding roads, the surroundings gradually shifted from the quaint charm of their town to a more dilapidated and run-down area. Trailer homes with peeling paint and overgrown yards lined the streets, and the air was filled with the distant barking of dogs and the occasional shout from unseen residents.

Dotty's trailer was easy to spot, thanks to the bright pink flamingos adorning her small front yard and the sign that read "Beware of Dogs (and Cats)" hanging crookedly on her door. Agatha and Emma exchanged a glance before Agatha reached out and knocked tentatively.

The door creaked open, and Dotty's face appeared, her

eyes narrowed with suspicion. "Who are you?" she asked, her voice raspy from years of smoking.

Agatha smiled warmly. "I'm Agatha, and this is my friend Emma. Tilda mentioned you might be able to help us with some information about Green Acres."

Dotty's eyebrows shot up in recognition. "Oh, right. Tilda said you'd be coming." She glanced over her shoulder nervously before ushering them inside. The trailer was cramped and cluttered, with cats and dogs of various sizes lounging on every available surface. The air was thick with the scent of pet food and cigarette smoke.

"Have a seat," Dotty said, gesturing to a lumpy couch that had seen better days. "But watch out for Mr. Whiskers. He's got a mean scratch if you sit on his tail."

As Agatha and Emma gingerly took their seats, trying to avoid the sleeping animals, a small terrier jumped up onto the couch beside Agatha, yapping excitedly.

"Well, hello there," Agatha said softly, gently pushing the dog away. "I'm sorry, but I can't play right now. We're here to talk to your mom."

The terrier tilted its head, seeming to understand, and hopped down from the couch, scampering off to join a group of other small dogs in the corner.

Dotty settled into a worn armchair across from them. She took a long drag from her cigarette before speaking, her voice low and conspiratorial.

"After I spoke to Tilda, I got curious and took a peek at the medication records," she began, her eyes darting around the room. "That's when I noticed something strange. There's this translucent green pill that Dr. Hartman insists on giving to Edna himself, but it's not documented anywhere in the official records."

Agatha leaned forward, her interest piqued. "Do you have any idea what pill that is, Dotty?"

Before Dotty could respond, a large tabby cat leaped onto her lap, demanding attention. Dotty absently stroked its fur as she continued, "I don't know for sure, but it's mighty suspicious, if you ask me. I've been working at Green Acres for a long time, and I've never seen anything like it."

Agatha opened her mouth to ask another question, but a small terrier leaped onto the couch beside her, yapping excitedly. She gently nudged the dog away, her brow furrowing as she tried to keep her mind on the conversation.

Dotty sighed, taking another drag from her cigarette. "Look, I shouldn't even be telling you this. If anyone finds out I talked, I could lose my job. And I need this job, you understand? I've got rent to pay and all these mouths to feed." She gestured to the various pets scattered around the trailer.

Emma spoke up, her voice reassuring. "We understand, Dotty. Your secret is safe with us. We won't tell a soul."

Dotty nodded, looking relieved. "Good. Because if anyone asks, I'll deny ever speaking to you. I can't risk it."

Agatha and Emma thanked Dotty for the information and carefully made their way out of the trailer, navigating around the sleeping animals. As they stepped outside, they breathed in the fresh air, glad to be away from the overwhelming scent of cigarettes and pet odor.

They climbed into Agatha's car, both lost in thought as they processed what Dotty had revealed. A loud knock on the driver's window startled them out of their reverie. They turned to see a young man with long blond hair and multiple gold crucifixes of different lengths hanging around his neck grinning at them, his face pressed close to the glass.

Agatha hesitated for a moment before rolling down the

92

window, her guard up. "Can I help you?" she asked, her voice cautious.

The man leaned in, his smile widening. "Hey, ladies! Can you give me a ride? I need to go see my father."

Emma shot Agatha a look that clearly said, "no way," her eyebrows raised in warning.

Agatha took a deep breath, trying to sound apologetic. "Sorry, but we're in a hurry. We can't give you a ride."

The man's hand shot through the window, making both women flinch. "Wait, wait! Before you go, I gotta ask – have you guys met Jesus?"

Agatha and Emma exchanged a confused glance, unsure of how to respond. After a brief pause, they stammered out a unified "no."

The man's grin turned eerie, his eyes gleaming with a strange intensity. "Well, then you better get ready, because you're gonna meet him today!"

Fear gripped Agatha's heart, and she quickly slammed the car into reverse, stomping on the gas pedal. The tires screeched as the car lurched backward, leaving the man standing in the dust.

Agatha shifted into drive and sped forward, her hands trembling on the steering wheel. The man attempted to chase after the car, his gold crucifixes glinting in the sunlight, but they quickly left him behind.

As they put distance between themselves and North Petunia Heights, Agatha and Emma couldn't help but let out nervous laughter, the adrenaline still coursing through their veins.

"That was too close for comfort," Emma said, her voice shaky. "I thought he was going to force his way into the car."

Agatha nodded, her heart still racing. "Me too. But at

least we got away unscathed. And now we have a new piece of the puzzle to work with."

"Well, that was... interesting," Agatha said, breaking the silence.

Emma nodded, twirling a strand of her red hair. "Dotty certainly had a lot to say about Dr. Hartman. But can we trust her?"

"Good question," Agatha mused, stopping at a red light. "She seemed genuinely worried about the patients at Green Acres."

Agatha drummed her fingers on the steering wheel. "We'll have to verify her claims somehow. Without tipping off Dr. Hartman or getting Aunt Edna into more trouble."

As they approached One Deadly Chapter, both women fell silent, pondering their next move in unraveling the mystery surrounding Green Acres.

Shortly after arriving back at the bookstore, Lorraine burst in, her eyes sparkling with excitement and her voice filled with urgency. "Bonjour, Agatha!" she exclaimed, her usual poise giving way to the weight of her discovery. "I think I saw something significant today."

Agatha, who had been lost in thought, trying to piece together the clues they had gathered so far, looked up sharply at Lorraine's sudden entrance. "What did you see?" she inquired, her curiosity piqued by the intensity in Lorraine's voice.

Lorraine took a moment to compose herself, smoothing down her perfectly coiffed hair and adjusting her stylish blazer. "I was helping in the laundry room this morning, and as I was putting laundry in the washer, I grabbed a pair of pink silk pajamas and," she paused, building the suspense with a dramatic flair.

Agatha leaned forward, her eyes sparkling with curiosity. "And? What did you find, Lorraine?" she prompted gently, trying not to betray her eagerness.

Lorraine's expression grew serious, her voice dropping to a conspiratorial whisper. "The pajamas had some drops of blood by the hem."

Agatha's eyes widened in surprise, and she exchanged a quick glance with Emma, who had been listening intently nearby. "Blood on the pajamas? Whose were they?" Agatha asked, her mind already racing with the implications of this new information.

Lorraine's face lit up, her excitement rekindled. "That's the thing - I went to check the name label inside, but it was missing! Torn right out! But I'm certain those were Beatrice's pajamas. I've seen her wear them before."

Agatha's brow furrowed as she processed this revelation. "Beatrice's pajamas with blood on them? That could be significant. Do you still have them?"

Lorraine's expression turned sheepish. "Well, I wasn't thinking about it at the time, and I washed them," she admitted, her voice tinged with regret.

Agatha sighed, a hint of disappointment in her tone. "That's unfortunate. Having the actual pajamas would have been helpful for further analysis."

Emma, ever the voice of reason, interjected, "It might not be as significant as we think. The blood could be from something as simple as a nosebleed."

Agatha nodded, considering Emma's point. "You're right. We shouldn't jump to conclusions without more information."

Lorraine, sensing the shift in the conversation, added, "But it's still worth keeping in mind, isn't it? I mean, it's a bit unusual to find blood on pajamas, even if it is from a nosebleed."

Agatha agreed, "Definitely. It's another piece of the puzzle, even if we don't have the physical evidence anymore. We'll just have to keep digging and see how it fits into the bigger picture."

Emma tapped her chin, her green eyes brightening behind her tortoiseshell glasses. "You know, Lorraine might be onto something here. We should ask around, see if anyone else noticed those pajamas. Could be a lead."

Agatha smiled, grateful for her friends' support and insights. "Good thinking, Emma. We'll keep our ears open and see if anyone else mentions anything about Beatrice's pajamas or her behavior that night."

Agatha's eyes widened. "Wait a minute," she said, snapping her fingers. "I just remembered something about that morning."

Lorraine leaned in eagerly. "Ooh, do tell!"

"When I saw Beatrice in Harold's room, she was wearing blue pajamas," Agatha explained. "Cotton ones with little moons and clouds on them."

Emma's brow furrowed. "But what about the pink silk pajamas Lorraine found?"

"Exactement!" Lorraine exclaimed. "The plot thickens, non?"

Agatha tapped her chin thoughtfully. "We're getting ahead of ourselves here. We don't know what Beatrice wore to bed that night."

Emma bit her lip, hesitating before speaking. "Maybe... she went to bed with the pink pajamas and changed after she... well, got them dirty with blood."

A hush fell over the group for a moment before Lorraine broke it with a dramatic gasp. "Mon Dieu! What a twist!"

Agatha shook her head, trying to lighten the mood.

"Let's not jump to conclusions. We need more information before we can make sense of this pajama puzzle."

"A pajama puzzle," Emma grinned, albeit a bit weakly. "Now that's a mystery I never thought I'd be solving."

Lorraine chimed in, "But this is progress, you two! We have new avenues to explore, new questions to ask. Every little detail brings us closer to the truth."

Agatha's face abruptly drained of color. "Oh no," she whispered.

"What is it?" Emma and Lorraine asked in unison, leaning forward.

Agatha swallowed hard. "I just remembered who owns a pair of pink silk pajamas exactly like the ones Lorraine described."

Emma's eyes widened. "Who?"

Agatha's voice was barely audible. "Aunt Edna."

11

WHISPERS ON TAPE

The next morning, Agatha took a deep breath as she walked through the cold, sterile halls of the jail. The clanging of metal doors and the murmur of distant conversations echoed around her. She approached the visitation room, her heart heavy with worry. The guard nodded and opened the door for her.

Inside, Aunt Edna sat at a small table, looking frail and lost. When she saw Agatha, her face lit up with a mix of relief and anxiety.

"Agatha, thank you for coming," Aunt Edna said, her voice trembling. "I don't know what happened, but I promise you, I went to Harold's room to make apologize to him."

Agatha sat down across from her, taking her aunt's hands in hers. "Aunt Edna, do you remember anything from that night? Anything at all?"

Aunt Edna nodded slowly, her eyes clearer than they had been in weeks. "Yes, I remember more now that I'm away from Green Acres. Before I went to Harold's room, I saw Beatrice in the kitchen. She was wearing pink silk pajamas.

We argued, and I... I threatened her and Harold. But after that, everything's still a blur."

Agatha's eyes widened. "Pink silk pajamas? Are you sure?"

Aunt Edna nodded. "Yes, I recall that she was wearing pink silk pajamas. I remember it clearly now."

Agatha felt a spark of hope. "You've been remembering things better since you left Green Acres, haven't you?"

Aunt Edna nodded again. "Yes, I think those little pills Dr. Hartman was giving me at night were making me feel very loopy. I feel so much better since I stopped taking them."

Agatha's eyes narrowed. "What were those pills for?"

"I don't know," Aunt Edna admitted. "But he started giving them to me the first night I spent at Green Acres."

Agatha nodded, squeezing her aunt's hands. "I promise I'll do everything I can to find out what really happened."

Agatha stood up, gathering her things. The stark walls of the jail's visiting room seemed to close in around her. She hesitated, her hand on her purse strap, as a sudden thought struck her.

"Oh, Aunt Edna," she said, trying to sound casual, "I just remembered. Don't you have pink silk pajamas as well?"

Aunt Edna looked up, surprise flickering across her tired face. "Pink silk pajamas?" She furrowed her brow, thinking. "Oh, those. Well, I did have a pair."

Agatha held her breath, waiting.

"But after I saw that Beatrice had copied me and bought an identical pair, I couldn't stand it," Aunt Edna continued, a hint of her old spirit returning to her voice. "So I donated mine to that thrift shop on Main Street."

Relief washed over Agatha. She smiled, squeezing her aunt's hand. "That sounds just like you, Aunt Edna."

"Why do you ask, dear?" Aunt Edna tilted her head curiously.

"Oh, no reason," Agatha said quickly. "I just thought they might be more comfortable than what they give you here."

As the guard signaled that visiting time was over, Agatha hugged her aunt tightly. "I'll be back soon," she promised, her mind whirling.

Walking out of the jail, Agatha's steps quickened with each passing moment. Her aunt's words echoed in her head: Beatrice had owned pink silk pajamas. This new piece of information fit perfectly into the puzzle she'd been trying to solve.

She fumbled for her phone, nearly dropping it in her haste. "Emma," she said as soon as her friend picked up, "you'll never guess what I just learned. We need to talk. Meet me at the bookstore in fifteen minutes?"

As she climbed into Eleanor, her trusty Ford Falcon, Agatha couldn't help but feel a glimmer of hope. They were one step closer to unraveling this mystery and clearing Aunt Edna's name.

Agatha and Emma settled into their usual spot at the café corner of One Deadly Chapter Books and Brew. Emma noticed the worried crease between Agatha's brows as she absently stirred her coffee.

"Agatha, what's troubling you?" Emma asked gently.

Agatha sighed, her shoulders slumping. "It's not looking

good for Aunt Edna, Emma. I overheard her threaten Beatrice and Harold, and the murder weapon... it was one of those knitting needles from that old competition. I just don't know what to think anymore."

Emma leaned in, lowering her voice. "Did you ask Aunt Edna about those pink silk pajamas Lorraine mentioned?"

"I did," Agatha nodded. "She said she used to have a pair but got rid of them when she found out Beatrice had bought the same ones. You know how competitive they are."

Emma's brow furrowed. "So the bloodstained pajamas Lorraine saw could actually be Beatrice's?"

"Possibly," Agatha mused. "Unless someone else at Green Acres has a similar pair."

"How can we find that out?" Emma asked, tapping her fingers on the table thoughtfully.

Agatha straightened, a spark of determination in her eyes. "We might have to ask around at Green Acres. If it'll help Aunt Edna, I'm willing to do whatever it takes."

She finished her coffee and dabbed her mouth with a napkin. "Want to take a trip to Green Acres with me?"

Emma nodded, already gathering her things. "Absolutely. Let's go."

Mike uncurled from his cozy spot by Agatha's feet, tail wagging as he sensed an adventure brewing. The trio made their way out of the café, with Mike trotting happily beside them.

Just as they reached the door, Detective Dawson approached, his expression stern. Agatha and Emma exchanged a quick, worried glance before turning to face him.

"Agatha," Dawson said, trying to sound firm but coming

off more like a worried uncle, "I hope you're not planning to get involved in this investigation. It's a police matter, and you know how these things can get complicated."

Agatha put on her most innocent smile. "Oh, Detective Dawson, you know me. I'm just going about my day, running my bookstore. No investigating here."

As she spoke, she casually crossed her fingers behind her back, catching Emma's eye. Emma bit her lip to keep from grinning.

"Uh-huh," Dawson replied, clearly unconvinced. "Just... be careful, okay? And if you happen to hear anything interesting, you'll let me know, right?"

"Of course, Detective," Agatha said sweetly. "You'll be my first call."

As Dawson walked away, shaking his head, Agatha and Emma shared a mischievous smile. They both knew that while they'd try to stay out of trouble, the allure of a good mystery was just too strong to resist.

"Ready for our completely normal, not-at-all investigative trip to Green Acres?" Agatha asked, her eyes twinkling.

Emma nodded, barely containing her excitement. "Lead the way, Miss Royale."

With Mike trotting happily beside them, the amateur sleuths set off, their minds already buzzing with theories and questions.

As they stepped out of the bookstore, Agatha paused, her eyes lighting up with an idea. "I know... let's ask Lindsey to see the security tapes again. Maybe we can spot what Beatrice was wearing that evening."

Emma nodded enthusiastically. "Good thinking! Last time we only focused on the hallway by Harold's bedroom. We should check the entire place, including the community room."

Just as they were about to head off, Emma's phone buzzed. She glanced at the screen and her face fell. "Oh no, it's the library. Sarah called out sick and they're asking if I can fill in for her."

Agatha couldn't hide her disappointment, but she put on a brave smile. "Don't worry about it, Emma. Duty calls. I can handle this reconnaissance mission solo."

Emma looked torn. "Are you sure? I feel terrible leaving you in the lurch like this."

"Absolutely," Agatha assured her, giving her friend a gentle push. "Go save the library from certain doom. I'll fill you in on all the juicy details later."

With a grateful smile and a quick hug, Emma hurried off to work. Agatha watched her go, then turned to Mike with a conspiratorial wink.

"Looks like it's just you and me, partner. Ready to do some sleuthing?"

Mike's tail wagged in response, and together they set off towards Green Acres, Agatha's mind already whirring with possibilities.

～

Agatha strolled into Green Acres, Mike trotting faithfully by her side. They approached the reception desk where Lindsey was buried in a mountain of paperwork.

"Hi Lindsey!" Agatha called cheerily. "Drowning in admin work?"

Lindsey looked up, her face brightening at the sight of Agatha and Mike. "Agatha! You two are a welcome distraction. What brings you here today?"

Agatha leaned in, lowering her voice. "I was hoping to take another look at the security footage from the night of the... incident. I want to see if anyone else was lurking around Harold's room. We might have missed something the first time."

Lindsey's eyes widened as she scanned the reception area. "Again?" she whispered, her voice unsteady. "Agatha, I could lose my job if anyone discovers I'm showing you this footage. Mr. Collins has tightened security recently..."

Agatha placed a reassuring hand on Lindsey's arm. "I understand your concern, Lindsey. I promise, no one will know you helped us. This could be crucial in solving Harold's murder."

Lindsey bit her lip, clearly torn between her fear and her desire to help. After a moment's hesitation, she sighed. "Alright, but we have to be quick, and if anyone asks, you didn't get this from me. Deal?"

"Deal," Agatha nodded solemnly. "Thank you, Lindsey. You're doing the right thing."

With a nervous glance over her shoulder, Lindsey stood up. "Let's go check it out before I change my mind."

As they walked to the security office, Mike padding quietly beside them, Agatha felt a mix of hope and nervousness flutter in her stomach. This could be their chance to spot something they'd missed before. Lindsey opened the door with a flourish, but her face quickly fell.

"Oh no," Lindsey exclaimed. "I completely forgot. Detective Dawson came by and took the footage a couple of days ago. I'm so sorry, Agatha."

Agatha's shoulders slumped. "Well, there goes that idea. Back to the drawing board, I suppose."

"Oh, fiddlesticks!" Lindsey exclaimed, snapping her fingers. "I wish I could be more help. I feel about as useful as a chocolate teapot right now."

Agatha couldn't help but chuckle. "Don't worry, Lindsey. You've been a peach. I guess I'll just have to put on my thinking cap and get creative!"

Lindsey's eyes suddenly lit up. "Hold your horses! I just remembered something. You know Ms. Patel, our resident gadget guru? Well, Ms. Johnson told me she's got more hidden cameras than a spy movie. Maybe she's caught something useful on her little tech treasures!"

Agatha's eyes sparkled with a glimmer of hope. "Oh, Ms. Patel might have something? That would be wonderful!"

"It's worth a shot," Lindsey nodded, her enthusiasm infectious. "Shall we pay her a visit?"

Agatha felt a flutter of excitement in her chest. "Absolutely. This could be just the clue we need to help Aunt Edna."

They made their way to Ms. Patel's room, their footsteps quickening with anticipation. Lindsey gave a soft knock, and the door opened to reveal a petite woman with silver hair and bright, inquisitive eyes.

"Lindsey, what a lovely surprise!" Ms. Patel beamed. Her gaze shifted curiously to Agatha.

"Hello, Ms. Patel," Lindsey smiled warmly. "I hope we're not intruding. This is Agatha Royale, Edna Ashton's niece."

Ms. Patel's eyes lit up with recognition. "Ah, Edna's niece! I've heard so much about you. Please, do come in!" She ushered them into a room that looked like a cozy tech haven.

Agatha stepped forward, her voice gentle but earnest. "It's wonderful to meet you, Ms. Patel. We were hoping you might be able to help us with something about... well, about what happened to Harold."

Ms. Patel's expression softened. "Oh, that dreadful business. I might have something that could help." She shuffled over to her desk, filled with gadgets. "I always keep my little recorder close. You'd be amazed at what it picks up!"

Agatha watched with anticipation as Ms. Patel rummaged through a drawer filled with various gadgets. "Ah, here we are," she said, pulling out a small, sleek device. "I often leave this running in the hallway. You'd be surprised what you can hear through these old walls."

She pressed play, and a soft static filled the room. Agatha and Lindsey leaned in, straining to catch any familiar sounds. Soon, hushed voices became audible, seemingly coming from the corridor outside.

Agatha's eyes widened. "That sounds like Nurse Amanda," she whispered, her pulse quickening. "Can you make it any clearer, Ms. Patel?"

With a deft touch, Ms. Patel adjusted the volume. Amanda's terse tone cut through the background noise. "I told you to take care of it. We can't afford any loose ends."

Agatha and Lindsey exchanged startled glances. Agatha's mind whirled with possibilities. Who was Amanda speaking to? What did she mean by "loose ends"?

"The woman is definitely Nurse Amanda," Agatha mused, her brow furrowed in concentration. "But that man's voice... it's familiar, but I can't quite place it. Does either of you recognize it?"

Lindsey shook her head. "It's too distorted to say for sure. The audio quality isn't great."

"You're right," Agatha sighed. She turned to Ms. Patel with a hopeful expression. "Ms. Patel, would you mind if I borrowed this tape for a bit? I'd like to listen to it more closely, see if I can pick up on anything we missed. I promise I'll bring it back tomorrow."

Ms. Patel hesitated, clearly reluctant to let the recording

out of her possession. After a moment of internal debate, she relented. "Okay Agatha. But please, be careful with it. Bring it back first thing tomorrow."

As Agatha stepped out of Green Acres, clutching the precious tape, a thought made her pause mid-stride. "Oh, fiddlesticks!" she exclaimed, smacking her forehead lightly. "I haven't owned a cassette player since leg warmers were in fashion. How on earth am I going to listen to this?"

She tapped her chin thoughtfully, then snapped her fingers. "Wait a minute! If anyone in this town still has a working cassette player, it's got to be Lorraine. That woman never throws anything away!" A smile spread across her face as she fished out her phone. "Time to give our resident Francophile a call!"

Lorraine's cheerful voice chirped through the phone on the third ring. "Allô, Agatha! Don't tell me you've stumbled onto another mystery already?"

Agatha couldn't help but smile. "Hello, Lorraine. Am I that predictable? Actually, I have a bit of an unusual favor to ask. You wouldn't happen to have a cassette player tucked away somewhere, would you? I've got some old recordings that might hold a clue or two."

"Mon Dieu! A cassette player?" Lorraine exclaimed, a hint of amusement in her voice. "I haven't heard that request since... well, since 1985! But you're in luck, ma chérie. I'm sure I have one tucked away somewhere."

Agatha breathed a sigh of relief. "Oh, Lorraine, you're a gem. Mind if I pop over?"

"But of course!" Lorraine replied cheerfully. "We'll make an adventure of it. Who knows what other treasures we might uncover in the process?"

Half an hour later, Agatha was elbow-deep in a dusty box of Lorraine's old knick-knacks. "Voilà!" Lorraine crowed triumphantly, brandishing a clunky tape player. "I knew this little guy was hiding somewhere. Ah, the memories! I used to make the best mixtapes back in the day. I was the queen of cassettes!"

Agatha grinned as she took the recorder. "Merci beaucoup, Lorraine. Hopefully this helps me crack the case wide open."

"Bonne chance, Nancy Drew!" Lorraine called after her. "And don't forget to spill the tea later, chérie!"

That evening, Agatha settled into her plush armchair, Mike dozing at her feet. She grabbed the phone and dialed her best friend. "Emma? It's Agatha. You've got to get over here, pronto. I think there's a major break in the Green Acres case."

Minutes later, Emma burst through the door, her eyes alight with curiosity. They huddled around the tape recorder as the static voices filled the room. Emma frowned, trying to place the male voice. "I don't recognize him. Do you have any idea who it could be?"

"Not yet," Agatha said, her determination growing. "But I intend to find out."

The next morning, Agatha marched into Green Acres with Mike trotting happily beside her, ready to uncover the truth. She spotted Lindsey at the front desk and hurried over.

"Lindsey!" Agatha said in an excited whisper. "I listened to the tapes again, but I still can't identify the man. Any ideas?"

"Shhh, keep your voice down!" Lindsey warned, her eyes darting around the lobby. She subtly tilted her head towards the corner, where Nurse Amanda stood deep in conversation with a well-dressed man in his thirties.

Agatha followed her gaze, curiosity piqued. "Who is that?" she breathed.

Lindsey gave a barely perceptible nod, her voice low and urgent. "That's Devin Jensen, A pharmaceutical rep and Harold's nephew. I'm almost certain he's the mystery voice on the tape.

12

THE NEPHEW

Agatha's eyes narrowed as she observed Devin and Nurse Amanda from across the lobby. Their easy laughter and intimate body language seemed out of place, considering the circumstances. Devin's uncle Harold had passed away mere days ago, yet here he was, all smiles and flirtation.

She leaned closer to Lindsey, keeping her voice low. "That's Devin Jensen? Harold's nephew?"

Lindsey nodded, her expression uneasy. "Yes, that's him."

"Interesting," Agatha murmured. "He doesn't exactly look like a man in mourning, does he?"

As Devin whispered something in Amanda's ear, eliciting another burst of giggles, Agatha's mind raced. The recording she'd heard, Harold's sudden death, and now this oddly cheerful nephew – the pieces were starting to form a troubling picture.

"I think I'll go introduce myself," Agatha said, straightening her jacket.

Lindsey's eyes widened. "Agatha, wait—" She glanced

nervously around the lobby before continuing in a hushed tone. "If they find out I helped you gather this information, I could lose my job. I can't risk it."

"Don't worry," Agatha reassured her. "I'll be discreet. You won't be involved."

Lindsey bit her lip. "Just... be careful, okay?"

With a reassuring pat on Lindsey's arm, Agatha made her way across the lobby. As she approached, Devin and Amanda's laughter faded, their expressions shifting to polite curiosity.

"Hello there," Agatha said warmly. "I don't believe we've met. I'm Agatha Royale, Edna's niece."

Devin's brow creased, a hint of confusion crossing his face before recognition dawned. "Oh, right. Edna Ashton. I'm Devin Jensen." His handshake was firm, his smile stretched a bit too far. "Nice to meet you, Ms. Royale."

"I wanted to offer my condolences," Agatha continued. "Losing family is never easy."

Something flickered behind Devin's eyes, but his smile never wavered. "That's very kind of you. Uncle Harold will be missed."

Before Agatha could respond, Amanda cut in, her voice dripping with disdain. "You have some nerve. Your aunt Edna kills Harold, and now you're here offering condolences to his nephew? That's rich."

Devin's eyebrows shot up as he glanced rapidly between Agatha and Amanda

Agatha stood her ground, her voice calm but firm. "My aunt hasn't been convicted of anything, Nurse Amanda. And kindness costs nothing."

Turning back to Devin, she asked, "How long will you be staying in town?"

"Oh, just long enough to settle his affairs," Devin

replied smoothly, clearly eager to end the conversation. "Now, if you'll excuse us, Amanda and I have some business to discuss."

As the pair walked away, Agatha's suspicions only deepened. Devin Jensen was hiding something, and she was determined to find out what. She glanced back at Lindsey, who quickly averted her gaze.

Time to do some digging, Agatha thought, her resolve hardening. *There's more to this story, and I intend to uncover it – for Aunt Edna's sake.*

Agatha was making her way through the lobby of Green Acres when a stern voice stopped her in her tracks.

"Ms. Royale, a word please."

She turned to see Mr. Roger Collins, the facility manager, striding towards her with a tight-lipped expression. His normally well-groomed appearance seemed slightly disheveled, as if he'd been running his hands through his hair in frustration.

"Mr. Collins," Agatha greeted, trying to keep her tone neutral. "How can I help you?"

He gestured to a quiet corner of the lobby. "Let's speak privately, shall we?"

Once they were out of earshot of the residents and staff, Collins turned to face her, his eyes narrowed. "Ms. Royale, I'll get straight to the point. Your snooping around is becoming a problem. You're making Green Acres look bad, and I can't allow that to continue."

Agatha opened her mouth to protest, but Mr. Collins held up a hand to silence her.

"I understand you're concerned about your aunt, but let me remind you, we have legal protections in place. If you continue to harass our staff or disturb our residents with your amateur detective work, we could pursue legal action against you for defamation."

His words hung in the air for a moment before he continued, his voice lowering. "It's not enough that your aunt committed a crime here. Now you're dragging our reputation through the mud as well."

Agatha felt a flash of anger at the mention of her aunt. "My aunt is innocent, Mr. Collins. I'm merely trying to—"

"Trying to what?" he interrupted. "Play detective? Leave that to the professionals, Ms. Royale. For your own sake, and for the sake of your aunt, I strongly suggest you cease this disruptive behavior immediately."

With that, Roger Collins turned on his heel and walked away, leaving Agatha standing there, her mind racing. She knew she couldn't back down now, not when she was getting closer to the truth. But it was clear she needed to be more careful, more discreet in her investigation.

As she watched Mr. Collins disappear down the hallway, Agatha realized she needed a fresh approach—one that would allow her to continue her investigation without raising suspicions. She needed a cover, a reason to be at Green Acres regularly without arousing Collins' ire.

The confrontation with Mr. Collins left Agatha shaken, but more determined than ever. As the afternoon sun cast long shadows across the town, she retreated to the familiar confines of her own bookstore, One Deadly Chapter Books and Brew. The bell chimed softly as she entered, the scent of fresh coffee mingling with the aroma of ink and paper.

Agatha leaned against the weathered oak counter, its surface marked by countless coffee rings and the occasional imprint of book corners from customers eagerly flipping through their new purchases. Celeste was busy restocking shelves while Emma sat at a small table near the window, reading a book.

As she stood there, Agatha's mind wandered back to her encounter with Mr. Collins. *Why was he so defensive?* she wondered. *What does he have to hide? His reaction only makes me more certain that something's not right at Green Acres.*

"You look like you've had quite the day," Emma observed, setting aside her book.

Agatha sighed, recounting her run-in with the facility manager. "I just need to find a way to spend more time at Green Acres," she mused, her fingers tracing the grain of the wood absently. "And without giving Mr. Collins any more reasons to be suspicious," she added silently.

Emma nodded, her brow furrowed in concentration. "It's tricky. You can't exactly hang around all day without a reason—" Emma's expression brightened as an idea struck her. "Agatha, I've just had a thought," she said excitedly. "I remember hearing at the library that Green Acres is looking for volunteer librarians."

Agatha's eyebrows shot up in surprise. "Really? That could be perfect."

Emma nodded. "Yes, and if I offer to join you, it would make our presence there seem less suspicious. We could volunteer together."

Agatha's face lit up with a smile, the worry lines softening. "Emma, that's a brilliant idea. We'd have legitimate reasons to be at Green Acres regularly, access to different areas of the facility, and opportunities to observe Mr. Collins and the staff without arousing suspicion."

"I'll call them first thing tomorrow," Agatha declared, her mind already racing with possibilities.

Emma nodded enthusiastically, a spark of adventure in her eyes. "Count me in. It'll be like we're characters in one of your mystery novels!"

Celeste, who had been quietly listening while arranging books, spoke up. "Don't worry about the shop, Agatha. I can manage things here while you're out playing detective."

"That's great Celeste," She looked pensive. I think I'll have to spend quite a lot of time over there to get some clues."

Before she could elaborate further, the bell above the door chimed merrily, announcing Lorraine's arrival. The vivacious Francophile breezed in, her arms laden with shopping bags, her floral perfume wafting through the cozy bookstore. "Mon amis, ça va?" Lorraine trilled, her bright red lipstick accentuating her wide smile.

Agatha couldn't help but chuckle at her friend's exuberant entrance. "We're doing well, Lorraine. How about you? Anything new happening in town?" She raised an eyebrow, knowing Lorraine was always a fountain of local gossip.

Lorraine's eyes sparkled with mischief as she set her bags down with a dramatic flourish. "Well, besides a murder at Green Acres, you mean?" She winked exaggeratedly. "As it happens, I do have some intriguing news..."

Lorraine leaned in conspiratorially, her eyes twinkling with the joy of sharing a juicy piece of gossip. "Have you ladies heard about the new resident of that old Victorian on Maple Street? You know, the one that's been empty since forever?"

Agatha and Emma exchanged glances before shaking their heads in unison.

"Don't keep us in suspense, Lorraine," Agatha prompted, her curiosity piqued. "Have you met her?"

"Sadly, non," Lorraine sighed dramatically. "But I've uncovered something rather intriguing about our new neighbor." She paused, savoring the moment. "Her name, mes chéries, is Gemma Jameson."

Agatha's brow furrowed as recognition dawned. "Gemma Jameson? Wasn't that—"

"Harold's ex-wife?" Lorraine finished with a triumphant nod.

"Now that you mention it," Agatha mused, tapping her fingers on the counter, "I distinctly recall Aunt Edna telling Beatrice, 'If Harold truly loved you, he wouldn't have married Gemma.'" She shook her head, remembering her aunt's sharp tongue.

Emma, who had been quietly absorbing the information, finally spoke up. "But why on earth would she move back here of all places?"

Agatha's gaze drifted to the display window, where the late afternoon sun cast long shadows across the quaint Main Street. Her green eyes narrowed with determination. "I don't know," she said slowly, "but you can bet I'm going to find out."

13

THE NOTE

The next morning, the bell above the bakery door chimed as Agatha stepped inside. The warm aroma of fresh pastries enveloped her, making her mouth water. Eliza looked up from behind the counter, her apron dusted with flour and smudges of dough, clearly having had a busy morning getting things ready for the day.

"Morning, Eliza," Agatha called out, inhaling deeply. "Smells heavenly in here as always."

Eliza's face lit up with a smile. "Agatha! Good to see you. What brings you by so early?"

"I need some pastries," Agatha replied, examining the display of delicious pastries. She sighed, "How have you been?"

"I've been doing great. Every day," Eliza said softly, "I wake up grateful. To be here, to be free, doing what I love." She gestured around the cozy bakery. "After everything... well, you know."

Eliza's expression shifted, her eyes widening. "Oh, Agatha, I'm so sorry. I didn't mean to—your aunt—"

Agatha waved off the apology. "Don't worry about it.

We're working on getting her out too." She leaned in, lowering her voice conspiratorially. "Actually, I'm on my way to see someone who might have some answers."

"Gemma Jameson?" Eliza asked, eyebrows raised.

Agatha blinked in surprise. "How did you—"

"Small town," Eliza shrugged, moving to rearrange a tray of scones. "She's been in a few times. Bit of a closed book, that one."

"Any insights?" Agatha pressed gently.

Eliza pursed her lips, considering. "Well, she's not exactly chatty. Reminds me a bit of Dolores, actually. Same... intensity."

Agatha grimaced. "Wonderful. Well, I was hoping to bribe her with some of your famous scones. Got any recommendations?"

"For a tough nut like her?" Eliza grinned, reaching for a box. "Let's go with the maple pecan. If that doesn't soften her up, nothing will."

As Eliza packed the scones, Agatha steeled herself for the encounter ahead. "Thanks, Eliza. Wish me luck."

"Good luck," Eliza called as Agatha headed for the door. "And Agatha? Whatever happens with your aunt... we're all rooting for you."

Agatha nodded gratefully, the weight of the warm scone box in her hands. With a deep breath, she stepped out into the morning, ready to meet Gemma Jameson.

Agatha clutched the white bakery box, its warmth seeping through the cardboard and filling the air with the aroma of freshly baked pastries. She emerged from the bookstore, where she'd stopped to collect Mike. As the door swung shut behind her, the familiar tinkle of the bookstore's bell faded. With Mike's leash looped securely around her other hand, they set off towards Gemma's.

The late morning sun cast dappled shadows through the oak trees lining the street, their leaves rustling gently in the breeze. As they neared Gemma's Victorian home, its faded yellow paint and intricate gingerbread trim coming into view, Agatha suddenly froze mid-step. Mike let out a small whine of confusion.

With a quick tug on the leash, Agatha ducked behind a large azalea bush, its glossy leaves providing ample cover. Her heart raced as she watched Gemma's ornate front door creak open. To her astonishment, Nurse Amanda stepped out, her white uniform stark against the weathered porch. Gemma followed close behind, her face etched with worry.

Agatha strained to hear their hushed conversation, catching only fragments of urgent whispers. She observed their animated gestures, noting the furtive glances they cast up and down the quiet street. After a few tense moments, Nurse Amanda nodded curtly and strode away, her usually cheerful demeanor replaced by a grim expression.

As Amanda hurried off, something fluttered from her pocket, landing on the sidewalk. Agatha's heart quickened. She waited, holding her breath, but Amanda didn't seem to notice the loss.

Once Amanda had turned the corner and Gemma had retreated inside, Agatha cautiously approached the dropped item. It was a small piece of paper, folded twice. She quickly scooped it up, glancing around to make sure no one had seen her.

With the paper safely tucked in her pocket, Agatha let out a breath she didn't realize she'd been holding. She glanced down at the pastry box, its edges creased from her anxious grip. With a sigh, she flipped open the lid, the sweet aroma of cinnamon and butter wafting up. She plucked out a scone, its golden crust still warm, and took a contemplative bite.

"Well, Mike," she murmured, brushing a few crumbs from her lips, "I guess we won't be visiting Gemma today after all." Mike looked up at her with curious eyes, his tail wagging hopefully for a taste of the scone.

Agatha turned and headed back to the bookstore, Mike trotting loyally beside her. The note seemed to burn a hole in her pocket. Don't build your hopes up, Agatha. It's probably just a grocery list or something mundane, she thought, trying to temper her expectations.

As she entered the bookstore, she breathed a sigh of relief when she realized there were no customers inside. She waved at Celeste, who was organizing books in the Agatha Christie section, and paced behind the counter. Taking a seat, she reached into her pocket and held the note in her hand for a moment before pulling it out.

With a dramatic flourish, she unfolded the paper and read it slowly: "Everything seems to be working out as we planned. I love you..." Her brow furrowed. "Who could this be from?" she muttered, looking pensive. Realization dawned on her. "Oh my gosh, it's probably from Devin. I bet they're in this together."

The bell above the door chimed softly as Tilda Morrison burst in, the cool morning air following her inside. Agatha looked up from behind the counter, where she'd been sorting through a new shipment of mystery novels. She was startled to see Tilda looking so disheveled, her usually neat auburn hair windswept and her cheeks flushed.

"Good morning, Tilda," Agatha greeted, setting aside a

book by Louise Penny. "What brings you to our humble bookshop so early? Looking for a thrilling new mystery to dive into?"

Tilda's eyes darted around the store nervously before settling on Agatha. She took a deep breath, her hands fidgeting with the strap of her purse. "I wish I was here for a book, Agatha. But... I've discovered something. Something troubling."

Agatha's brow furrowed with concern. She gestured towards a cozy reading nook in the corner of the store. "Why don't we sit down? You look like you could use a moment to catch your breath."

As they settled into the plush armchairs, Agatha leaned forward, her voice low. "What did you find out, Tilda?"

Tilda glanced over her shoulder before whispering, "I saw Nurse Amanda and Beatrice coming out of the medication room together at Green Acres."

"Beatrice was in the medication room?" Agatha echoed, her eyebrows raised. "That's odd. Residents aren't supposed to be in there, are they?"

"Exactly," Tilda nodded vigorously. "That's what got me worried." She paused, swallowing hard. "And I'm scared, Agatha. I think Nurse Amanda might have seen me watching them."

Agatha reached out and patted Tilda's hand reassuringly. "I understand your concern, but I doubt Amanda would do anything to harm you, even if she did spot you."

Tilda's eyes widened. "But Agatha, if she's involved in Harold's death... what's to stop her from coming after me?"

Agatha sat back, considering this. After a moment, she changed tack. "Tilda, did you know that Harold's ex-wife is living here in Bristol Lake now?"

"Yes," Tilda replied, looking somewhat confused by the

shift in conversation. "I've seen her visiting Green Acres a few times."

"And you don't find it strange that she would move here?" Agatha pressed gently.

Tilda shrugged. "Not really. They remained friends after their divorce. It's not uncommon."

Agatha nodded slowly, her mind working. "I see. Still, it strikes me as a bit suspicious, given the circumstances."

She stood up, smoothing down her cardigan. "Thank you for sharing this with me, Tilda. I appreciate you trusting me with this information. Why don't you take a look around the shop? Perhaps a good book might help take your mind off things for a while."

Tilda drifted towards the cozy mystery shelves, her fingers trailing along the spines of well-loved books. Agatha made her way back to the counter, her mind swirling with the new information. She couldn't help but steal glances at Tilda, watching as the woman pulled out a book, leafed through its pages, then slid it back into place.

The cheerful jingle of the bell above the door broke Agatha from her reverie. She looked up, expecting to see Mrs. Thompson or perhaps Gladys stopping by for their weekly fix of whodunits. Instead, her breath caught in her throat as she locked eyes with a familiar face—one she hadn't expected to see today, or any day for that matter. Gemma Jameson, Harold's ex-wife, stood in the doorway, her presence as startling as a plot twist in one of Agatha's beloved mysteries.

Gemma stood hesitantly at the entrance, her eyes darting around the shop before settling on Agatha. She was a petite woman in her early seventies, with a full head of silver hair that caught the morning light. Despite her advanced years, her blue eyes were sharp and alert. Her simple, well-worn cardigan and slacks spoke of comfort rather than fashion, but there was an undeniable air of dignity about her.

"Agatha?" Gemma's voice wavered as she called out. "I hope I'm not interrupting anything."

Agatha moved from behind the counter, offering a warm smile. "Not at all, Gemma. Is everything alright?"

Gemma stepped forward, lowering her voice. "I need to speak with you about Harold. It's... it's rather important."

Agatha nodded, gesturing towards the reading nook. "Of course. Why don't we sit down and talk?" She glanced over at Tilda, who was watching the exchange with poorly disguised curiosity. "Tilda, would you mind giving us a moment?"

Tilda nodded, clutching a book to her chest. "Certainly. I'll just... continue browsing." She disappeared behind a tall bookshelf, though Agatha suspected she wouldn't stray far.

As they settled into the armchairs, Gemma leaned forward, her weathered hands clasped tightly in her lap. "Agatha, I hope you don't mind me coming to you like this. I've only recently moved back to Bristol Lake, but word travels fast in small towns. The locals can't stop talking about how you solved that dreadful business at the French Boulangerie. Even out of town, your reputation as an amateur sleuth has spread."

Agatha felt a blush creep up her cheeks. "Oh, well, I wouldn't say I'm a sleuth exactly. It was just a strange set of circumstances."

Gemma's eyes sparkled with a mix of hope and desperation. "Be that as it may, you uncovered the truth when no one else could. And that's precisely why I'm here, Agatha. I need your help with something... delicate."

Agatha leaned in, her curiosity piqued. "What kind of help, Gemma?"

Gemma took a deep breath. "It's about Harold.

Agatha nodded, a mix of pride and concern crossing her face. "I've been fortunate to help in a few cases, yes. But Gemma, with the police investigating Harold's murder and their focus on my Aunt Edna, why come to me?"

Gemma's eyes darted nervously to the door before returning to Agatha. "That's precisely why I'm here, dear. The police seem so certain about your aunt's involvement, but something doesn't sit right with me. I know you're close to the case, but I also know you'll look at this objectively. You see, there's something I haven't told the police yet."

"What is it, Gemma?" Agatha prompted gently, leaning in.

Gemma took a shaky breath. "The night before Harold died, he called me. He sounded... odd. Excited, but nervous too. He said he had something important to tell Beatrice, something that would change everything."

"Did he give you any hint about what it was?" Agatha asked, leaning forward slightly.

Gemma shook her head, her silver hair catching the light. "No, he was being very secretive. Said he needed to handle it delicately. But the way he talked, Agatha... it was like he was planning some kind of grand gesture."

Agatha's brow furrowed. "A grand gesture?"

"Yes," Gemma nodded, her eyes distant with memory. "He mentioned needing to 'make things right' and 'start fresh.' I assumed it was just Harold being Harold, you know how he could be. But now, with everything that's happened..." She trailed off, leaving the implication hanging in the air.

After a moment, Gemma's voice took on a thoughtful tone. "You know, he started to tell me something else over the phone. I asked if it was about Beatrice, and he said no.

Then there was this long pause - I could practically hear him overthinking. Finally, he just mumbled that it was nothing."

She let out a soft chuckle. "That was so typical Harold. Even over the phone, I could tell when he was holding something back. We may have been divorced, but we still knew each other's quirks. He always came around to telling me things in his own time."

Agatha reached out and patted Gemma's hand gently. "I'm so sorry, Gemma. That must have been difficult for you. But I have to ask, why haven't you told the police about this call?"

Gemma's eyes, though misty with unshed tears, held a determined gleam. "I was afraid, Agatha. Afraid that if I mentioned Beatrice, they might start suspecting me of trying to frame her out of jealousy or bitterness. But I know your aunt isn't guilty, and I can't stand by while an innocent woman is accused. I need someone who will look at this with fresh eyes, someone who isn't bound by official proce-dures. I need to know the truth about what happened to Harold. And I'm convinced there's more to Beatrice's story than anyone knows."

14

A BITTER TRUTH

The clock on Eleanor's dashboard blinked 7:45 AM as Agatha pulled into the Green Acres parking lot. She'd barely slept, but there was no time to waste. As she switched off the engine, movement near the entrance caught her eye.

Lindsey stood just outside the main doors, shifting from foot to foot. When she spotted Agatha, she raised her hand in an urgent wave, glancing over her shoulder as if worried about being seen.

Agatha frowned, her hand pausing on the car door handle. Lindsey was usually the picture of calm efficiency. Seeing her so agitated sent a ripple of unease through Agatha's stomach.

Stepping out of Eleanor, Agatha hurried across the lot, her sensible shoes crunching on the gravel. "Lindsey? Is everything alright?"

"Agatha, thank goodness you're here," Lindsey said, her voice a mix of excitement and nervousness. "We might have stumbled onto something interesting."

As they walked to a small office, Lindsey explained, "You know those old cameras we thought were broken? Turns out they weren't totally kaput. We found some footage on them."

"Oh?" Agatha raised an eyebrow, intrigued.

"Yeah, but here's the thing," Lindsey continued, lowering her voice, "I haven't actually watched it yet. Could be nothing, but... I don't know, it just felt like something you should see before we hand it over to the police. You know, in case it's important for your... um, unofficial investigation?"

She gave Agatha a small, conspiratorial smile. "I mean, it's probably just hours of empty hallways, but who knows? Maybe there's a clue hiding in there somewhere."

Inside the office, Lindsey pulled up the footage on a computer. Agatha's eyes were starting to strain from staring at the grainy security footage. She was about to give up when something caught her attention.

"Wait," she said, leaning closer to the screen. "Lindsey, can you rewind that last bit?"

Lindsey obliged, her fingers moving swiftly over the keyboard. "What did you see?"

"There," Agatha pointed at a figure moving quickly down the hallway. "Can you zoom in on that?"

As the image enlarged, Agatha's breath caught in her throat. The figure was clearly Beatrice, her face partially obscured but still recognizable. But what made Agatha's heart race was what Beatrice was holding – a pair of gleaming gold knitting needles.

"Oh my god," Agatha whispered. "That's Beatrice coming out of Harold's room. And those are Aunt Edna's knitting needles!"

Lindsey leaned in, her eyes widening. "You're right. The

timestamp shows this was just minutes before Harold's body was discovered."

Agatha sat back, her mind whirling. Could Beatrice, who had been so quick to accuse Aunt Edna, actually be the killer? The evidence seemed damning, but something didn't quite add up.

"We need to show this to Detective Dawson," Agatha said firmly. "But let's keep this between us for now. If Beatrice really is the killer, we don't want to tip her off."

As they saved the footage, Agatha couldn't shake the feeling that while this discovery was significant, it wasn't the whole story. She knew she had to tread carefully with this new information.

"Lindsey, thank you for showing me this," Agatha said, standing up. "Let's not mention this to anyone else just yet. I need to think about our next move."

Lindsey nodded, her expression a mix of excitement and concern. "Of course, Agatha. Just... be careful, okay?"

Agatha smiled reassuringly, but as she left the office, her mind was racing. This new piece of evidence had just complicated everything, and she knew the real challenge was only beginning.

The morning sun cast long shadows across the hallway as Agatha made her way to the community room. Her footsteps echoed in the quiet corridor, matching the rapid beating of her heart. The image of Beatrice leaving Harold's room, gold knitting needles in hand, played on repeat in her mind.

Pausing at the doorway, Agatha took a deep breath to

steady herself. The familiar scent of Earl Grey tea wafted from the room, a stark contrast to the tension she felt.

Inside, Beatrice sat alone by the window, cradling a delicate porcelain teacup in her hands. Sunlight streamed through the lace curtains, casting a pattern on the carpet. The usual bustle of the community room was absent, leaving an eerie quiet broken only by the soft ticking of the old grandfather clock in the corner.

"Beatrice?" Agatha called softly, stepping inside.

Beatrice looked up, her eyes tired and lined with worry. The usual sharpness in her gaze was replaced by something Agatha had never seen before – vulnerability.

"Oh, Agatha," Beatrice sighed, setting down her cup with a soft clink. "Come to accuse me of something else? Or perhaps you're here to gloat about how the mighty have fallen?"

Agatha winced at the bitterness in Beatrice's voice. She hesitated, then slowly lowered herself into the armchair across from the older woman. Her fingers fidgeted with the hem of her sweater as she wrestled with how to broach the subject. Finally, she took a deep breath.

"Beatrice, there's something I need to ask you about," Agatha began, her voice gentle but uncertain. She paused, studying Beatrice's face. "I... I saw something on the security footage. It was you, leaving Harold's room. And you were carrying..." she trailed off, then forced herself to finish. "You were carrying Aunt Edna's gold knitting needles."

The color drained from Beatrice's face. Her hands shook, almost imperceptibly, as she reached for her teacup again, more for something to hold onto than to drink. "I suppose there's no point in denying it," she said finally, her voice barely above a whisper.

Agatha leaned forward, her heart racing. "So you did kill Harold?" she asked, dreading the answer.

Beatrice's eyes widened in shock, the teacup rattling against the saucer. "Kill Harold? Good heavens, no!" She set the cup down firmly, shaking her head. "It's not what you think, Agatha. I... I was trying to help Edna."

Agatha sat back, surprise and confusion warring on her face. "Help Edna? How?"

Beatrice took a deep breath, her gaze drifting to the window as she began her story. "That morning, I was walking past Harold's room. The door was ajar, which was unusual. I knocked, but there was no answer."

She paused, collecting herself. Agatha waited patiently, sensing the importance of what was to come.

"When I pushed the door open, I saw them." She paused, taking a deep breath to steady herself. "Harold was on the bed, clearly... gone. And Edna was collapsed on the floor beside him. One of those blasted gold knitting needles was clutched in her hand, and the other..."

Beatrice's voice faltered, and she swallowed hard before continuing in a whisper, "The other was... you know... in Harold's chest."

Agatha felt a chill run down her spine at Beatrice's words. "Oh, Beatrice," she said softly, "that must have been terrible to see."

Beatrice nodded, her eyes distant. "I'll never forget that sight as long as I live."

Agatha's breath caught in her throat. "What did you do?"

"I panicked," Beatrice admitted, her voice barely above a whisper. "I knew how it would look. I know I accused her initially..." She paused, shame coloring her features. "But after the shock wore off, I realized how ridiculous that was.

Edna and I may have our differences, but I've known her for decades, Agatha. She's not a murderer."

Beatrice's eyes met Agatha's, pleading for understanding. "So I... I thought if I could just get rid of the needles, maybe..."

"You tried to hide the evidence," Agatha finished, understanding dawning.

Beatrice nodded miserably. "I picked up the needles, careful not to leave fingerprints. But as I was leaving, I heard voices in the hallway. I was afraid someone would see me, so I... I snuck back in and put them where I found them."

As Beatrice's story unfolded, Agatha felt a mix of relief and embarrassment wash over her. She had been so quick to suspect Beatrice, to see the worst in her. And yet, here was a side of Beatrice she had never imagined – someone who, despite their rivalry, would risk everything to protect Edna.

But a nagging question tugged at the back of Agatha's mind. How did Beatrice explain putting the needle back in Harold? The thought made Agatha's stomach churn. She opened her mouth to ask, then closed it again, the words sticking in her throat. The implications were too grim, too shocking to voice aloud.

Instead, Agatha found herself saying, "That must have been terribly traumatic for you, Beatrice. I'm so sorry you had to go through that."

Beatrice nodded, seemingly oblivious to Agatha's internal struggle. "It was awful, dear. Simply awful." She paused; her eyes distant with the memory. Then, her voice thick with emotion, she continued, "I know Edna and I don't always get along. But she's not capable of murder. I couldn't bear to see her life ruined over something I knew she couldn't have done."

Agatha reached out and squeezed Beatrice's hand, touched by her unexpected show of loyalty. "Thank you for telling me this, Beatrice. It helps us understand what really happened that night." She sat back, processing this new information. The pieces of the puzzle were shifting, rearranging themselves in her mind. "We need to tell Detective Dawson about this," she said finally.

Just then, the door burst open with a dramatic flourish. Lorraine swept in, her colorful scarf trailing behind her like a banner. "Mon Dieu! Agatha, there you are!" she exclaimed, her eyes widening in surprise as she spotted Beatrice. "I've been looking everywhere for you, ma chérie. I thought perhaps you'd dashed off to solve another mystery without me!"

Lorraine's gaze darted between Agatha and Beatrice, curiosity sparkling in her eyes. "Oh là là, what's this? A secret meeting? How intriguing!"

Despite the tension of the moment, Agatha couldn't help but chuckle. Trust Lorraine to bring a touch of the absurd to even the most serious situations. "Not quite, Lorraine," she said, standing up. "But we do need to take a little trip to the police station."

Lorraine's eyes widened with excitement. "Ooh, a field trip! Shall I bring snacks? I have some lovely cheese and crackers that would be perfect for a stakeout."

"This isn't a stakeout, Lorraine," Agatha explained patiently. "We need to share some important information with Detective Dawson."

"Ah, well, one should always be prepared," Lorraine said sagely. "You never know when a simple conversation might turn into a thrilling chase through the streets!"

Beatrice, who had been quiet during this exchange,

suddenly let out a snort of laughter. "Oh, Lorraine," she said, shaking her head. "Never change."

Agatha slid behind the wheel of her 1962 Ford Falcon, the familiar creak of the door a comforting sound in the tense silence. Beatrice settled into the passenger seat, her eyes roaming over the vintage interior.

As they pulled out of the Green Acres parking lot, Beatrice's expression softened, a hint of melancholy crossing her face. "You know," she said, her voice gentle, "being in this car brings back so many memories. I had a new '62 Falcon back in the day. It was beautiful, gleaming white with red interior."

She ran her hand along the dashboard, lost in thought. "So many good memories of my younger days," she continued, a wistful smile playing on her lips. Then her smile gave way to a fleeting look of nostalgia. "Harold and Edna... we used to go on drives together in that car. Better days, you know."

Beatrice sighed, and Agatha noticed a glimmer of tears in her eyes. "Believe it or not, we were all good friends once, back in our younger days. Life has a way of complicating things, doesn't it?"

Agatha nodded, unsure of what to say. This vulnerable side of Beatrice was new to her, and it made her see the older woman in a different light.

The rest of the drive to the police station was tense, filled with nervous anticipation. Agatha's mind raced with possibilities. Would Dawson believe Beatrice's story? And if he did, where did that leave them in solving Harold's murder?

As they approached the station, Agatha couldn't help but wonder about the complex history between Beatrice, Harold, and her Aunt Edna. It seemed there were still many layers to this mystery, both past and present, waiting to be unraveled.

At the station, Detective Dawson listened to Beatrice's account with a mix of skepticism and interest, his strong features set in a thoughtful frown. His dark eyes, usually warm and inviting, were now sharp and focused as he absorbed each detail of her story.

"That's quite a story, Mrs. Belafonte," he said when she finished, his deep voice tinged with a hint of concern. "We'll need to verify it, of course. You understand that this could be seen as tampering with evidence?"

Beatrice nodded solemnly. "I know. I'm prepared to face the consequences of my actions. But please, you must believe me about Edna's innocence."

Dawson sighed, rubbing his temples. "Let's not get ahead of ourselves. We'll review the security footage again, interview the staff. If your story checks out, we'll... reassess the situation."

The next few hours were a blur of activity. Agatha and Beatrice waited anxiously as Dawson and his team pored over security footage, interviewed staff members, and pieced together the timeline of that fateful morning.

Finally, as the sun was beginning to set, Dawson called them back into his office. "Well, ladies," he said, his voice gruff but not unkind, "it seems Ms. Belafonte's story checks out. The additional footage confirms her movements that morning, and several staff members corroborate hearing voices in the hallway at the time she mentioned."

Agatha let out a breath she hadn't realized she'd been holding. Beside her, Beatrice's shoulders sagged with relief.

"So what happens now?" Agatha asked.

Dawson leaned back in his chair. "Now, we're back to square one. Ms. Belafonte, I'll need to have a more in-depth conversation with you about your actions that morning. But for now, you're free to go. And Mrs. Royale," he fixed Agatha with a stern look, "I trust you'll leave the investigating to the professionals from here on out?"

Agatha nodded, though they both knew it was a promise she was unlikely to keep.

As they left the station, the cool evening air a welcome relief after the stuffy interrogation room, Agatha turned to Beatrice. "I'm sorry I jumped to conclusions," she said softly. "I should have known better."

Beatrice smiled wryly. "Well, I suppose I haven't given the best first impression. Your aunt has probably told you plenty about me."

Agatha nodded, a small smile tugging at her lips. "I guess we both had some preconceptions to overcome."

As Agatha guided the Falcon back towards Green Acres, a thoughtful silence fell between them. The streetlights flickered on, casting intermittent glows across the dashboard. Agatha's mind was already racing ahead, sifting through the facts of the case. Beatrice was innocent, but that meant the real killer was still out there. And she was more determined than ever to uncover the truth.

"You know," Beatrice said suddenly, breaking the silence, "I've always admired your aunt's spirit. Even when we were at each other's throats, I respected her tenacity."

Agatha glanced at her, surprised by the admission, before turning her eyes back to the road. "I think she'd say the same about you, though she'd probably never admit it out loud."

Beatrice chuckled. "No, I suppose not. We're both too stubborn for our own good."

As Agatha guided the Falcon into the Green Acres parking lot, she felt the weight of unanswered questions pressing down on her. She put the car in park and turned to Beatrice.

"Beatrice," Agatha began, her voice tentative, "do you have any idea why anyone would want to kill Harold?"

Beatrice's brow furrowed, her gaze distant as she considered the question. After a moment, she let out a soft sigh.

"Harold was a man of means, Agatha," she said, her voice tinged with a mix of admiration and something harder to define. "He had his fingers in many pies, so to speak. Businesses, investments... who knows what else." She gave a subtle shake of her head. "In a world like that, well... anything is possible."

Agatha nodded slowly, absorbing this information. As they stepped out of the car, she knew that while one mystery had been solved today, a far larger one still loomed before them. The real investigation was only just beginning.

15

SHADOWS OF DOUBT

Agatha sat in her bookstore, the scent of books and freshly brewed coffee filling the air, but she barely noticed. Now that Beatrice had been cleared, her mind raced back to the cryptic note she had seen Amanda drop: 'Everything seems to be working out as we planned. I love you...'

Mike lay at her feet, his tail thumping occasionally against the worn wooden floor, a comforting presence as she sifted through her thoughts.

"I can't shake this feeling, Mike," Agatha murmured, absently scratching behind his ears. "Nurse Amanda is hiding something crucial. That note... who was it from? And what exactly were they planning?"

She leaned back in her chair, her brow furrowed in concentration. "First, she acts suspiciously around Aunt Edna, then this mysterious note... There's more to Amanda's story than meets the eye, and I'm going to find out what it is."

As the day wore on and customers trickled in and out, Agatha's mind raced with possibilities. By closing time, she had made up her mind. She would follow Amanda after her shift at Green Acres.

"Celeste," Agatha called to her assistant as she locked up the store. "I might be a bit late opening tomorrow. Something's come up."

Celeste raised an eyebrow. "Another mystery, Agatha? Do be careful."

Agatha smiled reassuringly. "Always am. It's probably nothing, but I need to check it out."

That afternoon, Agatha stepped away from the bookstore and popped into the Bristol Lake Post Office with a few outgoing packages—mostly online orders from out-of-town mystery lovers who had discovered her bookstore's social media.

The post office was quiet, except for the sound of an ancient ceiling fan and the rhythmic clack of Marlene Briggs's keyboard. The town's longest-working postal clerk looked up with her signature skeptical squint.

"Well, look who's still alive after that Green Acres debacle," Marlene muttered, sliding a roll of stamps across the counter.

Agatha smiled politely. "News travels faster than the mail around here."

"Everyone in town's talking about the murder at Green Acres," Marlene added with a shake of her head.

She snorted. "Earl Whitman came in yesterday with a theory about sabotage. He says Beatrice used to dabble in odd herbal remedies—claims she knows which herbs could put someone to sleep for a week. Like, the apothecary kind you'd see in a Victorian murder plot."

Agatha raised an eyebrow. "Sounds like someone's been bingeing true crime again."

Marlene leaned closer, eyes glinting. "Just keep your

eyes open, sweetie. That place has secrets. And Earl? He's more observant than folks give him credit for."

As Agatha stepped out into the sunlight, she tucked the stamps into her bag and whispered to Mike, "We're definitely going to need a bigger notebook."

As twilight settled over Bristol Lake, Agatha positioned herself near the entrance of Green Acres, Mike by her side. The air was cool and crisp, carrying the faint scent of approaching autumn. She pulled her cardigan tighter around herself, her eyes fixed on the facility's doors.

After what felt like hours, but was likely only forty-five minutes, Nurse Amanda emerged. Her uniform was still crisp, her face a mask of professional detachment. Agatha's heart quickened.

"Let's go, Mike," she whispered, gently tugging on his leash. They followed at a distance, keeping to the shadows cast by the streetlights.

Amanda walked briskly, her sensible shoes clicking against the pavement. Every so often, she would pause, glancing over her shoulder. Agatha would duck behind a parked car or a hedge, holding her breath until Amanda resumed her journey.

As they moved further from the town center, the streets became less familiar. Old warehouses and abandoned storefronts loomed on either side. Agatha's unease grew with each step.

Finally, Amanda approached a rundown storage facility. The sign, barely legible, read "Lakeview Storage." Amanda looked around furtively before slipping inside one of the units.

Agatha waited, counting to sixty in her head before approaching. The metal door was thin, and she could hear Amanda's muffled voice from within.

"...can't keep this up much longer," Amanda was saying, her voice tinged with anxiety. "Someone's bound to notice..."

Agatha leaned closer, straining to hear more, when suddenly Mike let out a low growl. She turned to see a figure in a dark coat approaching the unit. Panicking, she ducked behind a stack of old crates, pulling Mike close.

The figure entered the unit without knocking. Agatha's heart pounded as she listened to the heated exchange that followed.

"You promised it would be over by now," Amanda hissed.

"Complications arose," a voice replied, its tone low and indistinct. "He was onto us. We had to act."

"But framing that old woman? It's too risky!"

"It's done. Just keep your mouth shut and stick to the plan."

Agatha's mind reeled. *They were talking about Harold's murder and Aunt Edna's framing. But why? What was this plan?*

After a few more minutes of tense conversation, the figure left, followed shortly by Amanda. Both looked agitated as they hurried away in opposite directions.

Agatha waited until their footsteps faded before approaching the unit. The door was slightly ajar. Taking a deep breath, she slipped inside.

The small space was cluttered with boxes and papers. A musty odor permeated the air, making Agatha's nose wrinkle. Her eyes darted around, taking in the chaos until they landed on a folder labeled "Harold."

With trembling hands, she opened it. Inside were documents that seemed to detail a complex financial scheme. Agatha's eyes widened as she caught glimpses of names she recognized from Green Acres, including Amanda's.

"Oh, Harold," Agatha whispered. "What did you stumble into?"

She was about to delve deeper into the documents when a sudden noise from outside startled her. Heart pounding, Agatha quickly replaced the folder exactly where she'd found it. As much as she wanted to investigate further, she knew taking the documents would be theft – and possibly destroy crucial evidence.

The walk home was a blur, Agatha's mind racing with the implications of what she'd glimpsed. Once safely inside her cottage, she sat at her kitchen table, absently petting Mike.

"I think we're onto something big here, boy," she said, excitement and uncertainty mingling in her voice. "But we need more evidence. What I saw... it's not enough to prove anything yet."

Agatha spent a restless night pondering what she'd seen. The scheme seemed to involve falsified records and misappropriation of funds, but she needed more details. And a nagging doubt gnawed at her: Was Amanda really involved in Harold's death? Or was there a bigger picture she was missing?

As dawn broke, Agatha sat up in bed, determined. She had a lead, but she needed to be careful and gather more evidence. The truth about Harold's death – and the safety of her aunt – depended on her next moves.

Agatha decided she needed to confront Amanda directly. It was risky, but she needed answers. She picked up her phone and dialed Green Acres.

"Hello, this is Agatha Royale. I'd like to schedule a meeting with Nurse Amanda today. It's about my aunt's care," she lied smoothly. "Yes, this afternoon would be perfect. Thank you."

As she hung up, Agatha looked at Mike, who wagged his tail in response. "Well, old boy," she said, scratching his chin, "looks like we're in for an interesting day. Let's hope we're not walking into a trap."

The morning sun streamed through her house windows, illuminating the scattered papers on her kitchen table. Mike padded around her feet, sensing her nervous energy.

"What do you think, Mike? Should I bring some of these notes with me?" Agatha mused aloud, shuffling through the papers. She decided against it, not wanting to show her hand too early. Instead, she tucked a small notebook and pen into her favorite floral tote bag.

Before heading out, Agatha called Emma for moral support. The phone rang twice before Emma's cheerful voice answered.

"Emma, it's Agatha. I hope I'm not catching you at a bad time?"

"Not at all! I was just about to start on a new watercolor. What's up?"

Agatha hesitated, then plunged in. "I'm going to confront Nurse Amanda about Harold's death. I've uncovered some... well, let's just say some very interesting information."

Emma's tone turned serious. "Agatha, are you sure that's wise? Maybe you should take this to the police first."

"I need to be certain, Emma. I can't risk ruining Amanda's life if I'm wrong. But... if I don't call you by 3 PM, could you check on me? I'll be at Green Acres."

"Of course," Emma agreed, concern evident in her

voice. "But please, be careful. This isn't one of your mystery novels."

Agatha chuckled softly. "I know, I know. I'll be careful, I promise."

After hanging up, Agatha gave herself a once-over in the hallway mirror. Her silver hair was neatly pinned back, and she had chosen a comfortable but smart outfit – a pale blue blouse and navy slacks. She wanted to look professional but approachable.

The drive to Green Acres was short but tense. Agatha rehearsed what she would say to Amanda, trying to anticipate her reactions. As she pulled into the parking lot, she spotted Tilda heading into the building.

Agatha pushed open the doors of Green Acres, her nose immediately wrinkling at the peculiar blend of lemon-scented cleaner and artificial flowers. The reception area hummed with life – a gaggle of residents gossiped in plush armchairs while staff members zipped by like honeybees in a particularly busy hive.

Spotting Lindsey's familiar face at the front desk, Agatha plastered on her best 'I'm-definitely-not-here-to-snoop' smile and sauntered over. Her fingers drummed a silent rhythm against her thigh as she approached, mind already racing with how to wheedle information out of the receptionist without seeming too obvious.

"Morning, Lindsey!" she chirped, leaning casually against the counter. "Looks like it's all hands on deck today, huh?"

Lindsey looked up, her face brightening. "Agatha! Good to see you. How are you holding up? Any news about your aunt?"

Agatha's smile faltered. "It's been tough, but I'm doing

what I can to clear her name. Actually, I was hoping to catch Nurse Amanda. Is she available?"

A flicker of surprise crossed Lindsey's face. "Oh, yes. She mentioned you were coming. She's in her office. Shall I let her know you're here?"

"That would be great, thanks."

As Lindsey made the call, Agatha's eyes roamed the room. The sight of the residents going about their daily lives made her heart ache, thinking of her aunt Edna languishing in jail for a crime she didn't commit. Her resolve strengthened; she had to get to the bottom of this.

Moments later, Nurse Amanda appeared, looking visibly nervous despite her attempts to maintain a professional demeanor. "Ms. Royale? Please follow me to my office."

As they walked down the corridor, Agatha noticed Amanda's tense posture and the way she kept glancing over her shoulder, as if expecting someone to be following them.

Amanda's office was small but tidy, with a desk, two chairs, and a filing cabinet. A few potted plants added a touch of life to the sterile environment.

Amanda gestured for Agatha to sit, then closed the door quickly, checking to make sure it was securely shut. "Now, how can I help you today?" Amanda asked, her voice tense but controlled.

Agatha took a deep breath. "Nurse Amanda, I'm here to talk about Harold's death and my aunt's involvement."

Amanda's posture stiffened. "Ms. Royale, I understand this is difficult for you, but the evidence against your aunt is quite clear."

"Is it?" Agatha pressed, noticing how Amanda's hands tightened on the arms of her chair. "I believe there's more to this story."

Amanda's eyes narrowed. "I was there, Ms. Royale. I

saw your aunt with those gold knitting needles in her hands – the murder weapon. She was in the room with Harold's body. What more evidence do you need?"

Agatha leaned forward. "But that doesn't make sense. My aunt loved Harold. She would never—"

"Love can make people do terrible things," Amanda interrupted, her voice cold. "Your aunt was jealous of Harold's relationship with Beatrice. Everyone knew it."

"I don't believe that," Agatha said firmly. "And I think you know more than you're letting on. What about the financial irregularities at Green Acres? The ones Harold was investigating?"

Amanda's face paled visibly. "I... I don't know what you're talking about. This is about your aunt, not some imaginary financial scheme."

Just then, Amanda's phone buzzed. She glanced at it, her expression changing to one of panic. "I'm sorry, Ms. Royale, but I have to go. We're done here."

As Amanda hurriedly gathered her things, a small object tumbled from her pocket. Agatha's eyes zeroed in on it – a pill bottle. Before she could get a better look, Amanda snatched it up, shoving it back into her pocket with lightning speed.

"Amanda," Agatha said softly, "I think you need to tell me everything. It's the only way to ensure justice is served – for everyone involved."

Before Amanda could respond, there was a sharp knock at the door. It opened to reveal Roger Collins, his eyes narrowed as he took in the scene.

"Is everything alright in here?" he asked, his tone deceptively light.

Amanda straightened up, forcing a smile. "Yes, Mr. Collins. Ms. Royale was just leaving."

Amanda ushered Agatha out but paused at the door. She leaned in close, her voice barely above a whisper. "Tomorrow afternoon. Mr. Rogers will be out. We can talk then." Her eyes darted nervously down the hall. "Watch your step, Agatha. This goes deeper than you know."

Agatha left Green Acres, her mind whirling. Amanda's odd behavior, that mysterious pill bottle, the hushed conversation - nothing added up. As she slid into her car, a thought struck her: in this place, even the wallpaper seemed suspicious.

16

THE BREAK-IN

The bell above the door of One Deadly Chapter Books and Brew chimed softly as Agatha locked up for the evening. She'd spent the day juggling customers, organizing new arrivals, and sneaking moments to jot down notes about her ongoing investigation. The crisp autumn air was a welcome relief after the stuffy warmth of the bookstore.

"Come on, Mike," she called to her faithful companion, who had been napping in his bed behind the counter. The miniature schnauzer stretched lazily before trotting to her side.

As they made their way home, the setting sun cast long shadows across the quiet streets of Bristol Lake. The scent of fallen leaves and wood smoke from nearby chimneys filled the air, a reminder that winter wasn't far off.

After a long and exhausting day, Agatha breathed a sigh of relief as she approached her front door. She'd been so lost in thought about the case that her walk home had passed in a blur. As she fished for her keys in her oversized handbag, a sudden chill ran down her spine. Something felt off.

Mike's ears perked up, sensing his owner's unease. Agatha hesitated, then slowly pushed open the door. Her heart sank at the sight that greeted her...

Pushing the door open, Agatha was met with an unsettling sight that confirmed her worst fears. The living room was in complete disarray. Cushions were tossed haphazardly across the floor, books were scattered everywhere, and her favorite reading lamp lay toppled on its side, the shade cracked.

Agatha's heart skipped a beat as the realization hit her: someone had broken into her home. The sense of violation was overwhelming, and for a moment, she stood frozen in the doorway, unable to process what she was seeing.

"Mike, stay close," she murmured, her voice unsteady. The miniature schnauzer obediently followed her, his ears perked up in alert. His presence was comforting, a reminder that she wasn't entirely alone in this moment of shock and vulnerability.

With shaking hands, Agatha pulled out her phone and dialed Detective Dawson's number. As it rang, she took a deep breath, steeling herself for the conversation ahead.

"Detective Dawson," his gruff voice answered.

"Detective, it's Agatha Royale," she said, trying to keep her voice steady. "I'm afraid there's been another break-in at my house."

There was a pause, then a weary sigh. "Ms. Royale, are you certain? This isn't related to another one of your... investigations, is it?"

Agatha's lips curved into a faint smile at his tone, despite the situation. "I'm afraid it might be, Detective. I think you'll want to see this for yourself."

"I'll be right there," Dawson replied, his voice now all

business. "And Agatha? Try not to touch anything before I arrive."

"Of course," she agreed, ending the call. While waiting for Detective Dawson to arrive, Agatha paced on her front porch, occasionally peering through the windows at the chaos inside. She debated whether to go in and start cleaning up but decided against it, not wanting to disturb any potential evidence.

Detective Dawson arrived promptly, his cruiser pulling up with a soft crunch of gravel. His demeanor was calm and professional as he assessed the situation, a stark contrast to Agatha's nervous energy.

"Agatha, it might be best if you wait out here while we secure the house," he suggested, but Agatha was already moving towards the door.

"I appreciate your concern, Detective, but this is my home. I'm coming with you," she said firmly, her tone leaving no room for argument.

Detective Dawson sighed, knowing better than to try and dissuade her. "Alright, but stay close and don't touch anything."

Agatha nodded, following the detective into her house with Mike at her heels. The familiar rooms now felt alien, violated by an unknown intruder. She watched as the police team methodically went through each room, noting with a mix of frustration and admiration their thorough approach.

In the living room, Agatha's eyes darted from one over-turned object to another, her mind racing to catalog what might be missing. She noticed a detective carefully lifting a lamp for fingerprints and felt a sudden urge to start putting things back in order. But she restrained herself, knowing that preserving evidence was crucial.

"Detective Dawson," Agatha called out, drawing attention to a drawer left cracked open. "That drawer – I always keep it closed. Could you check it, please?" Dawson nodded, approaching the drawer with gloved hands. As he opened it fully, Agatha's heart sank. "My manuscript," she whispered, more to herself than anyone else.

The detective turned to her, eyebrow raised. "Something missing?"

Agatha nodded, her voice tight with emotion. "Yes, my manuscript. It was right there, in that drawer."

"Manuscript? What kind of manuscript?" Dawson inquired.

"It's a mystery novel I've been working on," Agatha explained, her voice trembling. "I just finished it recently."

The detective's features eased. "I see. Well, can't you just print another copy?"

Agatha shook her head vigorously, tears welling up in her eyes. "No, you don't understand. It was typewritten. I write on my old typewriter and hadn't had a chance to transfer it to my computer yet. It was the only copy I had."

"How much work are we talking about here?" Dawson asked, beginning to grasp the gravity of the situation.

Agatha leaned against the wall, suddenly feeling weak. "Hundreds of pages, Detective. I've been working on this book for over a year. Countless hours of writing, revising, perfecting every sentence. And now... it's all gone."

Detective Dawson's brow furrowed in sympathy. "I'm sorry, Agatha. That's a significant loss. Was there anything particularly valuable about this specific manuscript? Anything that might make someone want to steal it?"

Agatha shook her head, forcing a bewildered expression. "It's just a work of fiction, Detective. A small-town mystery novel," she explained. Then, with a weak attempt at humor, she added, "Maybe someone's desperate to be the first reader? Though I doubt I have secret fans for an unpublished book." She sighed. "This is the third time someone has broken into my house," Agatha continued, shaking her head in disbelief. "Hard to believe it's a coincidence."

Detective Dawson's expression sharpened. "You're right, it's not likely to be a coincidence. If I recall correctly, the other two times were when you were involved in crime investigations you shouldn't have been mixed up in." He paused, fixing Agatha with a stern look. "Agatha, have you been investigating Harold's case? Trying to clear your Aunt Edna's name?"

Agatha hesitated, crossing her fingers behind her back. "Well... maybe a little," she admitted reluctantly, trying to downplay her involvement. "But not much, really. Just asking a few questions here and there."

Dawson sighed, pinching the bridge of his nose. "Agatha, I've told you before how dangerous this can be. Leave the investigating to the professionals."

"I know, I know," Agatha said, trying to change the subject. "But why would anyone want to steal my manuscript because of that?"

"Good question," Dawson mused. "Did you tell anyone about your manuscript?"

Agatha thought for a moment. "Well, I mentioned it to a few people at the bookstore. And now that I think about it, I remember Lorraine telling me she'd chatted with Nurse Amanda about it during one of her volunteer visits to Green Acres. You know how Lorraine loves to talk about town gossip. She probably couldn't resist mentioning that I was writing a mystery novel."

Dawson nodded slowly. "I see. Though it's hard to imagine why someone would steal an unpublished manuscript."

Agatha shrugged, trying to appear nonchalant. "Maybe they're just really eager for new reading material?"

"Hmm," Dawson replied, not entirely convinced. "Well, we'll look into all possibilities, Agatha. But please, for your own safety, stay out of the Harold case. Let us handle it."

"Of course, Detective," Agatha agreed, though her crossed fingers told a different story. "Thank you for your help."

"We'll keep you updated on any developments," Dawson assured her. "And Agatha? Maybe consider making backup copies in the future. Just a thought."

As the police wrapped up their investigation and filed out, Agatha sank onto her couch, a heavy sigh escaping her lips. The house felt eerily quiet now, the aftermath of the break-in leaving a lingering sense of violation.

Mike padded in from the kitchen, his nails clicking softly on the hardwood floor. He'd just lapped up some water, droplets still clinging to his whiskers. Agatha reached out, running her fingers through his soft fur, seeking comfort in the familiar gesture.

Her mind whirled with questions. *Who would break in just to steal my manuscript? And why?* A chilling realization struck her. *Whoever took it knew I only had one copy.* This wasn't just a random burglary; it was targeted.

As she gazed into Mike's earnest brown eyes, searching for some sort of reassurance, she noticed something odd.

"Hey, what've you got there, buddy?" she asked, her brow furrowing.

Mike cocked his head, looking rather pleased with himself. Whatever it was, he clearly thought he'd made a great discovery.

Gently, Agatha reached for his muzzle. "Come on, let's see what treasure you've found."

She carefully extracted a small, metallic object from between his teeth. Bringing it closer to her face, she squinted, trying to make out what it was in the fading evening light.

"Well, I'll be," she murmured, turning the object over in her palm. "It's a pin. A nursing graduation pin."

17

THE NURSING PIN

Agatha's eyes widened as realization dawned. "Amanda... Nurse Amanda," she whispered, her voice barely audible. "Could this be hers? It must be hers."

She studied the pin in her hands, turning it over and over, watching as the last rays of sunlight caught its polished surface. The weight of the discovery settled in her stomach, a mix of excitement and dread.

Without taking her eyes off the pin, Agatha reached for her phone and dialed Emma's number. Her fingers trembled as she pressed the buttons.

After a few rings, Emma's breathless voice came through. "Hey, Agatha!"

"Hi Emma, are you busy?" Agatha asked, trying to keep her voice steady.

"I literally just walked in the door," Emma replied, still sounding winded. "What's going on? Everything okay?"

Agatha took a deep breath. "Well... someone broke into my house today."

"Again?" Emma exclaimed. "No way. This is getting ridiculous!"

"I know," Agatha sighed. "I just got home and found the place ransacked."

"Oh my god, Agatha!" Emma's voice shot up an octave. "Are you alright? Did they take anything?"

"I'm fine, just shaken up," Agatha assured her. "And they only took one thing... my manuscript."

There was a pause on the other end of the line. "What? Your first draft? Please tell me you made copies of it. I know it was typewritten, but you can make copies of type-written manuscripts, right?"

Agatha winced, feeling a fresh wave of regret. "I didn't make any copies, unfortunately. I thought about it, but didn't have the time with the investigation, the bookstore, and everything else going on."

"Oh, Agatha," Emma's voice was filled with sympathy. "That's awful. I'm really sorry to hear this." She paused for a moment. "I don't mean to be insensitive or anything, but... why would anyone want your manuscript? It's not like you're a bestselling author or anything."

"Believe me, I've been asking myself the same question," Agatha replied, her free hand absently stroking Mike's fur. "But then... well, Mike found something on the floor. A nursing graduation pin. And I think... I think it belongs to Nurse Amanda."

"Are you sure it's hers?" Emma's voice was cautious. "That's a pretty serious accusation, Agatha."

Agatha bit her lip, her mind racing back to her visit to Green Acres. "I'm pretty sure I saw it on her lapel when I saw her at Green Acres. It was distinctive – I remember thinking how shiny it looked."

"But why would Nurse Amanda break into your house

and steal your manuscript?" Emma asked, voicing the question that had been nagging at Agatha.

"I don't know," Agatha admitted, her gaze drifting to the window where the last light of day was fading. "But I intend to find out. Something's not right here, Emma. I can feel it in my bones."

"Agatha," Emma's voice took on a warning tone, "please be careful. If Nurse Amanda is involved in something shady, it could be dangerous."

"I know, I know," Agatha sighed. "But I can't just let this go. Not when Aunt Edna's freedom is at stake."

As she hung up the phone, Agatha looked down at Mike, who was gazing up at her with his big, trusting eyes. "Well, boy," she said, scratching behind his ears, "looks like we've got ourselves a real mystery on our hands."

The nursing pin glinted in the lamplight, a silent promise of secrets yet to be uncovered. Agatha turned it over in her palm, her mind racing with possibilities. Just as she was about to put the pin away, her phone buzzed with a text message. It was from an unknown number. With a furrowed brow, Agatha opened it, her heart pounding in her chest.

The message read: "If you ever want to see your manuscript again, stay away from Green Acres. Persist, and you won't just lose your novel. The next body they find won't be Harold's."

Agatha's eyes narrowed as she read the message. Instead of fear, she felt a surge of determination. Whoever sent this clearly didn't know her very well. She placed the phone next to the nursing pin on the coffee table, a small smile playing on her lips.

"Well, Mike," she said, her voice steady and resolved,

"looks like we've got an early morning ahead of us. Green Acres won't know what hit them."

∾

The next morning, Agatha set out for Green Acres with a sense of purpose, the crisp autumn air filling her lungs as she walked. She'd called Emma and Lorraine to meet her there, feeling safer with her friends by her side.

As they approached the entrance, they saw Nurse Amanda hurrying out, looking flustered.

"Nurse Amanda," Agatha called out, her voice steady. "Could we have a word?"

Amanda turned, surprise flickering across her face. "Agatha, what are you doing here? And with a whole entourage, I see."

Emma stepped forward, a warm smile on her face. "We're just here for moral support. And maybe a cup of that famous Green Acres coffee I've heard so much about?"

Lorraine nodded enthusiastically. "Oh yes, I've been dying to try it!"

Amanda's posture relaxed slightly, but her eyes remained wary. "I... I'm actually in a hurry. I have an important errand to run."

Agatha exchanged a quick glance with her friends before turning back to Amanda. "It won't take long. I just have a few questions about... recent events." She hesitated for a moment, then reached into her pocket. "And I was hoping you might be able to tell me something about this."

With a flourish that would have made a magician proud, Agatha produced the nursing pin. She held it up, letting it catch the sunlight. Amanda's eyes widened, a mix of recog-

nition and something else—was it fear?—flashing across
her face.

"Where did you get that?" Amanda asked, her voice
barely above a whisper.

Agatha smiled, the kind of smile that didn't quite reach
her eyes. "Oh, you know how it is. One minute you're
tidying up, the next you're finding all sorts of interesting
trinkets. Now, about those questions..."

Amanda's eyes widened. She looked around nervously
before leaning in. "Not here," she whispered. "Meet me at
the old oak tree in Willow Park... tomorrow is my day off. I
can meet you in the morning. I'll explain everything then."

The next morning, Agatha, Emma, and Lorraine gathered at
One Deadly Chapter Books and Brew. They indulged in
steaming cups of coffee and Eliza's heavenly pastries, forti-
fying themselves for the day ahead.

"Nothing like a good croissant to prepare for a clandes-
tine meeting," Lorraine quipped, licking a spot of chocolate
from her finger.

With a mix of anticipation and nerves, the trio set off for
Willow Park. As they approached, the old oak tree came
into view, standing tall and proud at the far end. Its gnarled
branches stretched out like welcoming arms, casting playful
shadows across the sunlit grass.

"Well, ladies," Agatha said with a wry smile, "shall we
go see what secrets Amanda has hidden up her sleeve?"

"Look," Lorraine whispered, pointing. "Is that someone
taking a nap under the tree?"

As they approached, Agatha's stomach did a little flip.

Nurse Amanda lay motionless beneath the oak, looking far too still for comfort.

"Oh dear," Emma murmured, her eyes wide. "This doesn't look good."

Agatha knelt beside Amanda, her fingers hesitating before checking for a pulse. Finding none, she sighed heavily. "I'm afraid we'll have to raincheck that chat with Amanda. We need to call Detective Dawson."

"Don't tell me," Lorraine said, her usual pep subdued. "No touching anything, right? It's a crime scene now."

As they waited for the police, the three friends huddled together, the once-cheerful park now feeling a bit less inviting. Agatha couldn't help but think, "So much for a quiet morning in the park."

Detective Dawson arrived within minutes, his car's tires crunching on the gravel path. He stepped out, his face grim as he surveyed the scene. Officer Jenkins followed close behind, already unspooling crime scene tape.

"Agatha," Dawson said, his tone a mix of concern and exasperation. "I should have known you'd be involved somehow. What happened here?"

Agatha took a deep breath. "We found Nurse Amanda like this, Detective. We were supposed to meet her here this morning."

Dawson's eyebrows shot up. "Meet her? Why?"

"She said she had something important to tell me about... recent events," Agatha replied carefully.

The detective's eyes narrowed. "Recent events? You wouldn't happen to be referring to your aunt's case, would you?"

Before Agatha could respond, Dawson turned to Emma and Lorraine. "And you two are here because...?"

Emma stepped forward. "We're Agatha's friends. We came for moral support."

"Oui," Lorraine chimed in. "Safety in numbers, n'est-ce pas?"

Detective Dawson rubbed his temples, looking like he needed a strong coffee. "Okay, let me wrap my head around this. You three just happened to be here, right when our potential star witness decides to take a dirt nap?"

Agatha fought to keep a poker face, knowing she had to play her cards close to the chest. "Look, Amanda texted me saying she wanted to meet up. Said she had some juicy gossip or something."

Dawson's eyebrows did a little dance. "And she picked this lovely park for your little chit-chat because...?"

"Beats me," Agatha shrugged, choosing her words carefully. "She was being all mysterious about it. Didn't give me any details, just said it was important."

The detective studied Agatha's face carefully. "Well, this certainly complicates things. Amanda had recently approached us, saying she had important information about the night of Harold's murder. She was considering coming forward as a witness."

Agatha raised her eyebrows, doing her best to look surprised. "Oh? How curious," she said, her voice a touch too high. Meanwhile, her mind was buzzing like a hive of excited bees. The confrontation with Amanda and that mysterious Nursing Pin flashed through her thoughts, but she pushed them aside. Those were definitely not tidbits she wanted to share with Detective Dawson right now.

"I had no idea she was talking to the police," Agatha said, which was at least partially true.

Emma and Lorraine exchanged worried glances, sensing the tension.

As Officer Jenkins began taking their statements, Dawson pulled Agatha aside. "Look, I know you're trying to help your aunt, but this is serious. You're treading in dangerous waters here."

Agatha nodded solemnly. "I understand, Detective. But I can't help feeling that there's more to this than meets the eye. Amanda seemed scared when she asked to meet me."

Dawson's eyes showed a flicker of concern. "That's something we'll have to look into. But please, be careful. It seems like you might be getting close to something big, and clearly, someone's willing to go to extreme lengths to keep it quiet."

As they watched the crime scene investigators work, Detective Dawson approached the three friends. "Alright, ladies, we're not quite done here. I'm going to need you three to come down to the station for further questioning."

Emma and Agatha exchanged worried glances, but before they could respond, Lorraine let out a dramatic gasp.

"Le station de police?" Lorraine exclaimed, her eyes wide with panic. "But, Detective, I cannot go to jail! I'm too delicate for prison life!"

Dawson raised an eyebrow. "Ms. Dubois, it's just routine questioning, not an arrest."

But Lorraine was on a roll. "You don't understand! My skin care routine requires specific French products. How will I maintain my youthful glow behind bars?" She clutched at her face in mock horror.

Emma tried to stifle a laugh. "Lorraine, he said we're not being arrested."

"Oh, mon Dieu!" Lorraine continued, ignoring Emma. "And the food! I cannot survive on gruel and stale bread. I need my croissants and café au lait!"

Agatha, despite the gravity of the situation, found herself fighting back a smile. "Lorraine, please..."

Detective Dawson, looking both amused and exasperated, held up a hand. "Ms. Dubois, I assure you, there will be no jail cells involved. We just need to ask you a few questions at the station."

Lorraine paused her theatrics, eyeing the detective suspiciously. "You promise? No handcuffs? No mug shots?"

"No handcuffs, no mug shots," Dawson confirmed, shaking his head in disbelief.

"Well, in that case," Lorraine said, suddenly composed, "lead the way, Detective. But if anyone asks, I'm consulting on the station's interior design. A pop of color could really liven up those dreary interrogation rooms."

As they followed Dawson to his car, Emma leaned in to whisper to Agatha, "Only Lorraine could turn a murder investigation into a comedy routine."

18

A NEW SUSPECT

Two days had passed since Nurse Amanda's shocking death under the old oak tree. Agatha couldn't shake the feeling of unease that had settled over her like a heavy fog. Bristol Lake, usually a quaint and cheerful town, now seemed to hold secrets in every shadow.

Agatha adjusted her volunteer badge as she walked down the hallway of Green Acres. She'd taken on the role of assistant librarian, hoping to keep a close eye on things without arousing suspicion. As she rounded the corner towards the library, a movement caught her eye.

Hank, the burly linen delivery guy, was easing Mr. Collins' office door shut behind him. Agatha frowned. *What business did Hank have with the administrator?*

She slowed her pace, pretending to fumble with her phone while watching Hank from the corner of her eye. He clutched a small bundle of linens to his chest, glancing nervously up and down the hallway before hurrying away.

Something wasn't right. Agatha's heart quickened as she

approached Mr. Collins' now-closed door. She hesitated, hand hovering near the knob. Should she knock? Peek inside?

"Everything alright, Agatha?"

She jumped at the sound of Mildred's voice behind her.

"Fine," Agatha said quickly, dropping her hand. "Just... thinking about which books to recommend for the book club."

As they continued towards the library, Agatha's mind raced. Why was Hank in Mr. Collins' office? And what was with that nervous behavior? She made a mental note to keep a closer eye on the linen deliveries from now on. Something was off, and she was determined to figure out what.

Later that day as she organized the books in the small, cozy library, her mind wandered to Devin, Harold's nephew. She'd seen him a few times at Green Acres, always seeming a bit too friendly with the staff, especially Nurse Amanda.

Agatha was sorting through a pile of donated books when she heard the library door creak open. She looked up to see Tilda Morrison entering, her usually confident demeanor replaced by a nervous energy.

"Agatha," Tilda said in a hushed tone, glancing over her shoulder as if afraid of being overheard. "Do you have a moment? It's... it's important."

Agatha set down the book she was holding and nodded, gesturing to a quiet corner of the library. "Of course, Tilda. What's on your mind?"

They settled into two worn armchairs, partially hidden by a tall bookshelf. Tilda leaned in, her voice barely above a whisper. "I've been thinking a lot about what happened to Harold and Nurse Amanda. There's something you should know."

Agatha's heart quickened. "Go on," she encouraged gently.

Tilda took a deep breath, her hands fidgeting in her lap. "A few nights before Amanda died, I saw her meeting with someone. It was late, and they clearly didn't want to be seen."

"Who was it, Tilda?" Agatha asked, though she had a sinking feeling she already knew the answer.

"It was Devin," Tilda confirmed, her eyes wide. "Harold's nephew. They were talking in hushed tones, and they seemed... well, very secretive."

Agatha felt a chill run down her spine. "Are you absolutely sure it was Devin?"

Tilda nodded emphatically. "I'm positive. I recognized his coat – it's very distinctive, dark with a silver stripe on the sleeve. I've seen him wear it often when he visits Green Acres."

Agatha leaned back, processing this information. "Did you hear anything they were saying?"

Tilda shook her head, looking frustrated. "No, I was too far away. But their body language... Agatha, it looked serious. Like they were discussing something important and didn't want anyone to know."

"How did Amanda seem?" Agatha pressed. "Was she upset? Angry?"

Tilda furrowed her brow, trying to recall the details. "She seemed... tense. Anxious, even. At one point, she grabbed Devin's arm, like she was pleading with him about something."

Agatha nodded slowly, her mind racing. "Tilda, this is very important information. Have you told anyone else about this?"

"No," Tilda replied, shaking her head. "I... I was afraid. After what happened to Amanda, I didn't know who to trust. But I knew I could come to you, Agatha."

Agatha reached out and patted Tilda's hand reassuringly. "You did the right thing. Thank you for telling me. I promise I'll be discreet with this information."

Tilda visibly relaxed, relief washing over her face. "What do you think it means, Agatha? Do you think Devin could be involved in... in what happened?"

Agatha chose her words carefully. "I'm not sure yet, Tilda. But it's certainly something that needs to be looked into. For now, I think it's best if you don't mention this to anyone else. Can you do that?"

Tilda nodded solemnly. "Of course. I trust you, Agatha. Just... be careful, okay? I can't shake the feeling that there's something dangerous going on here."

As Tilda stood to leave, Agatha caught her arm gently. "Tilda, one more thing. If you remember anything else, no matter how small it might seem, please let me know."

"I will," Tilda promised. She hesitated for a moment, then added, "Agatha, do you really think you can figure out what's happening?"

Agatha managed a small, determined smile. "I'm certainly going to try, Tilda. For Harold's sake, for Amanda's, and for everyone at Green Acres. The truth has to come out."

Agatha furrowed her brow, a thought suddenly occurring to her. "Tilda," Agatha said, lowering her voice, "now that you mention it, don't you find it odd that Devin continues to visit Green Acres so frequently?"

Tilda looked confused. "What do you mean?"

Agatha elaborated, her voice low and thoughtful. "Well, think about it. Harold is dead. Devin's not a resident here, and as far as I know, he doesn't have any other relatives at Green Acres. So why does he keep coming back?"

Tilda's eyes widened as the implication sank in. "I... I hadn't really thought about it that way. You're right, it is strange."

"Exactly," Agatha nodded. "Most people would have no reason to keep visiting after their relative passed away. Unless..."

"Unless what?" Tilda asked, leaning in closer.

"Unless there's something – or someone – here that he's very interested in," Agatha finished, her mind already racing with possibilities.

Tilda looked around nervously before whispering, "Do you think it has something to do with Beatrice? Or... or maybe it's connected to what happened to Amanda?"

Agatha shook her head. "I'm not sure, Tilda. But it's certainly something worth looking into. Devin's continued presence here could be a key piece of the puzzle."

∾

After her volunteer shift at the library, Agatha settled behind the counter of her bookstore, her laptop open before her. The screen glowed, casting a pale light across her features as she lost herself in thought. She needed to find out more about Devin's background.

Hours ticked by as Agatha sifted through various articles and records. Her eyes widened as she stumbled upon an interesting tidbit: Devin worked for a pharmaceutical company. Further digging revealed an even more intriguing fact – Harold was the owner of this very company.

Curious about Devin's role, Agatha decided to do some digging into Harold's family history. After some determined clicking and scrolling, she discovered something that made her pause.

"Well, well," Agatha murmured, tapping her chin thoughtfully. "Isn't that interesting? Devin is Harold's only living direct relative."

She leaned back in her chair, her mind already spinning with possibilities. If Devin was Harold's only living relative, it was quite likely he'd be the main beneficiary of Harold's will. Of course, she couldn't be certain, but it certainly cast things in a different light.

Agatha jotted down this new information in her notebook, adding a small question mark next to it. This discovery didn't prove anything, but it definitely gave her something to think about."

As Agatha was jotting down her thoughts about Devin, the bell above the bookstore door chimed. She looked up to see Lorraine entering, a look of excitement on her face.

"Bonjour Agatha! You look deep in thought. What's got your mind spinning today?" Lorraine asked, approaching the counter.

Agatha hesitated for a moment, then decided to share. "I was just looking into Harold's family. Did you know Devin is his only living relative?"

Lorraine's eyes widened. "Mon Dieu! That's interesting, but... oh, that reminds me of something I heard!" She leaned in, lowering her voice conspiratorially. "Word is, Harold changed his will recently. They say he left everything to Beatrice, can you believe it?"

"What?" Agatha exclaimed, her earlier discovery

suddenly cast in a new light. "But how do you know this if the will hasn't been revealed yet?"

Lorraine shrugged. "You know how gossip spreads in this town. Apparently, someone overheard a conversation at the diner about Harold's plans. Can you believe it? Even with how secretive he was trying to be, our local grapevine still picked it up. Of course, it's all supposed to be hush-hush until the official announcement."

Agatha's mind raced with this new information, her heart pounding with a mix of fear and concern. If Harold had indeed left everything to Beatrice, it would give Devin a strong motive to want both Harold and Beatrice out of the way. A chill ran down her spine as she realized the implications.

"Oh no," she whispered, her eyes wide. "If Devin's behind this, Beatrice could be in real danger." She glanced around nervously, as if expecting to see Devin lurking in the shadows.

Agatha's fingers tightened around her bag strap. "I need to warn her," she murmured, "but how can I do that without tipping off Devin?"

She knew she needed to dig deeper into Devin's activities and find out if he was truly behind the recent events, all while keeping Beatrice safe.

Determined to find more evidence and protect Beatrice, Agatha decided to keep a close eye on Devin. She had a feeling that the answers she sought were within reach, but she had to be careful not to reveal her suspicions too soon. The weight of responsibility settled on her shoulders as she realized it wasn't just about solving a mystery anymore – it was about potentially saving a life.

The next morning, Agatha arrived at Green Acres, her tote bag filled with books and a thermos of coffee. As she chatted with residents and staff, her eyes kept drifting to Devin, noting his movements and interactions.

"Morning, Devin," Agatha called out, waving casually as she passed him in the hallway.

"Oh, hi Agatha," he replied, seeming distracted.

Agatha watched as Devin hurried away, his shoulders tense and his gait quick. Something about his demeanor piqued her curiosity.

Later that afternoon, as Agatha was tidying up the library shelves, she glanced out the window and spotted Devin leaving the building. His furtive glances and hurried pace stirred her detective instincts.

On impulse, she grabbed her cardigan and followed him, keeping a discreet distance. He led her to a small park nearby, where he settled on a bench, fidgeting and repeatedly checking his watch.

Agatha hesitated behind a nearby oak tree, her curiosity getting the better of her. Taking a deep breath, she stepped out and approached him.

Devin looked up, surprise flickering across his face. "Agatha, what are you doing here?"

Agatha plopped down on the bench next to Devin, offering a friendly smile. "Hope you don't mind if I join you. It's such a lovely day, isn't it?"

Devin nodded, looking a bit puzzled. "Yeah, it's nice."

"You know," Agatha said, her tone conversational, "I couldn't help but wonder why you're still in Bristol Lake. Most people can't wait to leave after visiting their relatives."

Devin chuckled nervously. "Are you writing a book about the town or something?"

Agatha laughed. "Oh no, just a nosy neighbor, I'm

afraid. It's just, well, with everything that's happened lately... I saw you talking with Nurse Amanda the other day. You two seemed friendly."

"Amanda?" Devin's eyebrows shot up. "We were just friends, really."

"Oh, of course," Agatha nodded, then added gently, "It's just, with losing your uncle and now Amanda... I hope you're doing okay?"

Before Devin could respond, a familiar voice called out, "Well, what do we have here? A park meetup?"

Agatha turned to see Detective Dawson approaching, a bemused expression on his face.

"Detective!" Agatha chirped. "Lovely day for a stroll, isn't it?"

Dawson's gaze shifted between Agatha and Devin. "Mmhmm. Agatha, could I have a word?"

"Oh, certainly," Agatha stood, brushing off her skirt. "Devin, thanks for the chat. Take care!"

Agatha followed Dawson a few steps away, her heart pounding. "What is it, Detective?"

"I appreciate your enthusiasm, but you need to leave the investigating to us," Dawson said firmly. "You're putting yourself in danger."

"I understand, but I'm close to finding out the truth," Agatha insisted. "Devin knows more than he's letting on."

Dawson sighed. "We're looking into it. But please, let us handle it from here."

Reluctantly, Agatha agreed. As she turned to leave, she caught sight of Devin striding purposefully along one of the park's winding paths towards the main gate. Their eyes met for a brief moment, and Agatha felt a chill run down her spine.

Devin's gaze was a mixture of suspicion and barely

concealed anger. His jaw was set, and his hands were clenched at his sides as he quickened his pace, disappearing behind a cluster of oak trees.

Agatha watched him go, her mind racing. That look confirmed her suspicions - Devin was definitely hiding something, and he wasn't happy about her poking around.

～

The next morning, Agatha decided to treat herself to one of Eliza's famous cinnamon rolls. With Mike trotting happily beside her, she made her way to the bakery, the smell of fresh pastries growing stronger as they approached.

As she reached for the door handle, it swung open, and Devin stepped out, followed by a well-dressed man Agatha didn't recognize. The stranger's crisp suit and polished shoes screamed "out-of-towner."

"Excuse us," the man said politely, as he and Devin brushed past.

Agatha watched them go, her curiosity piqued. She entered the bakery, the little bell above the door announcing her arrival.

"Morning, Agatha!" Eliza called from behind the counter, her cheeks dusted with flour. "The usual?"

"Please," Agatha nodded, then added casually, "Say, Eliza, who was that man with Devin? I don't think I've seen him around before."

Eliza leaned in, lowering her voice conspiratorially. "Oh, him? He said he was an attorney from California, here on business. Ordered our strongest coffee - must be jet-lagged, poor thing."

"An attorney from California?" Agatha mused, absently

scratching Mike behind the ears. "I wonder if he's Harold's lawyer. But why would he be in town now?"

Eliza shrugged, boxing up Agatha's cinnamon roll. "Who knows? But it sure is exciting to have a big-city lawyer in our little town, isn't it?"

Agatha nodded, her mind whirring with possibilities. "It certainly is, Eliza. It certainly is."

19

A RECIPE FOR DANGER

A couple of days later, Agatha woke to the cheerful chirping of birds outside her window. Stretching, she felt a sudden urge to inject some normalcy into her life, which had become a whirlwind of amateur sleuthing.

"What do you say we bake something special for Aunt Edna today, Mike?" she asked her furry companion, who responded with an enthusiastic tail wag.

With her visit to Green Acres scheduled for later, Agatha decided to try her hand at baking a special treat. It was a welcome distraction from the whirlwind of her investigation.

Agatha stood in her kitchen, surveying the battlefield of flour, sugar, and scattered chocolate chips. Mike sat at her feet, his head tilted curiously.

"Well, Mike," Agatha sighed, tightening her apron, "how hard can baking be? It's just following instructions, right?"

She flipped open a well-worn cookbook to "Chocolate Chip Surprise Cake" and began reading aloud. "Step one:

Preheat the oven to 350 degrees. Easy enough." Turning the dial, she realized her mistake. "Broil? That would've been a disaster," she muttered, correcting it quickly.

Mike let out a small, seemingly judgmental bark.

"Oh, hush," Agatha chuckled. "I'd like to see you do better with paws." As she mixed ingredients, a sudden sneeze sent flour puffing into her face. Coughing and waving her hand, she looked down at Mike. "Not. One. Bark." The doorbell rang just as she knocked over the vanilla extract. "Perfect timing," she muttered, nudging Mike away from the spill.

Emma stood at the door, eyebrows raised at the flour-covered Agatha. "Baking, or starting a new career as a ghost?"

"Very funny," Agatha replied, letting her in. "I'm making a cake for Aunt Edna. It's... going well."

Emma surveyed the chaos. "I can see that. Need a hand?" As they cleaned and baked, Agatha filled Emma in on her investigation.

"So you think Devin's behind the manuscript theft?" Emma asked, expertly folding in chocolate chips.

Agatha nodded, licking batter off her finger. "It's too coincidental. He was seen with Amanda, and now my manuscript's gone. I think he's trying to pressure me."

"That's a big accusation, Agatha," Emma cautioned. "Are you sure?"

"Not completely," Agatha admitted. "But my gut says he's hiding something big."

They managed to get the cake in the oven with only minor incidents – including Agatha nearly turning the mixer on high without the bowl in place.

As they waited, sipping tea, Agatha continued, "I'm

close to something, Emma. I just need to be careful. Devin can't know I'm onto him."

Emma nodded, then grinned as the timer dinged. "Well, detective, let's see if your baking skills are as good as your sleuthing."

The cake, surprisingly, turned out perfectly. As they enjoyed slices with their tea, Mike looking up hopefully, Agatha felt a moment of normalcy amidst the chaos of her investigation.

"We'll figure this out," Emma assured her. "For now, let's just enjoy this small victory. Who knew you could bake?"

Agatha laughed, tossing a small piece of cake to Mike. "Don't get used to it. I think I'll stick to selling books – it's less messy."

The late afternoon sun cast long shadows across the parking lot as Agatha pulled up to the city jail. Her fingers drummed nervously on the steering wheel as she glanced at the passenger seat, where Mike usually sat. His absence felt palpable, and she could almost see his soulful eyes pleading to come along.

"Sorry, buddy," she murmured to the empty seat. "Not this time."

The jail's entrance loomed before her, its grey concrete walls emanating a chill that had nothing to do with the weather. As Agatha pushed through the heavy metal doors, the familiar scent of disinfectant and stale coffee assaulted her nostrils. She was so lost in thought that she nearly collided with a tall figure in the lobby.

"Detective Dawson?" Agatha exclaimed, taking a step

back. "What brings you to this cheerful establishment? Visiting a wayward cousin, perhaps?"

Dawson's lips twitched in what might have been a smile. "Cute, Agatha. I'm here on official business, actually. Checking in on your aunt."

Agatha's eyebrows shot up. "Oh? And how is she? Still maintaining her innocence, I hope."

Dawson's face grew serious. "That's the thing, Agatha. The evidence against her is rock solid, but something doesn't sit right. It's like trying to fit a square peg in a round hole."

"I know exactly what you mean," Agatha nodded, her voice dropping to a near-whisper. "Did you know they offered her bond?"

"I did," Dawson replied, his brow furrowing. "And she turned it down. Said she felt safer inside. Now, why would an innocent woman say that?"

Agatha's mind raced. "Unless... unless she's afraid of something. Or someone."

A heavy silence fell between them. Agatha could almost hear the gears turning in Dawson's head.

"Detective," she began, her heart pounding, "there's something I need to tell you." She launched into a detailed account of her discoveries, her words tumbling out in a rush.

Dawson listened intently, his expression unreadable. When she finished, he let out a long breath. "Agatha, I appreciate your... enthusiasm. But you're making some pretty big leaps here. Those documents you saw? Could just be routine paperwork. Green Acres rents storage units all over town."

"But what about Devin and Amanda?" Agatha pressed,

frustration coloring her voice. "Their secret meetings, the timing of it all?"

Dawson's eyes softened. "Look, it's no secret those two were... close. And Devin has an alibi for Amanda's murder. A solid one."

Agatha's jaw dropped. "He does? But... where was he?"

"You know I can't disclose that, Agatha," Dawson said, his tone gentle but firm. "We're doing our job. If your aunt is innocent, we'll prove it."

Agatha ran a hand through her hair, her frustration palpable. "I understand, Detective. But you have to see it from my perspective. My aunt, my family, is sitting in a cell. I can't just... I can't do nothing."

Dawson studied her for a long moment. "I get it, Agatha. I do. Just... be careful, alright? And if you find anything concrete, you come to me first. Deal?"

Agatha nodded, a small smile tugging at her lips. "Deal."

As Dawson walked away, his footsteps echoing in the stark hallway, Agatha took a deep breath. Her visit with Aunt Edna awaited, and after that, she had a mystery to solve. One way or another, she was going to get to the bottom of this.

After a bittersweet visit with Aunt Edna, where the Chocolate Chip Surprise Cake had been an unexpected hit despite the stark surroundings, Agatha headed home to pick up Mike before making her way to the bookstore. The warmth of Aunt Edna's smile as she savored the homemade treat lingered in Agatha's mind, a small victory amid the turmoil of recent events."

The bell above the door chimed softly as Agatha entered One Deadly Chapter Books and Brew, the familiar scent of books and freshly brewed coffee enveloping her. Mike trotted in behind her, his nails clicking on the hardwood floor.

Celeste looked up from behind the counter, her bright smile a stark contrast to the dimming evening light outside. "Evening, Agatha! Oh, and hello to you too, Mike," she added, reaching down to scratch the dog's ears.

"How'd it go today?" Agatha asked, hanging her coat on the rack by the door.

Celeste's eyes lit up. "You won't believe it! A tour bus from upstate stopped by for the afternoon reading. We were swamped!" She gestured to the nearly empty shelves. "Sold more books today than we have all week."

Agatha's eyebrows shot up in surprise. "That's fantastic! Though I'm sorry I wasn't here for the reading."

Celeste chuckled, shaking her head. "Oh, you should've heard the disappointed sighs when I told them the 'famous' Agatha Royale wouldn't be reading today. You've got quite the fan club, you know."

"Famous? Hardly," Agatha scoffed, but couldn't hide her pleased smile. "I'll make it up to them next week, I promise."

As Celeste gathered her things to leave, she paused, her brow furrowing. "Oh, I almost forgot. Tilda Morrison stopped by. Said it was important she speak with you."

Agatha's heart skipped a beat. "Did she say what about?"

"No, but she seemed pretty anxious. Everything okay?"

"Just peachy," Agatha lied smoothly. "I'll catch up with her tomorrow when I'm volunteering. Thanks for letting me know."

After Celeste left, Agatha sank into the chair behind the counter, her mind whirling. She opened her laptop, fingers hovering over the keys. 'I should have asked

Dawson how Amanda died,' she thought, mentally kicking herself.

A quick search brought up an article from the Bristol Lake Gazette. Agatha's eyes widened as she read. "Poisoned?" she muttered. "But how...?"

The bell above the door jingled again, startling Agatha from her thoughts. Emma burst in; her cheeks flushed with excitement.

"Agatha, you'll never guess!" Emma exclaimed, practically bouncing on her toes.

Agatha couldn't help but smile at her friend's enthusiasm. "What's got you so worked up?"

"I got a new job!" Emma blurted out. "At the Gazette! Can you believe it?"

Agatha's jaw dropped. "The Gazette? But... what about the library?"

Emma's smile faltered. "Oh, I... I didn't mention I was looking, did I? I'm sorry, I just... I didn't want to jinx it, you know?"

Agatha nodded, understanding dawning. "No, no, I get it. Wow, Emma, that's... that's great news. Congratulations!"

As they chatted about Emma's new job, Agatha's mind drifted back to the article. "Hey, speaking of the Gazette, I just read that Amanda was poisoned. Isn't that odd? She made it all the way to the park to meet me, and then...?"

Emma's expression turned serious. "You don't think... could someone have known about your meeting? Set you up?"

A chill ran down Agatha's spine. "I hadn't even considered that. But who would want to set me up? And why?"

The jingle of the door's bell interrupted their conversation. Agatha and Emma turned to see Tilda Morrison burst in, her eyes wild with fear.

"Tilda!" Agatha exclaimed, rising from her seat. "What's wrong?"

"Agatha!" Tilda gasped, her voice trembling. "I... I need your help!"

Agatha rushed to her side, guiding her to a nearby armchair. "Tilda, what's happened? You look like you've seen a ghost."

Tilda's hands shook as she clutched at Agatha's arm. Her gaze darted nervously between Agatha and Emma, as if checking for eavesdroppers. When she spoke, her voice was barely above a whisper.

"Someone... someone tried to kill me."

Emma gasped, her hand flying to her mouth. Agatha leaned in closer, her heart racing. "What do you mean? Tell us exactly what happened."

Tilda opened her mouth to speak, but before she could utter another word, the lights in the bookstore suddenly flickered and went out, plunging them into darkness. In the silence that followed, they heard the unmistakable sound of footsteps approaching from the back of the store.

Tilda's grip on Agatha's arm tightened. "They've found me," she whispered, her voice filled with terror.

As Agatha's eyes adjusted to the darkness, she caught a glimpse of a shadowy figure moving between the bookshelves, drawing ever closer.

20

SCARED TO DEATH

Agatha, Emma, and Tilda huddled together in the darkness, their breath coming in short, panicked gasps. The air felt thick with tension as they strained their eyes, trying to make out shapes in the inky blackness. Suddenly, a shadowy figure loomed from behind a bookshelf, its outline barely visible in the dim emergency light.

The three women screamed in unison, their voices piercing the silence of the bookstore. To their surprise, the shadowy figure let out an even louder, more terrified shriek.

In that moment, the lights flickered back to life, revealing a familiar face.

"Mon Dieu! Please don't kill me!" Lorraine cried, her hands thrown up dramatically, a book clutched to her chest like a shield. "I'm too young and fabulous to die!"

"Lorraine?" Agatha exclaimed, lowering the heavy book she'd grabbed as an impromptu weapon. "What in the world are you doing here?"

Emma burst into nervous laughter, the tension breaking like a dam. "We thought you were an intruder!"

Lorraine blinked rapidly, looking disoriented. "I... I came for the book reading this afternoon. I must have dozed off in that comfy chair in the corner. Oh la la, I sleep like the dead sometimes!"

Tilda, who had been clinging to Agatha's arm, slowly relaxed her grip. "So... no one's trying to kill us?"

"Only with embarrassment, it seems," Agatha chuckled, though her voice still held a tremor of leftover adrenaline. "Lorraine, how did none of us notice you were still here?"

Lorraine shrugged, a sheepish smile playing on her lips. "What can I say? I'm small and quiet when I sleep. Unlike when I'm awake, non?"

As the four women's laughter echoed through the bookstore, dispersing the last of their fear, Agatha couldn't help but wonder: Was this just a comedic misunderstanding, or had someone really been after Tilda? And if so, were they still out there, waiting for another opportunity?

The night suddenly felt very long indeed, and Agatha knew that once the laughter died down, they'd have to address Tilda's frightening claim. But for now, she allowed herself to enjoy this moment of relief, grateful for Lorraine's inadvertent comic timing.

Lorraine glanced at her watch, her eyes widening comically. "Oh la la! Is that the time? I've been here since... well, since forever! Au revoir, mes amies. This sleeping beauty needs her actual bed!"

After Lorraine's dramatic exit, a heavy silence fell over the bookstore. Tilda, the earlier excitement fading from her eyes, looked nervous and on the verge of tears. "I... I wasn't joking earlier. Someone really did try to kill me."

Agatha leaned forward, her voice gentle but urgent. "Tell us exactly what happened, Tilda."

Tilda's hands shook as she spoke. "I was in my backyard, tending to my roses, when suddenly... bang! A bullet whizzed past my ear and hit the fence behind me. I... I could have died!"

Emma gasped, her hand flying to her mouth. Agatha was already reaching for her phone. "We need to call Detective Dawson right away."

~

An hour later, they stood in Tilda's backyard, watching as Detective Dawson examined the fence with a flashlight. The night air was cool and still, broken only by the occasional chirp of crickets and the murmur of police radios.

"Here," Dawson called out, pointing to a splintered hole in the wooden fence. "Definitely a bullet hole. Tilda, you're lucky it missed you."

Tilda shuddered, wrapping her arms around herself. "But who would want to shoot me? And why?"

Dawson's face was grim in the harsh beam of the flashlight. "That's what we need to figure out. Agatha, a word?"

As they stepped aside, Dawson lowered his voice. "This is serious. First Amanda, now this attempt on Tilda. Something bigger is going on here."

Agatha nodded, her mind racing. "Do you think it's connected to Aunt Edna's case?"

"It's possible," Dawson admitted. "But we can't jump to conclusions. For now, Tilda needs protection. And you," he fixed Agatha with a stern look, "need to be careful. Whoever's behind this clearly isn't afraid to use violence."

Agatha glanced at her watch and let out a small gasp. "Oh, would you look at the time! Emma, we'd better scoot if we want to be bright-eyed for our library stint at Green Acres tomorrow."

She turned to Dawson with a grateful smile. "Thanks for all your help, Detective. We really appreciate it."

Dawson's eyes twinkled with amusement. "Just doing my job, Agatha. Though I hope this volunteer gig of yours is more about shelving books than solving mysteries."

Agatha placed a hand over her heart in mock offense. "Detective Dawson, I'm shocked you'd even suggest such a thing. We're model citizens, aren't we, Emma?"

Emma nodded vigorously, fighting back a grin. "Oh, absolutely. Perfect angels."

Dawson chuckled, shaking his head. "Alright, alright. Just remember, leave the sleuthing to the professionals, okay?"

"Cross my heart," Agatha said, making the gesture with a wink.

~

The antique grandfather clock in the corner of Green Acres' library chimed four times, its deep resonance echoing through the book-lined room. Agatha looked up from the pile of returns she was sorting, surprised at how quickly the afternoon had slipped away. Around her, the last few library patrons were gathering their selections – large-print novels, colorful magazines, and the occasional non-fiction tome.

Mrs. Peterson, a sprightly octogenarian with a penchant for mystery novels, approached the checkout desk. "Agatha, dear," she said, her voice wavering with age but still full of enthusiasm, "I've finally decided to give that new cozy mystery author a try. The one you recommended last week."

Agatha smiled warmly, taking the book from Mrs. Peterson's gnarled hands. "I think you'll enjoy it, Mrs. Peterson. The twist at the end is quite something."

As Mrs. Peterson shuffled away, her new book clutched to her chest, Agatha noticed Mr. Johnson, a retired history professor, carefully returning a stack of World War II biographies to their proper places on the shelves. His movements were slow but deliberate, each book aligned perfectly with its neighbors.

Once the last patron had left, the library fell into a comfortable silence, broken only by the soft ticking of the clock. Emma, who had been helping a resident navigate the library's single computer, turned to Agatha with a furrowed brow.

"Is it just me," Emma whispered, leaning close over the checkout desk, "or has Beatrice been conspicuously absent since... you know, Harold's passing?"

Agatha paused in her sorting, realization dawning on her face. "You're right. I hadn't even noticed. Poor thing must be taking it hard, wanting privacy to mourn."

Emma shook her head, unconvinced. "Maybe, but this is an assisted living facility, not some suburban neighborhood where you can hole up for weeks. Has anyone actually seen her?"

Before Agatha could respond, the library door swung open with a bang. Roger Collins strode in, his face a storm cloud of irritation.

"Ms. Royale," he barked, his voice echoing in the quiet room. "This isn't one of your mystery novels. You have no business interrogating people here."

Agatha blinked, taken aback by his hostility. "I'm sorry? I don't understand—"

"Don't play coy," Collins interrupted, his eyes narrowing. "I've heard you've been bothering Devin, asking why he's here. That's none of your concern. You're just a volunteer, remember?"

Agatha and Emma exchanged a quick glance, a silent agreement passing between them. Now wasn't the time for confrontation.

"I apologize, Mr. Collins," Agatha said, her voice calm despite her racing heart. "I only want to ensure everyone's safety. It won't happen again."

Collins snorted, clearly unconvinced. He turned his sharp gaze to Emma. "That goes for you too."

Emma nodded meekly, though Agatha could see the fire in her friend's eyes.

As Collins began inspecting the shelves with exaggerated care, Agatha decided to take a risk. "Mr. Collins, how is Beatrice doing? We haven't seen her in a while."

Collins stiffened, his back to them. "She's in California. Visiting family."

"Oh, that's nice," Agatha pressed gently. "When is she due back?"

Collins whirled around, his face flushed. "How should I know? She's not a prisoner here, Ms. Royale. She comes and goes as she pleases."

The tension in the room was palpable. Agatha forced a smile, deciding discretion was the better part of valor. "Of course. Thank you for the information, Mr. Collins."

As Collins stomped out of the library, Emma leaned close to Agatha. "Well, that was... interesting," she murmured.

Agatha nodded, her mind racing. Collins' reaction to the question about Beatrice had been oddly defensive. It was clear there was more going on here than met the eye. But what?

As Agatha and Emma were preparing to leave the library, a hesitant knock on the door frame caught their attention. They looked up to see Lindsey, the receptionist, standing there, nervously glancing over her shoulder.

"Agatha, do you have a moment?" Lindsey asked in a hushed tone, her usually cheerful demeanor replaced by a look of concern.

Agatha nodded, intrigued. "Of course, Lindsey. What's on your mind?"

Lindsey stepped into the library, closing the door behind her. "It's about Devin... Harold's nephew. I've seen some things that don't seem right."

Emma and Agatha exchanged quick glances before Agatha gestured for Lindsey to sit down. "What kind of things?"

Lindsey leaned in, her voice barely above a whisper. "The night before Amanda died, I saw Devin arguing with her in the parking lot. It looked pretty heated. And then, just yesterday, I overheard him on the phone, talking about Beatrice's absence. He said something like, 'With her out of the way, everything falls to me.'"

Agatha's heart raced. "Did you hear anything else?"

"He's been asking a lot of questions about Harold's will," Lindsey continued. "Wanting to know if anyone's seen it, if it's been read yet. He seems... desperate."

"Have you told anyone else about this?" Emma asked.

Lindsey shook her head. "I was afraid to say anything. Devin's been spending a lot of time with Mr. Collins lately. I thought maybe they were working together on something. And I don't want to lose my job."

Agatha reached out, patting Lindsey's hand reassuringly. "You did the right thing, Lindsey. This could be important. Have you noticed anything else unusual about Devin's behavior?"

As Lindsey shared more details, Agatha's mind whirled

with possibilities. Could Devin have killed Harold to inherit his fortune, only to discover Beatrice was the true beneficiary? And now, with Beatrice mysteriously absent, was he planning to eliminate her too?

But even as suspicion built within her, a nagging worry took root. If Devin was indeed behind these crimes, how far would he go to keep his secrets? And by confiding in Agatha, had Lindsey just put herself in danger?

Agatha knew she needed to tread carefully. With Devin looking increasingly guilty, she had to find a way to protect Beatrice and uncover the truth without alerting the real killer to her suspicions.

21

SUSPICIOUS ENCOUNTERS

The bell above the door of the Bookstore chimed merrily as Lorraine burst in, her silk scarf trailing dramatically behind her. The scent of freshly brewed coffee and old books filled the air, a comforting aroma that usually brought Agatha peace. Today, however, her mind was too preoccupied with the case to fully appreciate it.

Agatha and Emma, already seated at their favorite corner table, looked up from their steaming mugs of coffee. The afternoon sun streamed through the large front window, casting a warm glow over the cozy bookstore.

"Mes amies!" Lorraine exclaimed, dropping into the empty chair with a flourish. "You won't believe the gossip I've uncovered!"

Agatha raised an eyebrow, exchanging a knowing glance with Emma. "Lorraine, we're supposed to be discussing the case, not gossiping."

"Ah, but ma chérie," Lorraine replied with a wink, helping herself to a biscotti from the plate between them, "sometimes gossip and cases are one and the same, non?"

Emma leaned in, her eyes sparkling with curiosity despite her attempts to appear serious. "Go on then, what's this earth-shattering news?"

As Lorraine launched into a convoluted tale involving Mr. Collins, a mysterious phone call, and a suspected toupee, Agatha found her mind wandering. The cozy atmosphere of her bookstore usually brought her comfort, but today, with the weight of unsolved mysteries pressing down on her, even the familiar surroundings couldn't ease her tension.

"Agatha? Hello? Earth to Agatha!" Emma's voice snapped her back to attention.

"Sorry," Agatha mumbled, taking a sip of her now-luke-warm coffee. "I was just thinking about Devin. Something doesn't add up."

Lorraine nodded sagely. "Oui, that man is more suspicious than a cat in a room full of rocking chairs."

Despite herself, Agatha chuckled. "That's not quite how the saying goes, Lorraine."

"Close enough," Lorraine shrugged, reaching for another biscotti. "The point is, he's hiding something. I can feel it in my bones."

Emma straightened in her chair, her expression turning serious. "Speaking of Devin, I saw him leaving Green Acres late last night when I was driving home from the library. He looked... nervous."

Agatha's interest piqued. "Nervous how?"

"He kept looking over his shoulder," Emma explained, her brow furrowing as she recalled the scene. "And he was carrying a stack of folders. As I was driving past, he must have spotted my car because he suddenly looked panicked."

"Folders?" Agatha repeated, her mind racing. "Could you see what was in them?"

Emma chuckled, shaking her head. "Agatha, I was driving by. Unless I've miraculously developed superhero vision, there's no way I could've seen what was in those folders from that distance."

"Right, of course," Agatha said, smiling sheepishly. "Did you notice anything else unusual?"

"Well," Emma continued, "in his rush to get to his car, he dropped one of the folders. Papers went flying everywhere. You should have seen him scrambling to gather them up. He looked absolutely frantic, like he was terrified someone might see what was on those pages."

The three friends fell silent for a moment, each lost in thought. The quiet hum of the bookstore around them seemed to fade away as they contemplated this new piece of information.

"We need to find out what was in those folders," Agatha finally said, her voice low and determined.

Lorraine's eyes lit up. "Ooh, are we going to break into Devin's house? I've always wanted to be a cat burglar!"

"No, Lorraine," Agatha sighed, though she couldn't help but smile at her enthusiasm. "We're not breaking into anyone's house. We need to be smart about this. Careful."

"Careful is my middle name," Lorraine declared, causing both Agatha and Emma to snort in disbelief.

As they continued their discussion, dissecting every interaction they'd had with Devin, Agatha couldn't shake the feeling that they were missing something crucial. The pieces of the puzzle were there, just out of reach, tantalizingly close to forming a complete picture.

Later that evening, as the sun dipped below the horizon, painting the sky in brilliant hues of orange and pink, Agatha set out for her evening walk with Mike. The air was crisp, carrying the faint scent of wood smoke from a neighbor's chimney.

Mike trotted along happily, his leash slack in Agatha's hand. As they rounded the corner onto Maple Street, Agatha's steps faltered. There, emerging from Gemma's quaint Victorian house, was Devin.

Agatha quickly ducked behind a large oak tree, her heart racing. Mike, sensing her tension, let out a low growl.

"Shh, Mike," Agatha whispered, peering around the trunk.

Devin glanced furtively up and down the street before hurrying to his car. In the fading light, Agatha could see the tense set of his shoulders, the way his hands clenched and unclenched at his sides. And there, tucked under his arm, were some folders – similar, she imagined, to the ones Emma had described.

As Devin's car roared to life and sped away, Mike barked sharply, straining at his leash.

"I know, boy," Agatha murmured, patting his head. "I don't trust him either."

Her mind whirled with possibilities. What was Devin doing at Gemma's house? What was in those folders? And how did it all connect to Harold's death and the strange happenings at Green Acres?

The next morning, Agatha recounted her sighting to Emma and Lorraine over scones and tea at the bookstore. The early morning light filtered through the windows, casting a soft glow over the bookshelves and giving the store an almost ethereal quality.

"Mon Dieu!" Lorraine exclaimed, nearly upending her

teacup. "Do you think they're... you know?" She waggled her eyebrows suggestively.

Emma rolled her eyes. "Lorraine, please. This is serious."

"I am being serious!" Lorraine protested. "Perhaps it's a torrid love affair gone wrong. Or maybe they're secret agents, plotting to overthrow the government!"

Agatha smiled at Lorraine's wild theories. "I think the truth is probably somewhere in between 'torrid affair' and 'government conspiracy'. But whatever it is, I intend to find out."

"So what's our next move?" Emma asked, always the practical one.

Agatha took a thoughtful sip of her tea. "I think it's time we had a chat with Gemma. Find out what she knows about Devin's late-night visits."

"Ooh, can I come?" Lorraine asked eagerly. "I can be the distraction if things get tense. I'm excellent at causing a scene."

"We know," Emma and Agatha said in unison, sharing a knowing look.

"Ladies," Agatha said, her voice serious, "we need to be careful. Whoever is behind all this has already possibly killed two people. We can't take any unnecessary risks."

Emma and Lorraine nodded solemnly, the gravity of the situation settling over them like a heavy blanket.

"We're with you, Agatha," Emma said softly. "All the way."

"Oui," Lorraine agreed. "We're in this together. Like the Three Musketeers, but with better fashion sense."

Agatha smiled at her friends, feeling a rush of affection for these women who had stood by her through thick and thin.

As they left the bookstore to head to Gemma's house, Agatha cast one last look around her beloved shop. The rows of books, the cozy reading nooks, the lingering scent of coffee – all of it represented the life she had built for herself in Bristol Lake. A life that had been turned upside down by murder and mystery.

Soon, Agatha, Emma, and Lorraine found themselves standing at Gemma's front door, their nerves evident as they waited for her to answer. A sliver of light appeared as the door inched open, revealing Gemma's cautious eyes peering out at them.

"Hello, how can I help you?" she asked, her voice polite but guarded.

Agatha stepped forward with a friendly smile. "Hi Gemma! It's good to see you again. I hope you don't mind, but I've brought some friends along - this is Emma and Lorraine."

Gemma glanced at each of them, her face hard to read. She smiled politely but didn't say anything right away, which made the air feel a bit thick.

"We thought we'd pop by for a quick hello," Agatha said, trying to break the ice. "Sometimes it's nice to have a little company, you know?"

Gemma's smile grew warmer, though there was still a hint of caution in her eyes. "That's kind of you. Would you like to come in for a bit?"

The trio followed Gemma into her living room, which was tastefully decorated with antique furniture and soft, muted colors. As they settled in, Gemma's gaze landed on Lorraine.

"Oh, you are the..." she made air quotes, "French woman from New Orleans."

Lorraine's cheeks flushed, and she looked down, clearly embarrassed. "Oui, that's me," she murmured.

Sensing Lorraine's discomfort, Emma quickly changed the subject. "So, what brings you to Bristol Lake, Gemma?"

Gemma paused, her expression becoming more somber. "That's a touchy subject. My ex-husband moved here, and I still saw him as a family member... my only family, so I moved here too."

"How sweet," Agatha added sympathetically.

Gemma offered them tea and excused herself to the kitchen. As she left the room, Emma kept an eye on the door while Agatha took the opportunity to look around. Lorraine remained seated, her fingers fidgeting nervously in her lap.

In the corner of the room, an antique desk caught Agatha's attention. Curiosity getting the better of her, she approached it and noticed a folder with papers protruding from its edges. She glanced at Emma for a moment before gently lifting the folder. Her breath caught in her throat when she saw the title: "Last Will and Testament."

22

UNRAVELING THREADS

Agatha whispered to herself, "What's this doing here?"

Emma's eyes widened, and she moved closer to Agatha. "Do you think it's Harold's?" she asked in a low voice.

Agatha carefully opened the folder and scanned the document. Her eyes widened as she read the details: Devin was listed as the primary beneficiary. But then, something else caught her attention—the signature line at the bottom was blank. The will was unsigned.

"It's unsigned," Agatha whispered, a mix of relief and confusion washing over her. "This changes everything."

Before they could discuss further, they heard Gemma returning. Agatha quickly closed the folder and stepped away from the desk, trying to look casual. Gemma entered the room carrying a tray with a teapot and cups.

"Here we go," Gemma said, setting the tray down on the coffee table. "I hope you like Earl Grey."

"Thank you, this is lovely," Agatha replied, taking a

cup. She shot a quick glance at Emma, who nodded subtly, understanding that they needed to tread carefully.

As they sipped their tea, the conversation turned to lighter topics, but Agatha couldn't shake the image of the will from her mind. She knew they had stumbled onto something significant, and they needed to find out more without arousing Gemma's suspicion.

~

The next morning, a crisp autumn chill hung in the air as Agatha unlocked the front door of One Deadly Chapter Books and Brew. Emma arrived moments later, her cheeks flushed from the brisk walk, carrying two takeaway cups.

"Morning," Emma called, unwinding her scarf. "I brought chai lattes. Figured you might not have the coffee ready yet."

Agatha's eyes lit up. "You're a lifesaver. Come on in, let's get warmed up."

As they settled in, the bell above the door chimed. Eliza Martin bustled in, carrying a box of fresh pastries.

"Good morning, ladies!" Eliza chirped, setting the box on the counter. "I've got your usual assortment today - scones, muffins, and those cinnamon twists you love, Agatha."

"You're an angel, Eliza," Agatha smiled, peeking into the box. "How's business at the bakery?"

"Oh, you know, same old," Eliza shrugged, but her eyes twinkled. "Though I did have a rather handsome new customer yesterday. Tall, dark, and mysterious type."

They chatted for a few more minutes before Eliza excused herself, needing to get back to her shop. As the door closed behind her, Agatha and Emma settled into their favorite corner, each with a steaming chai latte and a freshly baked scone.

Agatha took a sip of her latte, savoring the spicy-sweet flavor before speaking. "What do you make of the unsigned will?" She paused, her fingers tracing the rim of her cup. "What gets me is that Tilda told me rumors are that Harold changed his will."

Emma broke off a piece of her lemon scone, considering. "I honestly don't know... maybe Devin found out about the change and was preparing to forge a new will with him as the beneficiary?"

"Maybe," Agatha mused, "but why would it be at Gemma's house? Is Gemma Devin's accomplice?" She took a bite of her own scone, crumbs falling onto the table. "Maybe they're planning on sharing the inheritance," she said, her words garbled by the scone in her mouth.

Emma leaned back in her chair, brow furrowed. "Maybe... but why would they kill Harold before he signed the will?"

Agatha's eyes widened at the thought. She stood abruptly, retrieving her laptop from her bag. The device whirred to life as she set it on the table, fingers flying across the keys as she typed "Devin Jensen" into the search bar. Nothing meaningful appeared.

"Let's try something else," she muttered, typing "Novus Vitae Pharmaceuticals."

Emma leaned in, her shoulder brushing Agatha's as they both peered at the screen. "Bankrupt? Was this Harold's company?"

"Could be... let's see what else we can find out," Emma suggested, her voice eager.

Agatha's finger traced the lines on the screen as she read aloud. "Looks like they were working on a revolutionary medication that wasn't approved, and that destroyed their credibility and finances."

"Interesting," Emma murmured, moving closer. "Look at this picture. The bright yellow shirts with the 'Novus Vitae' logo embroidered on the chest - must have been their company uniform." Her eyes scanned the group photo. "Here's Harold."

Agatha leaned in, squinting. "Isn't this Devin?"

Emma studied the photo for a moment, her nose almost touching the screen. "Yes, it's him. He looks a little younger, but that's definitely him. Those yellow shirts really stand out, don't they?"

The bell above the door chimed, startling them both. They looked up to see Gary, the mailman, walking in with his usual cheerful smile. His cheeks were ruddy from the chilly morning air, and his uniform bore the creases of a long morning, giving him a comfortable, well-worn look.

"Good morning, ladies," he greeted warmly, his eyes crinkling at the corners. "Something smells absolutely divine in here."

Agatha smiled, gesturing to the pastry case. "Fresh from Eliza's bakery. Care for a scone, Gary? On the house."

Gary's face lit up. "Don't mind if I do! Those lemon ones are my weakness." As Agatha handed him a scone wrapped in a napkin, he pulled out an envelope from his bag. "Oh, nearly forgot. Got this for you, Agatha. Bit odd, this one - no return address."

Agatha took the envelope, turning it over in her hands with a puzzled expression. "That is strange. Thank you, Gary."

Gary nodded, taking a bite of his scone. "Mmm, heavenly as always. You know, in all my years as a postman, I've learned that letters without senders are either very good news or very bad news. Here's hoping it's the former for you, Agatha."

With a friendly wave and another word of thanks for the scone, Gary headed out, the bell chiming again as the door closed behind him.

Agatha examined the envelope more closely, turning it over in her hands. "No sender," she commented, her brow furrowing. As she continued to study the envelope, her eyes narrowed. "It's postmarked from Oxford Hills," she added, reaching for the letter opener behind the counter.

As she carefully slit open the envelope and read the contents, the color drained from her face. Her fingers hovered momentarily over the paper.

"What's wrong?" Emma asked, alarm creeping into her voice. "Who is it from?"

Wordlessly, Agatha handed over the letter. Emma's eyes widened as she read the message scrawled in angry red marker across the first page of Agatha's manuscript: 'If you want to see your manuscript again, stop digging where you shouldn't be digging. Accept that your aunt is a murderer and needs to pay for it.'

Emma's hand flew to her mouth, a soft gasp escaping her lips. Agatha sank back into her chair, one hand pressed against her chest as if to slow her racing heart.

After a moment of stunned silence, Agatha spoke, her voice low and thoughtful. "It was mailed from Oxford Hills."

Emma snorted, a hint of sarcasm creeping into her voice despite the tension. "Well, so much for trying to hide. Oxford Hills is only a 40-minute drive from here."

Agatha carefully placed the copy of her manuscript back in the envelope, her fingers lingering on the paper as if reluctant to let it go. She held the envelope in her hands, her expression hardening with determination.

"I need to find out what's going on more than ever," she said, her voice low but firm. She paused, her brow furrowing in concentration. "You know, now that I think about it... I think I've seen a yellow shirt like the one from the pharmaceutical company uniform. I just can't remember where."

Emma leaned forward, her eyes bright with interest. "Really? That could be important."

Agatha nodded, standing up with sudden energy. "I'm going to ask Detective Dawson about the security footage from Green Acres," she announced.

Emma raised an eyebrow. "Good idea, but let's hope he's willing to share. Dawson can be pretty tight-lipped about evidence."

"He has to," Agatha replied, determination clear in her voice. "This might be the break we need to crack this case wide open."

Agatha pushed open the heavy glass door of the Bristol Lake Police Station, the sudden rush of air-conditioned air a stark contrast to the warm autumn day outside. The steady hum of activity filled the space - phones ringing, printers whirring, and the low murmur of conversations. She paused for a moment, taking in the scene of officers bustling about their daily routines.

Shirley looked up from her computer, her dark ponytail swinging as she turned. A smile, part warmth and part mischief, spread across her face. "Well, well, if it isn't

Agatha Royale. I was beginning to think you'd forgotten about us little people down at the station."

Agatha approached the desk, her fingers drumming a nervous rhythm on her purse. "Hello, Shirley. It's been a while, hasn't it?"

"That's an understatement," Shirley chuckled. "I've been by the bookstore so many times, but you're never there. What gives?"

"I've been volunteering at Green Acres," Agatha replied, her voice tight.

Shirley's eyebrows shot up. "Ah, yes. I heard about that." She leaned forward, lowering her voice conspiratorially. "Must be tough, knowing your aunt... you know."

Agatha bristled. "There's no proof she actually did it, Shirley."

"Hmm," Shirley hummed, skepticism clear in her tone. "Wasn't she found with the body, holding the murder weapon? Seems pretty damning to me."

Agatha swallowed hard, fighting to keep her voice steady. "She was unconscious, you know."

"Was she?" Shirley's eyes narrowed. "That's not what I heard. Amanda told me she was asleep, even snoring. Probably tired from all that murdering."

"Nurse Amanda told you that?" Agatha's voice rose slightly, her surprise evident.

Shirley nodded, a hint of sadness crossing her face. "Yes, she did. Rest her soul. She was here almost every day with some new tidbit. Really wanted your aunt Edna put away for good."

Agatha's mind reeled at this information. "I had no idea Amanda was so involved," she muttered, more to herself than to Shirley.

Shirley leaned in closer, her voice dropping to a conspiratorial whisper. "Oh, that's not even the half of it. We got an anonymous tip that your aunt hired someone on the outside to shut Amanda up."

As soon as the words left her mouth, Shirley's eyes widened in alarm. She quickly backtracked, realizing she'd said too much. "I mean... what? I don't know what you're talking about. Forget I said anything."

"What? How do you know that?" Agatha pressed, leaning forward, her heart racing at this new revelation.

Shirley's cheeks flushed as she grabbed the phone, clearly flustered. "You can go now. Dawson will see you," she said hurriedly, effectively ending the conversation.

As Agatha made her way to Dawson's office, her mind whirled with the new information. She wanted to ask Dawson about it, but didn't want to get Shirley in trouble. She'd have to bide her time.

Agatha knocked on Detective Dawson's door, her heart pounding with anticipation.

"Come in," Dawson's gruff voice called out.

She entered to find him hunched over a stack of files, his brow furrowed in concentration. He looked up, a mixture of exasperation and amusement crossing his face.

"Agatha Royale. Why am I not surprised?" he said, leaning back in his chair. "What brings you here this time?"

Agatha took a deep breath. "Detective Dawson, I need to see the security footage from Green Acres on the day of Harold's death."

Dawson's eyebrows shot up. "And why, pray tell, do you need to see that?"

"I believe there might be something we've all missed," Agatha said carefully. "Something that could shed new light on the case."

Dawson sighed, rubbing his temples. "Agatha, we've been over this. The case is—"

"Not as clear-cut as it seems," Agatha interrupted. "Please, Detective. Just give me a chance to look."

Dawson sighed, rubbing his temples. "Fine. But this is the last time, Agatha. You're not a detective, and I can't keep indulging your amateur sleuthing."

Relief washed over Agatha. "Thank you, Detective. I promise, if I don't find anything, I'll stop pestering you about this case."

Dawson snorted. "Somehow, I doubt that." But there was a hint of fondness in his voice as he turned to his computer. "I'll pull up the footage here. You have thirty minutes," he said firmly. "Make them count."

Agatha leaned closer to the monitor, her eyes straining against the grainy footage. The usual comings and goings of staff and visitors played out before her, nothing seemingly out of place. She was about to sigh in frustration when a flash of bright yellow caught her eye.

Her heart quickened as she focused on a figure slipping out the back door. The yellow shirt stood out starkly against the dull gray of the building. Agatha's fingers flew to the controls, rewinding and pausing the footage.

"Detective Dawson," she called, her voice tight with excitement. "Can you enhance this image?"

Dawson leaned over, his brow furrowed as he manipulated the controls. The image sharpened slightly, enough for Agatha to make out a logo on the shirt. Her breath caught in her throat.

"Novus Vitae Pharmaceuticals," she whispered, recognition dawning. "That's Harold's company."

Dawson's eyebrows shot up. "Harold's company? Are you sure?"

Agatha nodded vigorously. "Positive. Emma and I were just researching it this morning. But why would someone from Novus Vitae be here on the day of Harold's death?"

She leaned in closer, squinting at the figure's face as Dawson further enhanced the image. The features slowly came into focus, and Agatha felt as if the floor had dropped out from under her.

"Oh my God," she breathed, her hand flying to her mouth. "It's Devin."

Dawson's head snapped towards her. "Devin? Harold's nephew?"

Agatha nodded, her mind racing.

"But that's impossible. He told me he wasn't even in town when Harold died. He said he didn't arrive until after..."

Her voice trailed off as she checked the timestamp. The date and time glared back at her: 2:47 PM on the afternoon of Harold's death.

Agatha sat back, her world tilting on its axis. This changed everything. But before she could voice her thoughts, a commotion outside Dawson's office caught their attention.

Shirley's voice carried through the door, sounding uncharacteristically flustered. "Sir, you can't go in there!"

The door burst open, and Agatha's heart nearly stopped as she saw who stood in the doorway, his face a mask of anger and fear.

"Devin," she whispered.

23

THE PLOT THICKENS

The fluorescent lights of the police station buzzed overhead as Agatha waited in the hall, her fingers nervously tapping against her thigh. She had hoped to stick around for Devin's conversation with Detective Dawson, but fate had other plans.

"I'm sorry, Ms. Royale," Detective Dawson had said, his face a mix of apology and firmness. "Mr. Jensen has requested to speak with me privately. I'm afraid I'll have to ask you to step out."

Devin had stood there, his face unreadable, but Agatha could have sworn she saw a flicker of something - triumph, perhaps? - in his eyes as she was ushered out of the office.

For what felt like an eternity, Agatha paced the sterile hallway, her footsteps echoing softly against the linoleum floor. Her mind raced with possibilities. What could Devin be telling Dawson? Was he spinning some tale to further implicate Aunt Edna? Or was he cleverly covering his own tracks?

Just as she was considering whether to give up and head home, the office door opened. Devin emerged, his face composed but his eyes darting around nervously. He barely spared Agatha a glance as he hurried down the hallway, his footsteps echoing in the quiet station.

Agatha watched him go, her suspicions deepening. Whatever had transpired in that office, she was certain of one thing: the case was far from closed.

As she left the police station, the cool evening air a welcome relief after the stuffy interior, Agatha noticed Devin's car still parked in the lot. Curiosity piqued, she decided to wait and see what he was up to. She found a secluded spot behind a large shrub near the entrance, feeling a bit foolish but unable to shake the feeling that something was off about Devin.

The sun was setting, casting long shadows across the parking lot, as Agatha waited. After about fifteen minutes, Devin finally emerged from the station. He looked furtively around, his eyes scanning the nearly empty lot, before pulling out his phone. Agatha held her breath, pressing herself closer to the shrub, straining to hear as Devin began to speak in hushed tones.

Her heart pounded in her chest as she listened, every instinct telling her that what she was about to hear could change everything...

"Yeah, it's me," Devin said, his voice low. "We're good. No one suspects my role in Harold's..." He paused, glancing around again. Agatha's heart raced, but Devin didn't finish the sentence.

Instead, he continued, "I'll have to deal with Agatha. She's getting too nosy for her own good. Gemma told me she caught her snooping around the will at her house. Pretended not to notice, of course."

Agatha's eyes widened. She hadn't realized Gemma had seen her that day.

Devin's voice grew harder. "Beatrice? What about her? She's been taken care of." There was a pause as he listened to the person on the other end. "Don't worry, she won't be a problem. I'll take care of Agatha too. Can't have her messing things up now."

As Devin ended the call and walked to his car, Agatha remained frozen in her hiding spot, her mind whirling. The implications of what she'd just heard were chilling. What did Devin mean by Beatrice being "taken care of"? And what was he planning to do about her?

With shaking hands, Agatha pulled out her own phone to call Emma. She needed to tell someone what she'd heard, even if part of her felt she might be overreacting. After all, this was Bristol Lake, not some big city crime novel. Surely Devin couldn't actually be planning to hurt her... could he?

As she dialed Emma's number, Agatha couldn't help but feel that she'd just stumbled onto something much bigger – and potentially more dangerous – than she'd initially thought.

Emma's cheerful voice came through the phone. "Agatha! I was just thinking about you. How did things go at the station?"

"Emma," Agatha said, her voice low and urgent. "You're not going to believe what I just overheard."

She quickly recounted what she'd heard from Devin, her words tumbling out in a rush. Emma listened intently, gasping at the appropriate moments.

"Oh my goodness," Emma breathed when Agatha finished. "Do you really think he was talking about... you know... hurting you?"

Agatha sighed, running a hand through her hair. "I don't know. It sounded pretty ominous, but this is Bristol Lake, not some crime-ridden metropolis. Still, the way he was talking about Harold and the will..."

"And Gemma's involved somehow too?" Emma mused. "This is getting complicated."

"Tell me about it," Agatha agreed. "What do you think we should do?"

Emma was quiet for a moment, thinking. "Well, we can't go to the police with just an overheard conversation. We need more evidence." She paused, then added, "What about that will you mentioned earlier? Harold's will? Could that give us any clues?"

"You're right," Agatha said, her mind racing. "The key is discovering who the beneficiary is in Harold's will. If it's Beatrice, that would certainly give Devin a motive."

"Exactly," Emma replied, excitement creeping into her voice. "But how do we find out without raising suspicion?"

Agatha tapped her fingers on the table, thinking. "Remember that attorney I saw leaving Eliza's bakery? The one from California? I bet he's Harold's lawyer."

"Oh, right!" Emma exclaimed. "But we don't know his name, do we?"

Agatha shook her head. "No, and he told Eliza he was just in town on business. He's probably back in California by now."

"So we're back to square one," Emma sighed. "How do we find out about a lawyer all the way in California?"

"Hmm," Agatha mused. "What about Gemma? She was his wife for years. She might know who his attorney was."

"Good thinking," Emma said. "But how do we ask her without raising suspicion?"

Emma's voice took on a mischievous tone. "Well, I happen to know that Gemma volunteers at the community center every Thursday afternoon. We could pay her house a little visit while she's out, see if we can find any correspondence from a law office in California."

Emma sighed, her enthusiasm deflating a bit. "Hold on a sec, Agatha. Why would Harold's attorney be sending mail to his ex-wife? That doesn't make much sense, does it?"

Agatha paused, realizing Emma had a point. "You're right. I didn't think that through." She drummed her fingers on the table, brow furrowed in concentration. After a moment, her eyes lit up. "Wait, I've got it. What about Beatrice? She was close to Harold. She might know who his attorney was."

Emma perked up. "Now that's an idea. Beatrice would be much more likely to have that information. Good thinking, Agatha."

Agatha's face fell as she remembered a crucial detail. "Oh, wait. Beatrice isn't even here. Remember? She's supposedly visiting family back home."

Emma groaned, slumping back in her chair. "Well, that's a problem. Back to square one, I guess."

They sat in frustrated silence for a moment before Agatha's eyes lit up. "Maybe not. I just had an idea."

"I'm all ears," Emma said, leaning forward.

"Aunt Edna," Agatha said, a hint of excitement in her voice. "She's known Beatrice her entire life. Odds are, she knows who Beatrice's family is and where they live."

Emma's eyebrows shot up. "That's... actually brilliant, Agatha."

Agatha tapped her chin thoughtfully. "I'll have to be careful, though. I don't want to worry her. Maybe we could frame it as concern for Beatrice? Say we wanted to send her a card or something?"

"That could work," Emma nodded, a smile spreading across her face. "Looks like we've got our next move."

24

DEVIN JENSEN

Agatha looked up from her inventory list when she heard the bell above the door chime. Her heart skipped a beat as she saw Devin standing in the doorway, dark circles under his eyes.

"Agatha," he said, his voice hoarse. "I need to talk to you. It's important."

Mike, lounging behind the counter, lifted his head and let out a low growl. Agatha patted him reassuringly, her mind racing with possibilities. Was this the moment of truth? Was Devin about to confess?

"Alright, Devin," she said, gesturing to a quiet corner of the store. "Let's talk."

As they settled into the worn leather armchairs, Agatha noticed Devin's hands trembling. He took a deep breath, as if steeling himself. The late afternoon sun cast shadows across the room, giving Devin's face an almost ghostly pallor.

"I know how this looks," he began, his eyes darting nervously around the room. "My behavior, the will, everything. But it's not what you think."

Agatha leaned forward, her eyes narrowing. The scent of Devin's cologne, usually so subtle, seemed overpowering in the close quarters. "Then what is it, Devin? Because from where I'm sitting, it looks pretty damning. Especially after that phone call I overheard."

Devin's eyes widened in surprise, but he quickly composed himself. "You... you heard that? I can explain. I've been investigating Mr. Collins. I think he's behind everything – the embezzlement, Harold's death, maybe even Amanda's murder."

The revelation hung in the air between them. Agatha's mind raced, piecing together the new information with what she already knew. Could it be true? Had she been wrong about Devin all along?

"That phone call you overheard," Devin continued, his words tumbling out in a rush now, "I was talking to a private investigator I hired. We were discussing the evidence we'd gathered against Collins."

Agatha's brow furrowed. "And Beatrice? You said she was 'out of the picture'."

Devin nodded, a look of relief crossing his face as he realized Agatha was listening, not judging. "She's with a relative in an undisclosed location. Harold arranged it before he died, worried that she might be in danger if his suspicions about Collins were true."

Agatha leaned back, processing this new information. "So you're saying Beatrice isn't just visiting family, she's in hiding?"

"Essentially, yes," Devin confirmed, his voice low. "We couldn't risk anyone finding out where she really was. It was safer if everyone, including you, believed she was just away visiting family."

As Devin spoke, he suddenly reached into his jacket

pocket. Agatha tensed, her mind racing with worst-case scenarios. Was he reaching for a weapon?

Before she could react, the bookstore door burst open. Emma and Lorraine, who had apparently been watching from outside, came charging in like a pair of mismatched superheroes.

"Sacrebleu! Unhand that pocket, you scoundrel!" Lorraine cried, her scarf fluttering dramatically behind her as she launched herself at Devin.

Emma, more practical but no less determined, grabbed a hefty copy of Agatha Christie's "The Complete Miss Marple Collection" from a nearby shelf, brandishing it like a medieval mace.

Devin, caught completely off-guard, yelped in surprise as Lorraine collided with him, sending them both tumbling onto the worn carpet. Emma stood over them, book raised threateningly.

"Wait! Stop!" Agatha shouted, torn between laughter and exasperation. "He's not attacking me!"

Lorraine, still sprawled across Devin, looked up in confusion. "He's not? But ma chérie, his hand was in his pocket! That's always suspicious in the mysteries!"

Red-faced and slightly squashed, Devin managed to extract his hand from his pocket. In it was... a folded document.

"I was just getting this," he wheezed, waving the paper weakly. "It's the real will."

Emma lowered her literary weapon sheepishly as Lorraine scrambled to her feet, attempting to straighten her now askew outfit with as much dignity as possible.

"Oh," Emma said, placing the weighty Christie collection back on the shelf. "Well, in that case, carry on."

Agatha took the paper, her eyes quickly scanning its

contents. She felt the weight of its importance as she read. "He left everything to Beatrice," she said, looking up at Devin with surprise.

"Exactly," Devin confirmed, leaning back in his chair. "That's why I've been so desperate to find it. Someone's been trying to get their hands on the estate, but we don't know who."

Agatha furrowed her brow, processing this new information. "How did you end up with the will?"

Devin leaned forward, lowering his voice. "It's quite a story. Apparently, whoever was after the estate had stolen the will, but they must have accidentally dropped it. Mildred, one of the residents, found it on the floor in the community room."

"Mildred found it?" Agatha's eyes widened in surprise. "And she gave it to you?"

Devin nodded. "She didn't know what it was, but she knew it looked important. She gave it to me because she trusts me, and she knew I was related to Harold."

Agatha sat back, her mind racing. "So someone went to all the trouble of stealing the will, only to lose it by accident. That's... quite a stroke of luck."

"Luck, or maybe something else," Devin said, his expression serious. "I can't help but wonder if someone wanted us to find it. But why? That's what I've been trying to figure out."

As the truth unfolded, Agatha felt a mix of relief and embarrassment wash over her. She'd been so sure of Devin's guilt, and yet... The realization that she'd been wrong all this time settled in her stomach like a lead weight.

"Why didn't you come to me sooner?" she asked, unable to keep a hint of hurt from her voice.

Devin's expression turned sheepish. "I wasn't sure who I

could trust. And... well, I was trying to play the hero, I suppose. Solve it all on my own."

Agatha couldn't help but chuckle, the tension of the moment breaking. "Well, Mr. Hero, I think it's time we pooled our resources. We've got a real villain to catch."

Devin nodded, then his face grew serious. "There's another issue, Agatha. I have to go home for a while, or I'll lose my job. That's why I decided to go to Detective Dawson and tell him everything. I can't leave this unresolved, but I can't stay here indefinitely either."

Agatha leaned back, considering this new information. "I see. So you're passing the baton, so to speak?"

"In a way, yes," Devin admitted. "I've done what I can, but I think it's time to let the professionals handle it. And... well, I trust you'll keep an eye on things here. You've proven to be quite the detective yourself."

Agatha smiled wryly. "I'll do my best. But Devin, are you sure it's safe for you to leave? If someone is after the estate, and they know you've been investigating..."

Devin shrugged, trying to appear nonchalant despite the flicker of worry in his eyes. "I'll be careful. Besides, maybe my departure will make whoever's behind this let their guard down. Could be just what we need to crack this case wide open."

"Devin, I... I'm sorry. I thought..."

He held up a hand, cutting her off. "You don't need to apologize, Agatha. I know how it looked. I probably would have suspected me too."

A comfortable silence fell between them, broken only by the ticking of the old clock on the wall and Mike's occasional snuffles from his bed behind the counter.

"So what now?" Agatha finally asked.

Devin straightened, a determined look in his eyes. "Now, you gather evidence. Concrete, irrefutable evidence. We need to prove what's really been going on and clear your aunt's name in the process."

Agatha nodded, her own resolve strengthening. "We'll need help. Emma and Lorraine – they've been invaluable throughout this whole ordeal."

"The more eyes you have on this, the better," Devin agreed. "But you need to be careful. Whoever's behind this is dangerous, and if they realize you're onto them..."

"They won't," Agatha said firmly. "We'll be discreet." She paused, then added, "Thank you for sharing all this with me, Devin. I'll keep you posted on any developments."

Devin nodded, relief evident in his face. "I appreciate that, Agatha. And please, don't hesitate to reach out if you need any help or information. Just because I'm leaving doesn't mean I'm out of this completely."

"I will," Agatha assured him. "Safe travels, Devin. And be careful yourself."

As Devin turned to leave, Agatha called out, "Oh, Devin? One last thing, if you don't mind."

He paused at the door, raising an eyebrow. "Sure, what is it?"

"I was wondering about Amanda," Agatha said, trying to keep her tone casual. "Were you two... close?"

Devin's lips quirked into a half-smile. "We had a bit of a thing, yeah. Nothing serious though."

Agatha nodded, filing away this tidbit. "Thanks, Devin. Take care."

With a small wave, Devin stepped out, the bell chiming softly behind him.

~

Later that evening, as Agatha walked Mike along their usual route, her mind whirled with the day's revelations. The cool evening air carried the scent of blooming jasmine, a stark contrast to the turmoil of her thoughts.

"What do you think, Mike?" she mused aloud. "Have we been barking up the wrong tree this whole time?"

Mike looked up at her, his brown eyes wise and understanding. He gave a soft "woof" as if in agreement.

Agatha smiled, scratching behind his ears. "You're right. We can't dwell on our mistakes. We need to focus on finding the truth, wherever it leads us."

As they rounded the corner back towards home, Agatha's resolve strengthened. Tomorrow, she'd gather Emma and Lorraine. Together, they'd get to the bottom of this mystery, no matter what.

After arriving home, Agatha settled Mike for the evening and made herself a cup of chamomile tea, hoping it would help her relax after the day's revelations. She sat at her kitchen table, her laptop open before her.

Her fingers hovered over the keyboard as she typed "Roger Collins" into the search box. Her eyes drifted to the threatening letter propped against her typewriter, the words seeming to mock her.

"There's no way I'll leave Aunt Edna in jail for a crime she didn't commit," she muttered, her jaw set with determination. Glancing at her trusty typewriter, she added, "If I have to, I'll rewrite the book. I remember most of it anyway."

Taking a deep breath, she hit enter.

The search results loaded, and one headline immediately caught her eye: 'Local Nursing Home owner Accused of Corruption'

Agatha's heart raced as she clicked on the link. As she read, her eyes widened, and she realized that the case was far more complex than she had imagined. Roger Collins, it seemed, had secrets of his own – secrets that might just blow this whole case wide open.

25

UNSEEN CONNECTIONS

Agatha's fingers flew across the keyboard as she delved deeper into Roger Collins' past. Each click revealed a new layer of corruption, painting a picture of a man with a long history of questionable business practices.

"Local Nursing Home Mogul Faces Allegations of Embezzlement," one headline blared. Agatha's eyes widened as she read about the Collins family empire - a network of nursing homes spread across three states. Roger, it seemed, had been groomed from a young age to take over the family business.

But as she read on, a pattern emerged. One by one, the Collins nursing homes fell into financial ruin. Allegations of mismanagement, fraud, and money laundering dogged Roger's steps. Agatha's tea grew cold, forgotten, as she pieced together the story of Roger's fall from grace.

"Bankruptcy Claims Another Collins Facility," another article proclaimed. Agatha shook her head in disbelief. How had this man ended up running Green Acres?

The answer came in an obituary: "Millicent Collins, beloved aunt and philanthropist, leaves Green Acres Assisted Living to nephew." It seemed Roger had found a lifeline just when he needed it most.

But the most shocking revelation was yet to come. Agatha gasped as she read: "Roger Collins Serves Six Months for Tax Evasion." The man running Green Acres was an ex-con.

As she absorbed this information, a nagging thought kept resurfacing: Why would Harold, a wealthy man with means, choose to move into an assisted living facility in a small town like Bristol Lake? It didn't add up.

Agatha leaned back in her chair, her mind whirling. "What brought you here, Harold?" she murmured. "What did you know about Roger Collins?"

She glanced at the clock, surprised to see it was well past midnight. But sleep was the furthest thing from her mind. Instead, she opened a new search tab, determined to uncover any connection between Harold and Roger Collins.

As she typed, a new question formed: Was Harold's move to Green Acres really about retirement, or was he on some kind of mission? The more Agatha uncovered about Roger Collins' past, the more convinced she became that Harold's presence in Bristol Lake was no coincidence.

With renewed energy, Agatha dove back into her research. She was onto something big, she could feel it. And somewhere in this web of corruption and secrets lay the key to clearing Aunt Edna's name.

∼

The next morning, as Agatha arrived at Green Acres for her volunteer shift, she stopped dead in her tracks. There, sitting in the front area with Tilda, was Beatrice. Agatha blinked hard, certain she must be seeing things.

Beatrice looked apathetic, her normally bright demeanor dulled, dressed in somber black. Agatha's mind whirled, Devin's words from yesterday ringing in her ears: *Beatrice is with a relative in an undisclosed location. Harold arranged it before he died, worried that she might be in danger.*

Heart pounding, Agatha approached cautiously. Why was Beatrice back? And more importantly, was she safe? Trying to keep her voice steady despite her shock, Agatha managed, "Beatrice? I... I didn't expect to see you here."

Beatrice didn't respond, staring blankly ahead, her eyes clouded with sorrow. Agatha exchanged a worried glance with Tilda, who was hovering protectively near Beatrice.

Pulling up a chair, Agatha sat beside Beatrice. "How are you holding up?" she asked gently.

After a moment, Beatrice turned towards Agatha, her expression distant. "I'm... here," she murmured, her voice flat.

Tilda leaned in, her voice soft and filled with concern. "We're all here for you, Beatrice. You don't have to talk if you don't want to."

Beatrice gave a small nod, but her eyes remained unfocused. Agatha couldn't shake the feeling that something more was amiss, beyond just grief.

After a strained silence, Beatrice looked at Tilda. "Can we go back to my room now?"

"Of course, dear," Tilda said, helping Beatrice to her feet. She turned to Agatha, "I'll be right back."

As Tilda guided Beatrice away, Agatha watched them go, her mind whirling with questions. A few minutes later, Tilda returned, her face etched with worry.

"Agatha," Tilda said in a hushed tone, glancing around to ensure they were alone. "I'm really worried about Beatrice. She insisted on coming back, even though I tried to convince her to stay with her family a bit longer."

Agatha nodded encouragingly, hoping Tilda would reveal more.

"She's not herself," Tilda continued, wringing her hands. "It's more than just grief. She seems... confused sometimes. And she keeps talking about needing to find something important, but she can't remember what it is."

"That does sound concerning," Agatha agreed, her interest piqued. "Has she seen a doctor?"

Tilda nodded. "Yes, but they say it's just stress and grief. I'm not so sure. I can't help feeling there's more to it. I'm just so worried about her, Agatha. I don't know what to do."

Tilda excused herself with a worried glance at Beatrice. Agatha watched her go, then turned back to the quiet woman on the couch. Beatrice's blank stare and slumped shoulders were so unlike her usual self that Agatha felt a chill despite the warm room. She fiddled with her volunteer badge, her mind buzzing with questions. *Why was Beatrice back? What had caused such a drastic change in her?*

As Agatha made her way towards the library for her volunteer shift, a familiar figure caught her eye. Dr. Hartman, his white coat crisp and his stethoscope draped around his neck, was entering Beatrice's room. Agatha slowed her pace, her curiosity piqued.

Agatha's eyes widened as a sudden thought struck her. She leaned against the wall, her mind whirling like a merry-go-round on overdrive.

The medication they've been giving Aunt Edna... those little pills...

She shivered, rubbing her arms as if she'd caught a draft

in the stuffy hallway. Her gaze skipped over the faded wallpaper and worn carpet, seeing them with new eyes.

Huh, even the decor looks suspicious now. Get a grip, Agatha!

She shook her head, trying to organize her thoughts. *Could these pills be behind Beatrice's bizarre behavior? And what about Dr. Hartman – is he mixed up in all this?*

Agatha lingered near Beatrice's door, pretending to arrange some flowers in a nearby vase. She strained to hear any snippets of conversation from inside the room.

"Now, Beatrice," Dr. Hartman's muffled voice came through the door, "this new medication should help with those symptoms we discussed."

Agatha's heart raced. New medication? What symptoms?

A moment later, the door opened, and Dr. Hartman stepped out. He nodded curtly to Agatha before striding down the hall, his footsteps echoing in the quiet corridor.

Agatha waited a moment before knocking gently on Beatrice's door. "Beatrice? It's Agatha. May I come in?"

"Oh, yes, dear. Please do," Beatrice's voice called out, sounding a bit distant.

Agatha entered the room to find Beatrice sitting in an armchair by the window, a small pill bottle on the side table next to her.

"How are you feeling, Beatrice?" Agatha asked, taking a seat across from her.

Beatrice smiled vaguely. "I'm... I'm not quite sure, to be honest. The days seem to blur together lately."

As they chatted, Agatha noticed similarities between Beatrice's behavior and what she'd observed in Aunt Edna. The same confusion, the struggle to remember recent events, the occasional moment of clarity followed by bewilderment.

"Beatrice," Agatha said gently, "I couldn't help overhearing Dr. Hartman mention a new medication. Is everything alright?"

Beatrice's brow furrowed. "New medication? Oh, yes, I suppose so. He said it would help, but..." she trailed off, looking confused. "I'm sorry, what were we talking about?"

Agatha's concern deepened. The parallels between Beatrice and Aunt Edna were undeniable. As she left Beatrice's room, her mind whirled with possibilities. What was this new medication? And why were both Beatrice and Aunt Edna experiencing such similar symptoms?

One thing was clear: she needed to find out more about Dr. Hartman's role in all of this, and fast. As she slowly paced back towards the library, she thought about how to proceed. *Devin, maybe he'll be able to help me.* She checked her watch and calculated the time back in California where Devin was, then grabbed her phone and dialed his number. "Devin, it's Agatha Royale, can you talk?"

"Hey Agatha, how are you doing? Everything okay?"

Agatha sighed, "Well, Beatrice is back at Green Acres, and I'm worried. She's acting like she's stepped into the Twilight Zone."

"I was going to tell you she'd gone back," Devin replied. "I tried to convince her not to, but she was dead set on it."

"She's not herself," Agatha said, her voice tinged with concern. She paused, then asked, "Did she seem off-kilter at her relative's house? Any new meds in the mix?"

Devin hesitated. "I have to be honest. I wouldn't know. I didn't see her in person. Sorry, I can't be more help."

"No worries, thanks for trying," Agatha said. She

rubbed her forehead, feeling the gears in her mind turning. "Looks like I've got a mystery to unravel."

As she hung up, she muttered under her breath, "Dr. Hartman, you've got some explaining to do..."

26

ECHOES OF DECEPTION

The soft glow of the computer screen illuminated Agatha's face as she sat in the quiet corner of the Green Acres library. The gentle hum of the air conditioning and the occasional rustle of pages turning were the only sounds breaking the silence. Outside, the late afternoon sun cast long shadows through the windows, creating an almost ethereal atmosphere in the room.

Agatha's fingers flew over the keyboard as she delved deeper into Dr. Hartman's background. Her conversation with Devin had left her with more questions than answers.

"Dr. Gregory Hartman," she muttered to herself, scrolling through the search results. "Where did you come from, and what are you hiding?"

She found his medical school records easily enough - graduated with honors from a prestigious university. His early career seemed promising, with several published papers on geriatric care. Agatha made notes of the titles, planning to look into them later. But then, there was a gap. Three years where Dr. Hartman seemed to vanish from the medical community.

"Now, what were you up to during those years, Doctor?" Agatha mused, jotting down notes. She tried several search combinations, but the doctor's activities during that time remained frustratingly elusive.

As she dug deeper, she came across a news article from a small town newspaper. It mentioned a Dr. E. Hartman being involved in a controversial drug trial that was abruptly shut down. The details were vague, but it was enough to raise Agatha's suspicions further.

"Could this be our Dr. Hartman?" she wondered aloud, printing the article for later reference.

A knock on the door startled her. Agatha looked up to see Tilda peering in, a concerned expression on her face. The setting sun caught Tilda's hair, giving it an almost fiery glow. Agatha quickly minimized her browser window, not wanting to reveal the extent of her investigation just yet.

"Agatha? I hope I'm not interrupting," Tilda said softly, stepping into the room. She looked tired, Agatha noticed, with dark circles under her eyes and a slight droop to her usually upright shoulders.

"Not at all," Agatha replied, gesturing for Tilda to join her. "Is everything alright? You look exhausted."

Tilda sank into a nearby chair, her brow furrowed. She seemed to deflate as she sat, as if the weight of her concerns was physically pressing down on her. "It's Beatrice. I'm worried about her. She seems... different somehow."

Agatha's interest piqued. She leaned forward, giving Tilda her full attention. "Different how?"

"More confused, distant. It's not just grief anymore," Tilda explained, wringing her hands. The worry lines around her eyes deepened as she spoke. "This morning, she couldn't remember what day it was. And when I reminded her about her favorite TV show - you know, that British baking competition she never misses - she looked at me blankly. It's like... like pieces of her are slipping away."

Agatha nodded, her suspicions growing. She thought back to her aunt Edna's symptoms, noticing unsettling similarities. "Have you noticed any other residents experiencing similar changes?"

Tilda's eyes widened, a spark of realization lighting them. "Now that you mention it, yes. I've noticed some odd behavior from a few residents lately. Mrs. Peterson and Mr. Grayson, for example... they've been acting strangely."

"Can you tell me more about what you've observed?" Agatha prompted gently.

Tilda leaned in, lowering her voice as if afraid of being overheard. "Well, yesterday, Mrs. Peterson's granddaughter visited. The poor girl was in tears because Mrs. Peterson didn't seem to recognize her. She just sat there, patting the girl's hand and calling her 'dear.' It was so unlike her – she usually lights up when her family visits."

Tilda paused, her brow furrowing. "And Mr. Grayson... I found him wandering in the east wing yesterday, looking completely lost. When I asked if he needed help, he said he was trying to find the dining room. Agatha, he's lived here for five years and has never had trouble finding his way around before."

Agatha nodded, encouraging Tilda to continue.

"I don't know what's causing it," Tilda added, her voice laced with concern, "but these changes seem to have happened quite suddenly. It's... unsettling."

As they discussed the residents' symptoms, Agatha's mind raced. The pieces were starting to fall into place, but something still didn't quite fit. She couldn't shake the feeling that she was missing a crucial piece of the puzzle.

"Tilda," Agatha said carefully, deciding to shift the

conversation slightly, "what do you know about Mr. Collins' financial situation? Has he mentioned anything about the home's finances recently?"

Tilda looked surprised by the question, her brow furrowing. "Mr. Collins? I don't know him well at all, Agatha. There's no way he would be telling me anything about Green Acres' finances. It's not like we're friends or anything."

"I see," Agatha nodded. "What about his demeanor around the facility? Anything stand out to you?"

Tilda hesitated, glancing towards the door as if to ensure they were still alone. "Well, I'm not one to gossip, but..."

"But?" Agatha prompted gently.

Tilda lowered her voice. "I overheard him arguing on the phone about money. He seemed... desperate. Last week, I was walking past his office, and I heard him practically shouting into the phone. He was saying something about 'needing more time' and 'finding another way to raise the funds.' When he came out, he looked... well, haunted is the only word I can think of."

Agatha made a mental note to dig deeper into Mr. Collins' finances. Could his desperation be driving him to allow questionable medical practices at Green Acres? The thought sent a chill down her spine.

"What about Dr. Hartman?" Agatha asked, trying to keep her voice casual. "How would you describe his interactions with the residents and staff?"

Tilda hesitated, her fingers nervously playing with the hem of her uniform. "He's been... different. More secretive. He used to be gruff but caring, you know? He'd take time to chat with the residents, joke with the staff. Now, he barely speaks to anyone unless he has to. He's always rushing around with those new medication charts, and he gets this...

intense look when he's observing the residents. And the way he looks at some of them... it's almost like they're experiments, not people."

Agatha tilted her head, a question forming. "New medication charts? How do you know they're new? I thought you weren't part of the medical staff."

Tilda's eyes widened, caught off guard. She paused, her brow furrowing as if trying to find the right words. "Well, it's just... I've been here a while, you know? You start to notice things. The charts for some residents, including Edna and Beatrice, they're suddenly different colors now. Really bright, each one different. It's hard not to notice when you're around them all day, even if you're not medical staff."

Agatha nodded slowly, filing this information away. The detail about the different colored charts for specific residents, including her aunt Edna and Beatrice, seemed particularly significant. She made a mental note to look into this further, wondering what these color codes could mean.

"Thank you, Tilda. This is all very helpful," Agatha said, reaching out to pat Tilda's hand reassuringly. "Please, keep an eye on Beatrice and the others. And if you notice anything else unusual..."

"I'll come straight to you," Tilda promised, standing up. The worry was still evident in her eyes, but there was a glimmer of hope there too. "Be careful, Agatha. I can't shake the feeling that something very wrong is happening here."

As Tilda left, closing the door softly behind her, Agatha turned back to her computer. She had new leads to follow, and she wasn't going to let them slip away. She opened a new search tab, this time focusing more intently on Dr. Hartman's professional history. A name caught her eye: Novus Vitae Pharmaceuticals. It was mentioned in passing in an article about a controversial drug trial that Dr. Hartman had been involved with some years ago.

Agatha's pulse quickened. Novus Vitae - the same company Devin had worked for, the one he suspected was involved in the medication scheme. This couldn't be a coincidence.

"Now we're getting somewhere," Agatha murmured, quickly jotting down the information. As she scribbled her notes, a nagging question formed in her mind: *Why would a doctor with such a troubled history end up working in a small assisted living facility in the middle of nowhere?*

The more she uncovered about Dr. Hartman, the less sense his presence at Green Acres made. There had to be more to this story, and Agatha was determined to find out what it was.

As the sun dipped below the horizon, Agatha couldn't shake the feeling that she was on the verge of uncovering something big. But with each new piece of information, the puzzle seemed to grow more complex.

She leaned back in her chair, rubbing her tired eyes. The weight of the investigation was starting to take its toll, but she couldn't stop now. Not when she was so close to uncovering the truth.

Agatha glanced at the clock, surprised to see how late it had gotten. She quickly gathered her notes, making sure to clear her browser history before shutting down the computer. As she was reaching for her purse, the door of the library burst open.

Mildred stumbled in, her face ashen and eyes wide with fear. She was still in her nightgown, her silver hair disheveled.

"Agatha," Mildred gasped, her voice trembling. "Please, you have to help me."

Agatha rushed to steady the older woman, alarmed by her state. "Mildred, what's wrong? What happened?"

Mildred gripped Agatha's arm, her eyes darting around the room as if expecting someone to jump out at any moment. When she spoke, her words sent a chill down Agatha's spine.

"It's Dr. Hartman," Mildred whispered. "I think... I think he's trying to kill me."

27

A PILL TO REMEMBER

Agatha guided Mildred to a nearby chair, her mind racing. "Slow down, Mildred. Take a deep breath and tell me everything."

Mildred sank into the chair, her hands shaking. She took a shuddering breath before speaking. "I... I heard you were looking into Dr. Hartman. About Edna and Beatrice, and that new medication that's making them forgetful."

Agatha's eyebrows raised slightly, recognizing the information. *Gossip really does fly around here*, she thought. She gave Tilda an encouraging nod, hoping she'd continue.

"Well," Mildred said, her voice barely above a whisper, "tonight, Dr. Hartman brought me my medication himself. Can you believe it? In all my years here, I've never seen him do that. It's always been the medical assistant."

"That is odd," Agatha agreed, her suspicion growing. "What happened next?"

Mildred leaned in closer, her eyes darting to the door. "When he handed me the cup, I noticed something strange. There, right in the middle of my usual pills, was this... this translucent, green pill. I'd never seen anything like it before."

"A green pill?" Agatha echoed, her brow furrowing.

Mildred nodded vigorously. "Yes, and it gave me the most awful feeling. So I... I pretended to be clumsy. Knocked the whole cup right onto the floor."

Despite the tension, Agatha couldn't help but smile at Mildred's quick thinking. "Clever of you. Then what?"

"Well, while I was picking up the pills, I managed to hide that green one under my pillow. Dr. Hartman looked so flustered, kept asking if I was sure I'd gotten them all. When he left, I..." Mildred paused, looking almost guilty.

"What did you do with the pill, Mildred?" Agatha asked gently.

Mildred sighed. "I flushed it down the toilet. I was scared, Agatha. I didn't know what else to do."

Agatha felt a pang of disappointment at the lost evidence, but she understood Mildred's fear. "You did what you thought was best, Mildred. But why do you think Dr. Hartman is trying to kill you?"

Mildred's eyes filled with tears. "Because I remember, Agatha. I remember things that happened years ago, clear as day. And I've seen what's happening to Edna and Beatrice. I think... I think he wants to silence me."

As Agatha processed this information, her mind whirled with possibilities.

The green pill... Dr. Hartman's behavior... Mildred's clear memories...

It all pointed to something sinister at Green Acres. But without the physical evidence of the pill, how could she prove it?

I'm onto something, but I need more. This could be dangerous...

She took a deep breath, determined to unravel this mystery, no matter what.

"Mildred," Agatha said gently, squeezing the older woman's hand, "I believe you. But I need to understand what you think might be dangerous. Can you tell me more about that?"

Mildred's eyes widened, a mix of fear and excitement dancing across her face. "Oh, it's the medication, dearie. I've noticed... changes. And not just in mine." She leaned in closer, her voice dropping to a conspiratorial whisper. "Mrs. Johnson down the hall? She used to be sharp as a tack. Now she can't remember what day it is."

Agatha nodded, encouraging her to continue. "Have you noticed anything else unusual?"

Mildred's face suddenly lit up, her earlier concern momentarily forgotten. "Well, now that you mention it, I do remember the day I won the pie-eating contest at the county fair in 1952. Seventeen blueberry pies in one sitting!" She patted her stomach proudly. "My secret? A splash of vinegar in my water. Kept the nausea at bay."

Agatha couldn't help but chuckle, though her mind was racing with this new information. "That's... quite a memory, Mildred. But let's focus on the present. Do you think anyone else might have noticed something strange about their medication?"

Mildred's expression turned serious again. "It's not just that, dear. They're taking things away from us, bit by bit. Why, when I moved in here, I had an entire apartment to myself. Spacious living room, full kitchen, the works."

"And now?" Agatha prompted, curious.

Mildred huffed indignantly. "Now? Ever since Mr. Collins took over from his dear aunt Velma - rest her soul, terrible business with that plane crash - they've split my apartment in two! Can you believe it? Now I have what they call a 'kitchenette.' Hah! It's barely big enough to heat up a TV dinner."

She leaned in conspiratorially. "And don't get me started on the 'activities.' We used to have wine and cheese nights. Now it's prune juice and crackers. Crackers!" She shook her head in disbelief. "I tell you, Agatha, it's a slippery slope. First, they take away your wine, then your memories. What's next? Our dentures?"

Agatha bit back a smile, touched by Mildred's spirited complaint. But beneath the humor, she sensed a real concern. "I understand, Mildred. These changes must be frustrating. But do you think they're connected to what's happening with Edna and Beatrice?"

Mildred's face grew serious again. "I don't know, dear. But I do know that things aren't right here. And that green pill... well, I'm not taking any chances. I may be old, but I've still got all my marbles, and I intend to keep them!"

The morning after Mildred's startling revelation, Agatha arrived at Green Acres earlier than usual. The corridors were quiet, with only the soft shuffling of the night staff preparing to end their shift breaking the silence.

As she turned the corner towards the residents' wing, she nearly collided with Dr. Hartman. The doctor looked startled, clutching a clipboard to his chest.

"Ms. Royale," he said gruffly, his eyes darting around. "You're here early."

Agatha forced a smile. "Good morning, Dr. Hartman. Yes, I thought I'd get an early start today."

She couldn't help but notice the way Dr. Hartman's

knuckles whitened as he gripped the clipboard tighter. "Well, don't let me keep you," he muttered, brushing past her.

Agatha watched him hurry down the corridor, her suspicions growing. What was on that clipboard that had him so on edge?

Throughout the morning, Agatha discreetly observed the residents, paying close attention to those who had recently started new medications. She couldn't shake the uneasy feeling that something was terribly wrong.

During her lunch break, Agatha spotted Dotty, the nurse's assistant who had recently returned to work after Nurse Amanda's passing. Dotty looked tired; her usual cheerful demeanor subdued.

"Dotty," Agatha called softly, "how are you holding up? It must be difficult being back."

Dotty managed a weak smile. "It's... strange without Amanda. But the residents need us, you know?"

Agatha nodded sympathetically. "Have you noticed anything unusual since you've been back?"

Dotty glanced around before leaning in. "Actually, yes. Dr. Hartman, he's been acting odd lately. Always in the medication room, insisting on administering certain meds himself."

Agatha's heart raced. "Really? That does sound unusual."

Dotty nodded. "And the other day, I could've sworn I saw him swap out some pills from the dispensary. But when I asked about it, he got defensive. Told me to mind my own business."

As Dotty was called away to assist a resident, Agatha's mind whirled with this new information. The evidence against Dr. Hartman was mounting, but she needed more concrete proof.

Later that afternoon, as she was shelving books in the library, she overheard Dr. Hartman's voice from the adjacent office.

"I don't care what it takes," he was saying, his voice tense. "We need to keep this quiet. The plan has to work."

Agatha's blood ran cold. What plan? And what was Dr. Hartman trying to keep quiet?

As she left Green Acres that evening, Agatha knew she had to act fast. Tomorrow, she decided, she would take her findings to Detective Dawson. Whatever was happening at Green Acres, it was clear that the residents were in danger.

28

CROSSING THE LINE

The next morning, Agatha met Emma for coffee at the bookstore before heading to the police station. The aroma of freshly brewed coffee filled the air as they huddled over a corner table.

"Are you sure about this, Agatha?" Emma asked, concern etched on her face. "Detective Dawson was pretty clear about you staying out of the investigation."

Agatha nodded firmly. "I have to, Emma. The residents at Green Acres could be in danger. I can't just sit back and do nothing."

Celeste bustled about, preparing for the day's customers. "Don't you worry about a thing, Agatha," she called out cheerfully. "I've got everything under control here. You just focus on what you need to do at Green Acres."

Agatha smiled gratefully at her assistant. "Thanks, Celeste. I don't know what I'd do without you."

Turning back to Emma, Agatha lowered her voice. "Are you sure you're okay with coming to the police station with me?"

Emma nodded firmly. "Of course. Someone needs to keep you out of trouble," she added with a wry smile.

As they approached the police station, Agatha felt a flutter of nerves in her stomach. She took a deep breath, smoothing her cardigan as Detective Dawson greeted them with a raised eyebrow at the entrance to his office.

"Ms. Royale," he said, a hint of amusement in his voice. "I see you're determined to keep me on my toes."

Agatha offered a small smile. "I know you asked me to step back, Detective, but I've stumbled upon some information about Dr. Hartman that I think you should hear."

Dawson sighed, but his eyes held a glimmer of curiosity. "Alright, let's hear it. But remember, this isn't one of your mystery novels."

Emma chimed in, "We know it's serious, Detective. That's why we're here."

As Agatha shared her findings about Dr. Hartman's behavior, Dotty's account, and Mildred's experience with the green pill, she watched Dawson's expression change from skepticism to interest.

When she finished, he leaned back in his chair, tapping his pen thoughtfully. "I have to admit, that's quite a story. Thank you for bringing this to my attention."

"So, you'll look into it?" Agatha asked hopefully.

Dawson nodded. "We will. But I need you both to promise me you'll be careful. No more amateur sleuthing, at least for now. Deal?"

Agatha and Emma exchanged glances. "We'll do our best," Agatha said, though her mind was already buzzing with ideas for their next move.

As they left the station, Emma turned to Agatha. "You're not really going to stop, are you?"

Agatha smiled wryly. "Of course not. But we'll need to be more careful from now on."

As Agatha and Emma left the police station, neither noticed the figure lurking in the shadow of a large oak tree across the street. The person was of average height, face obscured by the brim of a dark baseball cap and large sunglasses. A non-descript grey hoodie completed the disguise.

The figure watched intently as the two women walked away, their animated conversation carried on the breeze. Once they were out of sight, a gloved hand reached into the hoodie pocket, pulling out a sleek smartphone.

After a moment's hesitation, the figure dialed a number, bringing the phone to their ear. "It's me," the person said, voice low and slightly muffled. "The Royale woman is asking questions. We may need to adjust our plans."

The figure listened for a moment, then nodded. "I understand. I'll keep an eye on things here. We can't let this unravel now - there's too much at stake."

With a soft sigh, the mysterious caller ended the call and slipped the phone back into their pocket. They cast one last glance in the direction Agatha and Emma had gone, then turned and walked away, disappearing into the shadows of the building.

Meanwhile, oblivious to the danger now stalking them, Agatha and Emma made their way back to One Deadly Chapter Books and Brew. The cheerful chime of the bell above the door announced their return.

Celeste looked up from the cash register, a concerned expression on her face. "How did it go?" she asked, noting their serious expressions.

Agatha sighed, sinking into one of the comfortable

armchairs. "Not great. Detective Dawson wasn't exactly thrilled with our amateur sleuthing."

Emma nodded, settling into the chair opposite. "That's putting it mildly. He practically ordered us to stay out of it."

"But you're not going to, are you?" Celeste asked, knowing Agatha all too well.

Agatha managed a small smile. "Of course not. We just need to be more careful."

As Celeste returned to helping a customer, Agatha and Emma huddled closer, speaking in hushed tones.

"So, what's our next move?" Emma asked.

Agatha's brow furrowed in concentration. "We need more concrete evidence. Something that Detective Dawson can't ignore."

"What about that green pill Mildred mentioned?" Emma suggested.

Agatha's eyes lit up. "That's it! If we could get our hands on one of those pills..."

Their plotting was interrupted by the jingle of the bell. They looked up to see Tilda rushing in, her face pale with worry.

"Agatha," she gasped, out of breath. "You need to come quickly. It's Beatrice. Something's terribly wrong."

As they arrived at Green Acres, Lindsey greeted them with a warm smile that quickly turned to curiosity when she noticed Agatha, Emma, and Tilda striding past her with purpose, heading towards the residents' rooms.

"Is everything alright?" Lindsey called after them, her brow furrowing with concern.

Agatha paused, turning back to explain. "We're not sure, to be honest. Tilda mentioned something might be wrong with Beatrice, so we're going to check on her."

Before Lindsey could respond, Tilda hurried ahead, her voice tinged with urgency. "Come on, Agatha! We need to see Beatrice now."

Agatha exchanged a quick glance with Emma, who nodded, and they hurried after Tilda. As they rushed down the hallway, the faded floral wallpaper blurring past, they were brought to an abrupt halt by Mr. Collins, who stepped out of a doorway, blocking their path.

"Well, well," he said, his voice dripping with sarcasm as he looked them up and down. "What's all the commotion about? Where's the fire?"

Agatha took a deep breath, trying to keep her irritation in check. "Tilda asked us to check on Beatrice. She's worried something might be wrong."

Mr. Collins's eyebrows shot up, and he turned to Tilda. "Wrong? What could possibly be wrong with her?"

Tilda shifted uncomfortably under his gaze. "I... I couldn't wake her for breakfast," she explained, her voice quavering slightly. "I tried everything, but nothing worked. For a moment, I was afraid she wasn't breathing." She paused, swallowing hard. "But she was. She was breathing just fine."

Mr. Collins's gaze swiveled back to Agatha, his eyes narrowing. "And how exactly does Ms. Royale fit into this situation? Last I checked, she wasn't on our medical staff."

Agatha opened her mouth to defend herself, but Mr. Collins held up a finger, silencing her. "If there's a genuine health concern, we'll have Dr. Hartman examine her." He turned to Lindsey, who had followed them down the hall. "Lindsey, please fetch Dr. Hartman immediately."

As Lindsey scurried off, Agatha felt a knot of dread forming in her stomach. She leaned close to Emma, whispering, "Oh no, not Dr. Hartman. What if he's the one who gave her some bizarre medication that put her in this state?"

Emma nodded subtly, her eyes conveying that she shared Agatha's concerns.

Moments later, Dr. Hartman approached, his white coat crisp and his expression stern. He gestured for Mr. Collins and Tilda to follow him, pointedly ignoring Agatha and Emma.

As they started down the hallway, Agatha and Emma moved to follow, but Dr. Hartman turned, fixing them with a cold stare. "You can wait here... or better yet, you can leave. This doesn't concern you."

Agatha and Emma watched in disbelief as the group disappeared into Beatrice's room, the door closing firmly behind them.

"Well, that's just great," Agatha muttered, running a hand through her hair in frustration. "Now we'll never know what's really going on."

"I know," Emma agreed, placing a comforting hand on Agatha's arm. "But maybe we can still figure something out."

As they waited, Agatha paced the hallway, her eyes fixed on Beatrice's door. The minutes ticked by agonizingly slowly.

Finally, Emma broke the tense silence. "You know, it can't be too bad. We haven't seen any ambulances or emergency personnel rushing in."

Agatha nodded, trying to take comfort in that observation. "You're right. Everything does seem oddly calm."

After what felt like an eternity, the door opened, and Mr. Collins, Dr. Hartman, and Tilda emerged. Agatha rushed forward, her heart pounding. "Is Beatrice okay? What's going on?"

Mr. Collins and Dr. Hartman brushed past her without a word, their faces unreadable. Dr. Hartman paused for a moment, shaking his head and giving Agatha a disapproving look before continuing down the hallway.

Tilda approached, a small smile on her face. "She's okay," she said softly. "She was just sleeping very deeply, but she's fine now."

Relief washed over Agatha. "That's wonderful news. Can we see her?"

"Of course," Tilda nodded, gesturing towards the room. "Come on in."

As they entered, they found Beatrice propped up in bed, looking surprisingly refreshed in a silk, light blue night-gown. She rubbed her eyes and beamed at them. "Well, hello there, darlings! What a lovely surprise!"

Agatha couldn't help but smile back, noticing how Beatrice's beauty still shone through, despite her age. "How are you feeling, Beatrice?" she asked gently.

Beatrice stretched her arms above her head, letting out a contented sigh. "Oh, I'm feeling just marvelous, dear. I can't remember the last time I slept so well!"

Agatha's smile faltered slightly. "Have you been feeling extra tired lately?"

Beatrice's brow furrowed in thought. "You know, I can't quite recall. But last night, Dr. Hartman gave me this wonderful little pill and some gummies. I slept like an absolute angel!"

Agatha and Emma exchanged worried glances. "A pill?" Agatha pressed gently. "Do you remember what it looked like?"

Beatrice's eyes lit up. "Oh yes, it was the most curious little thing. A small, translucent green pill. Looked almost like a piece of candy!"

As Beatrice chattered on about her restful night, Agatha's mind raced. What exactly had Dr. Hartman given her, and why? The mystery deepened, and Agatha knew she had to get to the bottom of it – for Beatrice's sake, and for all the residents of Green Acres.

As Beatrice continued to chat happily about her restful night, Agatha felt a chill run down her spine. Her mind raced back to her conversation with Mildred just a few days ago.

Dr. Hartman tried to give me this strange green pill, Mildred had confided, her voice barely above a whisper. *Said it would help me sleep, but I didn't like the look of it. Flushed it down the toilet when he wasn't looking.* The memory of Mildred's worried face and trembling hands made Agatha's stomach tighten. What exactly was in those green pills, and why was Dr. Hartman so insistent on the residents taking them?

Mildred's warning about Dr. Hartman and the translucent green pills suddenly took on new significance. As Beatrice described an identical pill, alarm bells rang in Agatha's head. She caught Emma's eye, seeing her own concern mirrored in her friend's face. There was no denying it now – something was definitely amiss at Green Acres.

As they left Beatrice's room, Agatha's mind buzzed with questions. *What exactly was in those green pills? And why was Dr. Hartman so eager to hand them out?*

She turned to Emma, keeping her voice low. "We need to find out more about those pills. Something doesn't add up here."

A terrifying thought struck her, stopping her in her tracks. She turned to Emma, her voice low and urgent.

"Emma," she whispered, "what if these pills aren't just for sleeping? What if they're the reason Aunt Edna can't remember anything about the night Harold died?"

29

CONNECTING THE DOTS

A gatha sat at her kitchen table, surrounded by a sea of notes. The morning sun streamed through the window, illuminating the organized chaos before her. She sipped her tea, brow furrowed in concentration.

"There has to be a connection," she muttered, tapping her pen against her chin.

Just then, Emma burst through the door, a paper bag in hand. "I brought scones!" she announced cheerfully. "Thought we could use a sugar boost for our investigation."

Agatha smiled gratefully. "You're a lifesaver, Emma. I've been staring at these notes for hours."

As they munched on still-warm scones, Agatha spread out her findings. "Look here," she said, pointing to a scribbled note. "Remember those green pills Beatrice mentioned? I'm starting to suspect they might not be just simple sleeping pills."

Emma leaned in, intrigued. "What do you think they could be?"

"I'm not sure," Agatha replied, her voice low. "But something about them doesn't sit right with me. And I have a hunch Nurse Amanda might have been involved somehow."

A heavy silence fell between them as the implications sank in.

"But Amanda's death..." Emma whispered, trailing off.

Agatha nodded grimly. "We know it wasn't an accident, but there's more to it. I'm certain she wasn't killed in the park. Someone moved her there."

As they continued to pore over the evidence, a knock at the door startled them. Agatha opened it to find Tilda standing there, looking slightly out of breath.

"Tilda! What brings you here?" Agatha asked, trying to keep the surprise out of her voice.

Tilda smiled, tucking a strand of hair behind her ear. "I was just out for my morning walk and thought I'd check in and say hello." She peered at Agatha, concern flickering in her eyes. "Is everything okay? You look like you've been up all night thinking."

Agatha hesitated for a moment before inviting her in. As Tilda settled at the table, Agatha noticed her gaze flicker briefly over the scattered papers.

"That's very kind of you to check in, Tilda," Emma said, offering her a scone. "We were just discussing some... concerns about the recent murders at Green Acres."

Tilda's eyebrows raised slightly. "Oh? Anything I might be able to help with? I'm very concerned for Beatrice's safety."

Agatha took a deep breath. "Actually, Tilda, I'm sure I've asked you before, but do you remember anything unusual around the time of Nurse Amanda's death? Any strange behaviors or incidents at Green Acres?"

Tilda's expression changed, a mix of concern and hesitation

crossing her face. She glanced around as if checking to see if anyone else might be listening. "Well," she began, lowering her voice, "there is something I haven't told anyone yet. The night before Amanda died, I overheard her arguing with someone."

Agatha and Emma exchanged glances. "Do you know who she was arguing with?" Agatha pressed gently.

Tilda nodded slowly. "It was Devin. I'm sure of it. And..." she paused, taking a deep breath, "I saw them leaving together that night. Devin was the last person I saw with Amanda."

Agatha's eyes widened. "Tilda, this is important information. Did you tell Detective Dawson about this?"

Tilda shook her head, looking down at her hands. "No, I... I was afraid. I didn't want to get involved. But I can't stop thinking about it. Do you think it's important?"

"It could be crucial," Agatha said, her mind racing. "Tilda, why didn't you tell us this before?"

Tilda looked up, her eyes meeting Agatha's with a mix of vulnerability and determination. "I was afraid, Agatha. I should have spoken up sooner, I know that now. But I trust you, and I want justice for Amanda. Everything is important now to protect Beatrice."

Agatha nodded, giving Tilda a reassuring pat on the arm.

As Tilda left, promising to let them know if she remembered anything else, Agatha turned to Emma. "What do you make of that?"

Emma shook her head, looking puzzled. "It's a lot to process. Devin being the last person seen with Amanda... that's a game-changer."

Agatha's brow furrowed. "I know. It's surprising, considering he spoke to Detective Dawson and gave me valuable information for the investigation. I can't imagine him harming Amanda."

"It does sound strange," Emma agreed. "What do you think we should do?"

"I'll try calling him," Agatha said, reaching for her phone. She dialed the number Devin had left, but her eyes widened as an automated voice informed her the number had been disconnected.

"That's odd," Agatha muttered. "His number's no longer in service."

Emma leaned in, her voice lowered. "A disconnected number right after we learn he was the last one seen with Amanda? That's suspicious."

Agatha nodded slowly, considering. "You're right, it is odd timing. But let's not jump to conclusions."

"What do you think we should do?" Emma asked. "We can't exactly drop by his place since he's not in California."

Agatha's eyes lit up. "What about Gemma? Harold's ex-wife? She seemed to know Devin pretty well. Maybe she has some insight or a way to reach him."

Emma smiled. "Good thinking, Agatha. It's worth a shot. Should we give her a call?"

"Or better yet," Agatha said, her eyes twinkling as she reached for Mike's leash, "why don't we pay Gemma a visit in person?"

Agatha and Emma, with Mike trotting beside them, approached Gemma's Victorian house. The well-manicured garden and freshly painted trim spoke of meticulous care, but there was something unwelcoming about the drawn curtains.

Agatha raised her hand to knock, but before her knuckles touched the wood, the door cracked open.

Gemma's face appeared in the narrow gap, her expression guarded.

"How can I help you?" she asked, her tone clipped.

Agatha, taken aback by the chilly reception, hesitated for a moment before speaking. "Hi Gemma, we were hoping to have a quick word. Have you been in touch with Devin recently?"

Surprise flashed across Gemma's face, quickly replaced by a neutral mask. "Devin is out of the country. He'll be gone for a while."

"Oh," Agatha said, exchanging a glance with Emma. "Do you know where exactly-"

"I'm sorry," Gemma interrupted, already closing the door. "I'm quite busy. Good day."

The door clicked shut, leaving Agatha and Emma standing on the porch, mouths agape.

"Well," Emma muttered, "that was... unexpected."

Agatha nodded, her brow furrowed. "Very. Let's head back and regroup."

As they walked back to Agatha's house, both women were lost in thought. Mike sensed their mood, padding along quietly beside them.

~

"What do you make of that?" Emma finally asked as they settled in Agatha's kitchen.

Agatha sighed, sinking into her favorite armchair. "I'm not sure, but Gemma definitely knows more than she's letting on. The question is, why is she being so secretive?"

Agatha poured steaming tea into two mismatched mugs, the comforting aroma of Earl Grey filling her cozy kitchen. She slid one mug across the worn wooden table to Emma, who wrapped her hands around it gratefully. Mike settled at Agatha's feet, his tail thumping softly against the linoleum floor.

"There has to be another clue somewhere," Agatha murmured, tapping her pencil against her notepad. She glanced at the envelope she'd received earlier. "Whoever sent me this must be connected to Harold and Amanda's deaths."

Emma nodded, her eyes sparkling with curiosity. "It's like a real-life mystery novel!"

Just then, Mike's ears perked up. He trotted to the door, tail wagging.

Agatha chuckled. "Looks like we have a visitor. Mike's better than any doorbell."

The actual doorbell chimed moments later. Agatha opened it to find Detective Dawson, his usual serious expression softened by a slight smile.

"Detective Dawson," Agatha greeted warmly. "What a surprise! Come in, please."

As Dawson entered, he glanced at Emma. "Actually, I was hoping we could speak privately for a moment, Agatha."

"Oh, anything you have to say, you can say in front of Emma," Agatha replied cheerfully. "She's been my partner in all this amateur sleuthing."

Emma, ever perceptive, stood up with a smile. "You know what? I think I'll go make us some tea. I'm sure we could all use a nice cuppa. Detective Dawson, how do you take yours?"

"Oh, uh, milk and sugar, please," Dawson replied, looking a bit flustered by the hospitality.

As Emma headed to the kitchen, Agatha turned to

Dawson. "Now, what brings you here, Detective? Any new developments in the case?"

Dawson sighed, running a hand through his hair. "It's about your aunt. Someone else has come forward with information about both murders."

Agatha's heart skipped a beat. She exchanged a worried glance with Emma before turning back to Dawson. "What did they say? Is it good news?"

The detective's grim expression said it all. "I'm afraid not. A witness saw your aunt entering Harold's room with those gold-plated knitting needles. Said she looked extremely upset."

Agatha felt the blood drain from her face. She sank onto the couch, her mind racing. After a moment, she looked up. "Wait a minute. Who was this witness? And what were they doing there so late at night?"

Dawson shifted uncomfortably. "It was the linen delivery man. He says they often run late due to their busy schedule."

"And you verified this?" Agatha pressed, her detective instincts kicking in.

"We did," Dawson nodded. "But there's more. The same witness also placed Devin with Amanda on the day of her death. It seems Devin was the last person seen with her."

Agatha's eyes widened. She remembered Tilda's account of seeing Devin with Amanda too. The pieces were starting to fall into place, but something still felt off.

"Detective," Agatha said slowly, "don't you find it strange that the same person witnessed two key moments in both murders? And that he just happened to be there both times?"

Dawson's brow furrowed. "What are you suggesting, Agatha?"

A stranger with access to the facility, showing up right when all this happens?" She tapped her fingers on the table, her mind racing. "I'm saying we might need to take a closer look. Maybe he saw something, or someone, that he's not telling us about."

Dawson nodded, his expression serious. "We're looking into everything, Agatha. But the linen delivery man has a rock-solid alibi. He was making deliveries across town at the time of the incident, and multiple witnesses confirm it."

After Detective Dawson left, Agatha sank into her favorite armchair, her brow furrowed in thought. Emma returned from the kitchen, two steaming mugs of tea in hand.

"Well, that was quite the revelation," Emma said, handing Agatha a mug. "What do you think?"

Agatha took a sip of tea, her mind whirling. "I'm not convinced, Emma. This linen delivery man's story seems too convenient. And it doesn't explain the strange behavior we've seen from Dr. Hartman."

Emma nodded, settling into the chair opposite. "You're right. Those green pills he's been giving to Beatrice... do you think they're connected to all this?"

"I'm almost certain of it," Agatha said, her eyes sparking with determination. "We need to confront Dr. Hartman about those pills. They might be the key to this whole mystery."

Emma sighed, running a hand through her hair. "But Agatha, we don't have any real evidence. Just suspicions and hunches. How can we approach him without looking like we're grasping at straws?"

Agatha set down her mug, a plan forming in her mind.

"We'll go to him, expressing concern about Beatrice's behavior. If we can get him talking about the medication, we might learn something crucial."

"That could work," Emma said, her eyes lighting up. "When should we do it?"

"Tomorrow morning," Agatha replied. "We'll catch him at Green Acres before he starts his day. It's time we got some answers."

As the evening light faded outside, Agatha and Emma spent the rest of the night refining their plan. Tomorrow, they would face Dr. Hartman and hopefully uncover the truth behind the mysterious green pills and their connection to the murders at Green Acres.

30

A BITTER PILL TO SWALLOW

The aroma of freshly brewed coffee wafted through the halls of Green Acres, mingling with the scent of disinfectant - a sure sign that the morning cleaning routine was in full swing.

Agatha stifled a yawn as she and Emma positioned themselves outside Dr. Hartman's office. The early hour meant fewer prying eyes, but it also meant confronting the doctor before her second cup of caffeine had kicked in.

"I hope he's a morning person," Emma whispered, smoothing down her blouse nervously.

Agatha nodded, squaring her shoulders as she raised her hand to knock. The muffled sounds of the facility coming to life - carts rattling down hallways, muted conversations, and the distant chime of a medication reminder - provided a fitting backdrop for the tense moment ahead.

"Ready?" Agatha whispered, her hand poised to knock.

Emma nodded, her face a mixture of determination and nervousness.

Just as Agatha was about to rap on the door, a familiar

voice chirped behind them. "Ooh là là! What's this? A secret rendezvous with the dashing doctor?"

They turned to see Lorraine, her eyes twinkling with mischief.

Agatha sighed, "Lorraine, this isn't the best time—"

"Nonsense, ma chérie! There's always time for a little excitement," Lorraine grinned, positioning herself between them.

Before Agatha could protest further, the office door swung open, revealing a startled Dr. Hartman.

"Ladies," he said, his eyebrows raised. "Is everything alright?"

Agatha took a deep breath. "Actually, Dr. Hartman, we need to talk. It's about those green pills you've been prescribing."

Dr. Hartman's face paled. He ushered them inside, closing the door behind Lorraine, who was practically bouncing with curiosity.

As they settled into chairs, Agatha's mind raced. She'd planned this conversation carefully, but now that the moment had arrived, doubt crept in. *What if I'm wrong about all this?* she thought, her fingers nervously twisting the strap of her purse. *Dr. Hartman seems so respected here. But those pills... something's not right.*

Pushing aside her hesitation, Agatha leaned forward, her eyes fixed on Dr. Hartman. The ticking of the clock on the wall seemed to grow louder in the tense silence.

"Dr. Hartman," she began, her voice steady despite her racing heart, "we know about your past with Novus Vitae Pharmaceuticals and the lawsuit. We also know about the green pills you gave Beatrice and tried to give Mildred."

The doctor's hands trembled slightly as he adjusted his glasses, a faint sheen of sweat visible on his brow. He opened his mouth, closed it, then tried again. "I... I don't know what you're talking about," he stammered, his eyes darting between Agatha and Emma.

Agatha felt a flicker of doubt. Was she wrong about him? She glanced at Emma, who gave her an encouraging nod.

Lorraine, unable to contain herself, gasped dramatically. "Oh, the plot thickens! It's just like in 'The Case of the Poisoned Prescription'!" She clasped her hands to her chest, eyes wide with excitement.

Emma, momentarily distracted from the tension, turned to Lorraine. "What case are you talking about?"

"Oh, ma chérie," Lorraine gushed, her eyes sparkling. "It's from this absolutely riveting mystery novel I just finished. The dashing detective confronts the suspicious doctor, just like our Agatha is doing now!" She leaned in conspiratorially. "Of course, in the book, the doctor turned out to be innocent. It was actually the gardener who—"

"Lorraine," Agatha interrupted gently but firmly, "perhaps we can discuss your book later?"

Emma shot Lorraine an apologetic look before turning her attention back to Dr. Hartman. Agatha took a deep breath, steeling herself for what she was about to say next.

The playful interlude had done nothing to diminish the gravity of the situation, and she could feel the weight of her next words hanging in the air.

"Dr. Hartman," she said, her voice low and intense, "did you have anything to do with Harold and Amanda's deaths?"

The room fell silent. Even Lorraine seemed to hold her breath, the gravity of the accusation finally sinking in. The only sound was the steady tick-tock of the clock and the faint hum of the air conditioning.

Dr. Hartman's face went through a range of emotions - shock, anger, fear - before finally crumpling in despair. "No!" he exclaimed, his voice cracking. "God, no. I would never..." He trailed off, burying his face in his hands.

Agatha watched him closely, her mind racing. Was this genuine distress or just an act? She'd seen enough guilty people try to feign innocence to know that appearances could be deceiving. But something about Dr. Hartman's reaction felt raw, unguarded.

As the silence stretched on, broken only by Dr. Hartman's ragged breathing, Agatha exchanged a glance with Emma. They'd come this far - now it was time to hear what the doctor had to say for himself.

Dr. Hartman took a deep breath. "The truth is, I suspected someone was drugging the residents. I've been replacing those pills with harmless vitamins and melatonin to protect them."

Agatha's eyes widened. "Drugging the residents? But why didn't you report this?"

"I didn't have concrete proof," Dr. Hartman replied, his voice strained. "I wasn't sure who was supplying the pills, so I hesitated to get a sample tested. And after what happened in my past... I was afraid no one would believe me without solid evidence." He paused, running a hand through his hair. "Or worse... they'd blame me."

He then reached into his pocket and pulled out two small bottles. "Here, look at these. These are the pills I've been replacing."

Agatha examined the pills, recognizing them immediately. They matched the description Beatrice, Mildred, and Aunt Edna had given her.

"To be honest," Dr. Hartman continued, his voice barely above a whisper, "the only two residents I saw having significant changes were your Aunt Edna and Beatrice. But I was closely monitoring the other patients' medications."

Agatha's brow furrowed. "But who was giving them the medications if not you?"

Dr. Hartman hesitated, then sighed. "I believe it was Nurse Amanda. She was very secretive before... you know, before what happened to her."

Lorraine leaned in, her usual joviality replaced by intense curiosity. "Mon Dieu! So we have mysterious pills, secretive nurses, and now a doctor playing detective. This is better than any soap opera!"

Lorraine clapped her hands together. "Mon Dieu! The plot twist we've all been waiting for!"

Agatha smiled at Lorraine's enthusiasm, even as her mind raced with this new information. She turned back to Dr. Hartman, her expression serious.

Dr. Hartman leaned forward, his voice barely above a whisper. "Listen carefully. Don't tell anyone about the pills yet. We don't know who might be watching or listening."

He glanced nervously at the door before continuing. "Even though I suspect Amanda was involved, someone is still tampering with the medications. I've been keeping a close eye on Beatrice's pills, and even Mildred's. We need to be extremely careful."

Agatha nodded, feeling a chill run down her spine. "What should we do next?" she asked softly.

"For now, act normal," Dr. Hartman advised. "We need to gather more evidence without alerting whoever's behind this. Can I count on your discretion?"

Agatha's jaw set with determination. "You can count on us, Dr. Hartman," she said softly. "We'll be as quiet as church mice, but keep our eyes wide open."

As they left the office, Agatha felt a mix of relief and

frustration. They'd cleared Dr. Hartman, but now faced a new mystery. Her mind raced with possibilities. *Could Mr. Collins be behind this?* She wondered. *We know he's having financial problems. Maybe he's making money with an unauthorized drug trial?*

She turned to Emma, keeping her voice low. "What if Mr. Collins is involved? It would explain the secrecy and the mysterious pills."

Emma's eyes widened. "That's a disturbing thought, but it makes sense. And how does the linen man fit into all this?"

Agatha shrugged, her brow furrowed. "I have no idea," she admitted. "But something tells me he's mixed up in this somehow."

Emma nodded, her eyes thoughtful. "It's like putting together a jigsaw puzzle without knowing what the picture is supposed to be."

"Exactly," Agatha agreed. "And I have a feeling we're still missing quite a few pieces."

Lorraine linked arms with Agatha and Emma. "Well, mes amies, shall we go dust for fingerprints? Or perhaps disguise ourselves as potted plants to spy on Mr. Collins?"

Despite everything, Agatha found herself chuckling. Trust Lorraine to find humor in even the most serious situations.

31

THE DISCOVERY

Exhaustion weighed heavily on Agatha's shoulders as she approached her beloved bookstore. After the events at Green Acres, she craved the sanctuary of familiar spines and the aroma of freshly ground coffee beans.

"Morning, Agatha!" Celeste called from behind the counter, her hands busy arranging a tray of still-warm scones. "We've got a busy day ahead. The tour bus just pulled up!"

Agatha hung up her coat, surveying the shop with a mix of pride and anticipation. "Thanks for the heads up, Celeste. Let's make sure they all leave with a good book and a full stomach!"

As if on cue, the door swung open, and a group of chattering tourists streamed in. Agatha smoothed down her cardigan and plastered on her best welcoming smile.

"Welcome to One Deadly Chapter!" she greeted warmly. "Feel free to browse, and don't hesitate to ask for recommendations. We've got a mystery reading in an hour, so make yourselves comfortable!"

As the visitors dispersed throughout the store, Agatha noticed Mr. Anderson, a silver-haired regular, perusing the new releases section. She made her way over to him, weaving between browsing customers.

"Good morning, Mr. Anderson," she said, her voice warm. "Finding any new mysteries to solve?"

Mr. Anderson's eyes crinkled with amusement. "Ah, Agatha! Just the sleuth I was hoping to see. I'm torn between these two." He held up a pair of hardcovers. "Which would you recommend for an old detective like me?"

Agatha chuckled, taking the books from him. "Well, let's see. 'The Vanishing Violin' is a classic whodunit, but 'Whispers in the Willow' has some unexpected twists that might keep you guessing."

Mr. Anderson leaned in conspiratorially. "I hear you've got quite the knack for solving real-life mysteries these days."

Agatha felt a flush of pride mixed with embarrassment. "Oh, Mr. Anderson, you flatter me. I just happened to be in the right place at the right time. Or the wrong place, depending on how you look at it!"

As the hour for the reading approached, Agatha made her way to the hastily arranged podium at the back of the store. The wooden crate draped with a tablecloth served as an impromptu stage, a testament to the bookstore's charm and resourcefulness. Chairs borrowed from the café area were filled with an eager audience, a mix of tourists and familiar local faces. She couldn't help but notice a few whispers and pointed looks her way as she stepped up to the makeshift platform.

"That's her, the amateur detective," she heard one tourist whisper excitedly to another.

Agatha cleared her throat, pushing aside the twinge of discomfort at being the center of attention. "Good morning, everyone. Thank you for joining us today. I'll be reading from 'The Silent Sonata,' a gripping mystery set in a small coastal town not unlike our own Bristol Lake."

As she read, Agatha found herself swept up in the story. The audience hung on her every word, gasping at the reveals and chuckling at the witty dialogue. For a moment, she allowed herself to imagine it was her own novel she was reading from, the manuscript that had been so cruelly stolen from her.

After the reading, as the crowd dispersed, Gladys approached Agatha. Her silver hair was neatly coiled in its usual chignon, and her eyes sparkled with the enthusiasm of a woman half her age.

"Agatha, dear, that was simply marvelous!" Gladys said, patting Agatha's arm. "But it's made me realize how much I miss our book club meetings. When are we going to have another one?"

Agatha smiled warmly at her neighbor and friend. "You know what, Gladys? I was just thinking the same thing. How about this Tuesday? I've been so caught up with everything going on with Aunt Edna, I completely lost track of time."

Gladys's face lit up. "Tuesday sounds perfect! I'll spread the word up and down our street. Will you be getting those delightful mystery scones from Eliza's?"

"You bet," Agatha chuckled. "It wouldn't be book club without Eliza's mystery scones, would it?"

"Oh, wonderful!" Gladys beamed, then lowered her voice. "And Agatha, dear, do be careful with all this investigating. We neighbors worry about you, you know."

As the afternoon waned, Agatha was just about to lock

up when the door opened, bringing with it a gust of cool evening air and Gary, the mailman.

"Evening, Agatha!" Gary called out cheerfully, his mailbag slung over his shoulder. "Got a special delivery for you."

Agatha's heart skipped a beat. "Oh? What have you got there, Gary?"

Gary pulled out a large manila envelope, his brow furrowing. "Here's an odd one for you, Agatha. No return address."

Agatha took the envelope, her curiosity piqued. What's this? she wondered, turning it over in her hands. The familiar weight made her breath catch. Could it be...?

"Thanks, Gary," she managed, her voice barely above a whisper. Her heart raced as she stared at the envelope. My manuscript?

Gary tilted his head, noticing her reaction. "Everything alright?"

Agatha nodded absently, still lost in thought. "Yes, I... I just need to open this."

"Well, before I head out," Gary said with a friendly smile, "mind if I grab a couple of those mystery scones? My wife's been raving about them since book club."

"Of course," Agatha replied, gesturing towards the display. "Help yourself. They're Eliza's best seller."

As Gary selected his scones, humming contentedly, Agatha couldn't resist. With trembling fingers, she carefully opened one corner of the envelope. A small note slipped out. Her eyes widened as she read the cryptic message: "Read these documents carefully."

"These smell heavenly," Gary said, heading for the door. "Thanks, Agatha. See you tomorrow!"

The bell above the door jingled as Gary left, leaving Agatha alone with her mysterious envelope.

Quickly, she tucked the note back inside and sealed the envelope. Whatever was inside, it clearly wasn't her manuscript. But it seemed important.

She slipped it into her bag, her mind whirling with possibilities. What documents? And who sent them? The contents would have to wait. Right now, Aunt Edna needed her, and Agatha wasn't about to let her down.

~

After leaving the bookstore, Agatha had paid a visit to Aunt Edna at the county jail. Despite the circumstances, Aunt Edna's irrepressible spirit had shone through, and they'd shared a few laughs over old family stories.

On the drive home, Agatha's thoughts drifted to Cecilia Morgan's case. The memory of that unsolved mystery tugged at her heart, but it also steeled her resolve. She wouldn't let Harold's death go unsolved, not if she could help it.

Mike greeted Agatha happily at the front door when she arrived home, his tail wagging furiously. He then headed straight to the kitchen and stood by the door, looking back at her expectantly.

"Need to go outside, buddy?" Agatha asked, smiling.

Mike barked softly in response. She opened the door, and he trotted out, heading to the plant beds in the backyard. Agatha watched Mike go, her gaze shifting toward the flower bed where, not long after she'd moved in, Mike had dug up Cecilia Morgan's skeleton. That discovery had led to her first big case. Now, with Harold's death, she felt that same pull to uncover the truth. She lingered on her memories for a while, the past mixing with the present, before heading back inside.

Her eyes fell on her purse on the table, next to her type-writer. She reached for her purse, then hesitated and pushed it away. "I need a break," she voiced aloud, opening the door to let Mike back inside.

Mike wagged his tail excitedly, his eyes bright and full of energy. He then paced towards his food bowl, looking back at her with anticipation.

"Alright, do you want to eat?" she asked, laughing as Mike jumped excitedly.

"I'm also going to eat a good dinner, start a new book, and relax this evening," she continued, pouring kibble into his bowl. "I think I'll start a romance today. I need a break from the real-life mystery I'm currently living."

Mike didn't understand her words, but he acted excited for her anyway, wagging his tail even more as he dug into his food.

～

Sunlight streamed through Agatha's bedroom window, rousing her from a fitful sleep. As consciousness crept in, so did the memory of yesterday's mysterious package. She'd left it unopened, too overwhelmed by the day's events to face another potential complication.

With a sigh, Agatha padded into the kitchen. The manila envelope sat on the counter where she'd left it, looking deceptively ordinary in the morning light.

"No more procrastinating," she muttered, reaching for the package.

As she tipped the envelope, a small note fluttered out along with a stack of documents. Agatha's heart raced as she unfolded the paper, her eyes widening as she recognized the handwriting.

"Devin," she breathed, then read the hastily scribbled message aloud: "Agatha, What I've uncovered about Green Acres is worse than we thought. These documents could help Edna, but be careful. Trust no one.

• Devin"

Her hands trembling slightly, Agatha spread the documents across her kitchen table. Financial records, email printouts, internal memos – all marked 'Confidential'.

"Oh, Devin," she whispered, "what have you gotten yourself into?"

Reaching for her phone, she dialed a familiar number. "Emma? Can you come over right away? Devin's sent us what might be our first big break in Aunt Edna's case."

Thirty minutes later, Agatha and Emma huddled in the living room, papers strewn about. The comforting scent of lavender couldn't mask the tension in the air.

Emma leaned forward, her brow furrowed as she studied a spreadsheet for the third time. "These documents are damning, Agatha," Emma said, tapping a highlighted section of a bank statement. "Mr. Collins has been siphoning money for years. But this isn't enough to prove he had anything to do with the murders."

Agatha nodded, her mind racing. "You're right. We need something more concrete, something that ties him directly to Amanda and Harold's deaths."

She paused, staring at the scattered papers, deep in thought. "Detective Dawson already thinks we're meddling. But maybe if he sees this, he'll realize we're onto something."

Emma looked up, hope flickering in her eyes. "You think he'll listen?"

Agatha took a deep breath, reaching for her phone. "It's worth a try. We need him on our side."

Agatha picked up the phone and dialed Detective Dawson's number. After a few rings, he answered.

"Detective Dawson, it's Agatha. We've found something important. Can you come over to review it?"

There was a brief pause. "Alright, Agatha. I'll be there shortly."

When Detective Dawson arrived, Agatha ushered him into the living room. His tall frame filled the doorway, and his expression was stern but not unkind.

"Thank you for coming, Detective," Agatha said, stepping aside.

Dawson entered, his gaze sweeping the room and landing on the documents spread out on the table. He sighed. "Alright, Agatha. What have you got for me?"

Agatha motioned for Dawson to sit down. "I think there might be some financial troubles at Green Acres," she said, fiddling with a pen on her desk.

Dawson raised an eyebrow. "Oh? And how do you figure that?"

"Well," Agatha began, "have you seen the place lately? They've turned those spacious apartments into cramped kitchenettes. And the whole building looks like it hasn't seen a fresh coat of paint in years."

"That doesn't necessarily mean anything, Agatha," Dawson said, leaning back in his chair. "Could just be poor management. You know how these places can be."

Agatha nodded, but her eyes sparkled with determination. "True, but I can't help thinking it might be connected to everything else that's been going on. Amanda's murder, Harold's death... it all seems to lead back to Green Acres somehow."

Dawson sighed, a hint of a smile on his face. "You and your hunches. Got any actual evidence to back that up?"

Agatha handed him the documents, watching as Dawson scanned them quickly. His expression remained skeptical.

"This is interesting, Agatha, but it's not enough for a murder charge," Dawson said, setting the papers down. "Where did you get these documents, anyway?"

Agatha hesitated for a moment. "Devin sent them to me."

Dawson's eyebrows shot up. "Devin? We've been trying to locate him for questioning. Any idea where he is?"

"No," Agatha admitted, "he just sent the documents anonymously."

Dawson sighed. "That's more suspicious than the documents themselves, Agatha. We need to find Devin."

Agatha furrowed her brow, deep in thought. Suddenly, she sat up straighter, her eyes widening with realization. "You know, I just had a thought. What if Harold kept records of his own? He seemed like the type to notice things, especially if there were financial troubles at Green Acres."

"Records?" Dawson asked, his interest piqued. "What makes you think he might have kept records?"

"Well, from what I've gathered, Harold was quite meticulous," Agatha explained, her voice gaining confidence. "And if he suspected something was amiss with the finances, he might have started documenting it. It's worth checking his room, don't you think? There could be something there that helps us understand what was really going on at Green Acres."

Emma nodded enthusiastically. "That's a great idea, Agatha. Harold's room might hold some crucial clues we've been missing."

Dawson rubbed his chin thoughtfully. "Well, Agatha, Harold's room is no longer an active crime scene. We've already conducted our initial investigation there." He paused, choosing his words carefully. "Officially, I can't authorize you to search the room or give you access. However, if you happen to notice anything of interest during your visits to Green Acres, I'd certainly be interested in hearing about it."

He leaned forward slightly, lowering his voice. "Just remember, you can look, but don't touch or remove anything without proper authorization. We need to maintain the integrity of any potential evidence."

```Agatha nodded, trying to contain her excitement. "Understood, Detective. We'll be careful."

"I mean it, Agatha," Dawson said, his tone serious but not unkind. "No funny business. I know how you get when you're on the scent of something."

"Cross my heart," Agatha replied, making the gesture. "You'll be my first call if we find anything interesting."

Later that afternoon, Agatha and Emma arrived at Green Acres. They approached the reception desk where Lindsey was sorting through some papers.

"Good afternoon, Lindsey," Agatha greeted warmly. "How are you holding up?"

Lindsey sighed, pushing a strand of hair behind her ear. "Hey, Agatha. Honestly? It's been a long week. I can't wait for the weekend." She offered a tired smile. "But thanks for asking. What brings you two in today?"

Emma leaned in, her voice low. "We were hoping to
```

check on something in Harold's room. Just to tie up some loose ends, you know?"

Lindsey's brow furrowed. "I'm not sure that's a good idea. Mr. Collins has been very particular about who goes into residents' rooms, especially since... well, you know."

Agatha leaned in, lowering her voice. "Lindsey, I understand your concern. We're looking for anything that might help clear Aunt Edna's name. Harold might have left something important behind."

Emma nodded, adding, "We won't disturb anything, I promise. We'll be quick and careful."

"And don't worry," Agatha reassured, "I spoke to Detective Dawson about this, and he said it was okay."

Lindsey's shoulders relaxed slightly. "Oh, well, if Detective Dawson approved... I suppose a quick look couldn't hurt. Just please, be careful. And if Mr. Collins asks, I knew nothing about this, okay?"

Lindsey still looked uncertain when Tilda walked by, catching the tail end of the conversation.

"I can help with that," Tilda offered, her voice low. "I have the master key, and if Detective Dawson okayed it, it should be fine."

Agatha and Emma exchanged surprised but grateful glances. As they walked to Harold's room, Tilda explained in hushed tones, "I've been helping the police catalog items. They've actually finished processing the room now. It's no longer part of the active investigation."

"I should check first," Tilda whispered, her hand on the doorknob. "Just to make sure everything's... appropriate."

Agatha and Emma exchanged curious glances but nodded in agreement.

Tilda slipped into the room, closing the door behind her. For a moment, all they could hear was the faint sound of drawers opening and closing, and soft footsteps moving about the room.

After what felt like an eternity, Tilda reappeared, her face flushed. "All clear," she said, holding the door open. "You can go in now."

When they entered, the room was much as they remembered: neat, with a faint smell of Harold's cologne lingering in the air.

"Thanks, Tilda," Agatha said. "We won't be long."

Tilda nodded. "I'll be down the hall if you need anything."

As Tilda left, Agatha and Emma exchanged glances.

"Now, where do we start?" Emma asked, looking around the room.

"Hold on a second," Agatha said, reaching into her purse. She pulled out a pair of disposable gloves and handed another to Emma. "We should put these on first. We don't want to contaminate anything."

Emma nodded, slipping on the gloves. "Good thinking. Detective Dawson would have our heads if we messed up any evidence."

"Exactly," Agatha agreed, snapping her own gloves into place. "Okay, now we're ready. Any ideas?"

Emma's eyes scanned the room before settling on a wooden desk in the corner. "Let's start with his desk," she suggested. "If Harold was keeping records, that's probably where he'd store them."

"Good call," Agatha said, moving towards the desk. "Let's see what we can find."

They began to carefully search through the drawers, flipping through old receipts, letters, and notes. It wasn't long before Emma's fingers brushed against something unusual.

"Look, Agatha, this drawer has a false bottom!"

Agatha hurried over as Emma pried it open, revealing a hidden compartment. Inside was a small, leather-bound journal.

"What's this?" Agatha said, carefully picking up a leather-bound book from the nightstand.

Emma leaned in for a closer look. "It looks like a journal," she whispered.

Agatha gently opened it, revealing pages filled with handwriting. "You're right," she nodded. "And judging by the dates, it seems to be Harold's recent thoughts."

As she flipped through the pages, Agatha's eyebrows raised. "The handwriting is incredibly neat. It's almost like he wanted to make sure anyone who found this could read it clearly."

Agatha cleared her throat and read aloud: "'Collins is a thief. I'm getting too close. He knows I'm onto him.'" She glanced at Emma. "Well, that's certainly dramatic."

Emma's eyes widened. "Oh my, he sounds terrified. Do you think he knew something we don't?"

"Probably," Agatha muttered, flipping through more pages. Her brow furrowed unexpectedly. "Huh, that's odd."

"What is it?" Emma asked, leaning in closer. "Did you find something?"

Agatha chuckled, gently pushing Emma back. "Easy there. It's probably nothing. Just thought the handwriting looked a bit different in some places. See here?" She pointed to a section. "It's like his penmanship changed mid-sentence."

Emma squinted at the page. "Hmm, maybe he was writing in a hurry? Or switched pens?"

"Could be," Agatha shrugged. "Or maybe he was just getting more anxious. Stress does funny things to people."

"Speaking of stress," Emma said, "what else does it say?"

Agatha's expression grew more serious as she continued reading. "It's not pretty, Emma. These entries get increasingly panicky. Listen to this: 'I can't sleep. Every noise makes me jump. Collins is watching me, I know it. If anything happens to me, it's him. He's the key to all of this.'"

Emma let out a low whistle. "Yikes. Sounds like poor Harold was afraid for his life."

"And he might have paid the ultimate price for it," Agatha added grimly.

Agatha's brow furrowed as she held the journal. "Wait a minute... why didn't the police mention this? Surely they would have found it during their investigation."

Emma's eyes widened. "You're right. That's odd. Do you think someone could have placed it here after the police finished?"

Agatha bit her lip, considering. "It's possible. Or maybe the police overlooked it somehow. Either way, we can't just hand it over to Detective Dawson without understanding more about where it came from."

"No, we can't," Agatha agreed, her brow furrowed in concentration. She tapped the journal thoughtfully. "I think we need to look into this further before we do anything else. There might be clues in here that could help us understand what really happened to Harold and why this journal wasn't found earlier."

Emma nodded, a spark of determination in her eyes. "Good idea. Should we take pictures of the pages? That way, we're not removing evidence, but we can still study it later."

"Perfect," Agatha smiled. "Let's do that, and then we

can go through it carefully when we're somewhere more private. We need to tread carefully here, Emma. This could be the breakthrough we've been looking for in Aunt Edna's case."

Agatha tapped her chin thoughtfully. "We need to find a link between Collins and Amanda's murder. That's the missing piece."

"And where do you propose we look for this missing piece?" Emma asked, raising an eyebrow.

A mischievous grin spread across Agatha's face. "Why, my dear Watson, isn't it obvious? We're going to take a little field trip to Amanda's office."

Emma groaned. "Why do I get the feeling we're about to break several laws?"

"Not break, Emma," Agatha said, her eyes twinkling. "Just... bend them a little. For justice!"

32

UNDER THE DESK AND OVER THEIR HEADS

Agatha turned to Emma, her brow furrowed in concentration. "We need more proof... solid proof, I mean. Something that'll make even Detective Dawson sit up and take notice."

Emma sighed, running a hand through her hair. "So, what now? It's not like we can dust for fingerprints or anything."

Agatha tapped her chin thoughtfully. "No, but we might have an advantage the police don't."

"Oh? And what's that?" Emma asked, raising an eyebrow.

"We know this place, these people," Agatha explained. "Little things that seem normal to the cops might stand out to us."

Emma nodded slowly, a small smile forming. "You know, you might be onto something there."

"Exactly," Agatha said, straightening up. "Ready to do some good old-fashioned snooping?"

"Lead the way," Emma chuckled, falling into step beside her.

Agatha cracked the door open and peered into the hallway, her heart racing with anticipation. After a thorough
scan, she turned back to Emma and gave an exaggerated
thumbs up. "Coast is clear. Operation Snoop is a go."

As they tiptoed down the hall, they kept their eyes
peeled for any sign of movement. Agatha glanced at Emma
and nodded, trying to look as inconspicuous as possible.

Suddenly, a door opened, and out stepped Mildred and
Mrs. Johnson, engrossed in animated conversation about
something in Mildred's hand.

Mildred spotted them and beamed. "Hello, my dears!"
she exclaimed, her smile bright enough to light up the dim
hallway. "Look what I did." She proudly displayed a pair of
tiny knitted baby shoes. "Mrs. Johnson here showed me
how to knit these for my grandkids."

Mrs. Johnson's eyebrows shot up. "Grandkids? Don't
you mean great-grandkids?"

Mildred's eyes narrowed playfully. "Yes, of course. I
meant to say great-grandkids. Slip of the tongue."

"Sure you did," Mrs. Johnson teased, her tone dripping
with sarcasm. "I think you just wanted them to think you're
younger than you are."

"Nonsense, Mrs. Johnson," Mildred retorted with a
wink. "Age is just a number, and I've decided mine is
unlisted."

The two women continued their banter as they headed
towards the community room, leaving Agatha and Emma
forgotten in their wake.

Agatha let out a relieved sigh. "Thank goodness they
didn't ask what we were doing in this hallway. I was already
cooking up a story about looking for a lost earring."

Emma chuckled. "I know, right? I was afraid we'd have

to follow them to the community room and spend the next hour discussing the finer points of knitting baby booties."

Agatha and Emma arrived at Amanda's old office, pausing outside the door.

"What if it's locked?" Emma whispered, eyeing the doorknob.

"Only one way to find out," Agatha murmured back.

They glanced up and down the hallway one last time. Seeing no one, Emma reached for the knob and turned it gently. To their surprise, it gave way easily.

They both let out a quiet sigh of relief.

"Well, that's convenient," Agatha said under her breath.

With a final nod to each other, they slipped inside, carefully shutting the door behind them.

"We need to be quick," Agatha whispered, her voice tinged with urgency. "Someone could walk in any moment, and I doubt 'We're conducting an unauthorized investigation' will go over well as an excuse."

Emma nodded, her eyes darting around the room. "Where should we start? It's not like there's going to be a folder labeled 'Incriminating Evidence' sitting on the desk."

Agatha pointed to a desk in the corner. "How about I tackle those drawers, and you search over there?" She motioned towards a small cabinet on the opposite side of the room.

After several minutes of fruitless searching, Emma sighed dramatically. "Gee, there's nothing here... I mean, nothing significant to the investigation at least. Unless you count an impressive collection of herbal tea bags as suspicious."

Agatha's gaze shifted to a printer by the desk, where a lime green notebook caught her attention. She grabbed it and began flipping through the pages. "Oh my, Emma, look at this!"

"What is it? The secret recipe for the mystery meat they serve on Tuesdays?"

"No, look," Agatha said, pointing at an open page. "It says 'Harold's net worth?' with a question mark."

Emma frowned. "That's it? 'Harold's net worth' with a question mark? What does that even mean?"

"I don't know, but don't you find it odd that a nurse in an assisted living facility would be wondering about a resident's net worth?"

"Yes, that's definitely strange," Emma agreed. "Some might even say it's incriminating. Or at least nosier than your average caregiver."

Before Agatha could close the notebook and return it to its spot, they heard the doorknob turning. Panic flashed across their faces.

"Quick! Under the desk!" Agatha hissed, already diving for cover.

Emma's eyes widened. "Are you serious? We're not exactly schoolgirls who can fit under-"

The door began to open, and Emma didn't finish her protest. She squeezed herself next to Agatha in the cramped space, their limbs tangled awkwardly.

"Ow! That's my foot!" Agatha whispered.

"Well, that's my ribs your elbow is trying to puncture," Emma retorted quietly.

They heard Mr. Collins' voice. "Is anyone in here? I'm sure I heard voices."

Agatha closed her eyes tightly, as if that would make them invisible. She could hear Mr. Collins' footsteps getting closer.

"This is ridiculous," Emma muttered. "We look like the world's worst hide-and-seek players."

"Shh!" Agatha hushed her, trying not to laugh despite the tension.

Suddenly, Mr. Collins' face appeared as he bent down to look under the desk. His eyes widened in surprise, mirroring the shocked expressions on Agatha and Emma's faces.

"What in the world are you two doing under there?" he demanded, his voice a mix of confusion and exasperation.

Agatha and Emma looked at each other, then back at Mr. Collins, their minds racing for a plausible explanation.

"Would you believe we're conducting a very thorough dust inspection?" Agatha offered weakly.

Mr. Collins' expression hardened as he helped Agatha and Emma out from under the desk. "Go on, let me hear your excuse for trespassing in a private office... for invading a deceased employee's privacy." His gaze fell on the lime green notebook in Agatha's hand. "Are you stealing from us now?"

Agatha bristled at the accusation. "Of course not!" she retorted, placing the notebook back on the printer with more force than necessary. She met Mr. Collins' gaze, her chin lifted defiantly. "It's rather ironic to hear you accuse us of stealing when you—"

"When I what?" Mr. Collins interrupted, his voice sharp.

Agatha realized this was the moment of truth. There was no going back now. She reached into her bag and pulled out the large envelope containing the papers she'd received from Devin. "I have evidence that you've been stealing money from Green Acres."

Mr. Collins' face paled. "What are you talking about?" He ran a hand over his bald head, a nervous gesture that didn't escape Agatha's notice. "I hope you're not trying to play one of your amateur detective games. I've heard about your... reputation."

"This is no game, Mr. Collins," Agatha said firmly, pulling the papers from the envelope and holding them out.

He snatched the documents from her hands, his eyes growing wider as he scanned the numbers and details. "This is insane," he muttered. "These documents are forged. They have to be."

Emma crossed her arms, skepticism written across her face. "Sure, they're fake. Maybe you'd like to try another excuse? That one's not very convincing."

Mr. Collins' shoulders slumped. "Look, I've had my problems, and yes, I'm in debt, but I'm not stealing from my own business. That would be financial suicide."

"I believe the term you're looking for is 'money laundering,'" Emma added dryly.

"No, you don't understand," Mr. Collins insisted, his voice tinged with desperation. "Wait here, please. I need to show you something."

Before they could protest, he dashed out of the office. Agatha and Emma exchanged puzzled glances.

"What do you think?" Emma whispered. "Is he running away or actually getting proof?"

"I'm not sure," Agatha replied, her brow furrowed. "But if he is guilty, why would he leave us alone with all this potential evidence?"

Mr. Collins returned moments later, slightly winded and clutching a folder. He pulled out several documents and thrust them at Agatha. "Look through these. Please."

As Agatha reviewed the papers, she felt the blood rush to her face. Embarrassment washed over her as she realized the truth. Mr. Collins had been telling the truth – while he was indeed in debt, he hadn't been stealing from Green

Acres. The documents she'd received from Devin were clever forgeries, exact copies of the originals she now held, but with altered numbers. It was clear that Devin had been trying to shift blame away from himself.

Mr. Collins handed her one more document. "Look at this. It's a promissory note for a loan Harold made to Green Acres – not to me personally, but to the company. Someone is trying to set me up." He sighed heavily. "I may be irresponsible with my personal finances, but I'm not a thief, and I'm certainly not a murderer."

Agatha looked up, her face etched with regret. "I'm so sorry, Mr. Collins. We jumped to conclusions, and that was unfair of us."

He nodded, accepting her apology. "It's alright. But now we have a bigger problem. Where's Devin? Why would he go to such lengths to cast suspicion on me if he wasn't guilty of something himself?"

"Probably murder," Emma said grimly.

Agatha's eyes widened as a realization hit her. "Oh my gosh, Emma! What did Devin and Amanda have in common?"

Emma frowned, confused. "What? I don't follow."

Mr. Collins looked equally perplexed, shrugging his shoulders.

"Gemma!" Agatha exclaimed. "Remember when I told you I saw Amanda leaving her house, and then we saw Devin there?"

Emma's eyes lit up with understanding. "That's right! And there's one small but crucial detail we're forgetting."

"Gemma is Harold's ex-wife," Agatha finished, the pieces falling into place.

"Exactly," Emma nodded. "I'd say she has a pretty strong motive to harm both victims. Her and Devin both."

Agatha's mind raced with the implications. "The real question now is, where is Devin? We need to find him before he disappears for good."

Mr. Collins looked between the two women, a mixture of confusion and admiration on his face. "I have to say, you two are quite the investigative team. But what do we do now? Should we take this information to the police?"

Agatha nodded slowly. "Yes, I think it's time to bring Detective Dawson into the loop. But first, we need to gather every bit of evidence we can.

33

UNVEILING TRUTHS

The late afternoon sun cast long shadows across the quiet street as Agatha and Emma approached Gemma's house. The air was crisp with the scent of fallen leaves, their rich autumn colors a stark contrast to the tension Agatha felt building in her chest.

Suddenly, Agatha's hand shot out, grabbing Emma's arm. "Did you see that?" she whispered; her eyes fixed on a window to the left of the front door.

Emma followed her gaze, squinting against the sun's glare. "See what? I don't—"

"The curtain," Agatha insisted, her voice low and urgent. "It moved. I swear I saw a figure standing there, and then the curtain closed as soon as we got closer."

Emma's brow furrowed as she studied the window. The curtain hung still now, innocuous and unrevealing. She shook her head, a small smile playing at her lips. "It must be your imagination running wild again, Agatha. Look," she said, pointing towards the garden. "There's Gemma, trimming her plants. Nothing suspicious about that."

Agatha's gaze lingered on the window for a moment

longer before she reluctantly nodded. "Yeah, I suppose you're right. My eyes must be playing tricks on me." But the nagging feeling in her gut refused to subside.

As they approached the gate, the earthy scent of fallen leaves and damp soil filled the air. Gemma knelt in her garden, pruning shears in hand, cutting back spent perennials and preparing her flowerbeds for winter. She seemed oblivious to their presence.

"Good afternoon, Gemma," Agatha called out, trying to keep her voice light and casual.

Gemma's head snapped up, her eyes narrowing in suspicion as she registered their presence. She stood slowly, brushing dirt from her gardening gloves. "Hello, ladies," she said, her tone polite but guarded. "How can I help you?"

Emma, ever the peacemaker, stepped forward with a warm smile. "Hello, Gemma. How have you been doing? We were just passing by and thought we'd say hello."

Agatha nodded, adding, "We hope we're not interrupting anything."

"Been doing fine," Gemma replied curtly, her gaze drifting back to her garden work as if silently willing the conversation to end.

Agatha, sensing their window of opportunity closing, decided to cut to the chase. "Gemma," she began, her heart racing, "have you heard from Devin by any chance?"

Gemma's brow furrowed in apparent confusion. "Devin? Which Devin?"

"Devin, Harold's nephew," Agatha pressed. "We saw him at your house a while back, remember?"

Recognition flickered across Gemma's face, quickly replaced by a mask of indifference. "Oh, that Devin. No, I haven't heard from him," she answered dismissively, already turning back to her roses.

Emma exchanged a quick glance with Agatha before trying again. "We're trying to get ahold of him. You wouldn't happen to know where he is, would you?"

Gemma's shoulders stiffened. "Of course I don't," she snapped, shaking her head. "Why should I know where he is?"

An uncomfortable silence fell over them, broken only by the soft snip of Gemma's pruning shears. Agatha opened her mouth to speak again when a familiar, jovial voice cut through the tension.

"Bonjour, mes chères amies!"

They turned to see Lorraine approaching from across the street, a bag of pastries swinging from her arm, her face beaming with its usual infectious cheer.

"How is everyone on this lovely afternoon?" Lorraine chirped, joining them at the gate. Her eyes sparkled mischievously as she turned to Gemma. "And how is your houseguest doing, ma chérie? Is he enjoying our quaint little town?"

Gemma's pruning shears froze mid-snip. "What houseguest?"

Lorraine's eyebrows shot up in surprise. "Why, the gentleman I saw arriving a couple of days ago with the suitcases. What was his name again?" She tapped her chin theatrically. "Ah, oui! Devin, that's it. Such a charming young man."

Agatha and Emma exchanged meaningful looks as Gemma's face drained of color. The garden and its autumn tasks suddenly seemed very far away from everyone's mind.

Gemma's face flickered with a mix of annoyance and resignation. She sighed deeply, setting down her pruning shears.

"Oh, alright. Yes, Devin is here. He's been feeling under

the weather since he arrived – jet lag and a touch of flu, I think."

Agatha's eyebrows shot up. "But why didn't you tell us when we asked?"

Gemma's eyes narrowed just enough to show her irritation. "Because, quite frankly, it's none of your business. Devin wanted to rest, and I didn't want the town's self-appointed detectives barging in on him."

Emma stepped forward, her voice gentle. "Gemma, we understand your concern, but this is important. We really need to speak with Devin."

After a moment's hesitation, Gemma nodded reluctantly. "Fine. Come in, but please, try not to exhaust him."

As they entered Gemma's house, Lorraine held up her bag of pastries. "Mes amis, perhaps we could share these lovely treats? A little sweetness to lift our spirits, non?"

Gemma shook her head, her expression tired. "No, thank you, Lorraine. I'm not really in the mood for sweets right now."

Lorraine's face fell for a moment, a flicker of disappointment crossing her features. Then, she quickly recovered, lifting her chin. "Ah, well, I was just being polite anyway. More for me, then!" She hugged the bag closer to her chest, a hint of defiance in her tone.

They found Devin in the guest room, looking pale and tired, but alert. His eyes widened in surprise at the sight of Agatha and Emma.

"Ladies," he said, sitting up straighter in bed. "To what do I owe this unexpected visit?"

Agatha took a deep breath. "Devin, we need to talk about the documents you gave me – the ones about Mr. Collins and Green Acres' finances."

Devin's face remained impassive, but Agatha noticed a slight twitch in his left eye. "What about them?"

"They're forgeries," Emma stated bluntly. "Very good ones, but fake nonetheless."

Devin's eyes widened in shock. "Forged? What do you mean?"

Agatha leaned forward, her expression serious. "Mr. Collins showed me the real documents. The ones you presented are not authentic."

Devin's face paled, and he sank back into his chair. "That's... that's impossible. I had no idea."

"If you didn't forge them," Agatha pressed gently, "where did you get them from?"

"From Amanda," Devin replied, his voice barely above a whisper.

Emma's eyebrows shot up. "Did she tell you where she got them?"

Devin shook his head. "I asked, but she was very secretive about it. All she would say was that it came from someone at Green Acres. She didn't want to tell me where it came from exactly, but she wanted me to know what was going on." He paused, his brow furrowing. "And she mentioned something else... she had suspicions about Mr. Collins."

Agatha leaned forward, her interest piqued. "Suspicions? What kind of suspicions?"

"She didn't go into detail," Devin replied, his voice lowering. "But the way she talked about him... it was clear she didn't trust him. She seemed to think he was involved in something shady at Green Acres."

As Devin finished explaining his interactions with Amanda, a thoughtful silence fell over the room. Agatha's eyes darted between Emma, Devin, Gemma, and Lorraine, her mind working overtime to process this new information.

"Thank you for your honesty, Devin," Agatha said, her voice carefully neutral. "I think we have a lot to consider."

Emma nodded in agreement, catching the subtle shift in Agatha's demeanor. "Yes, this certainly puts things in a new light."

As they prepared to leave, Lorraine piped up, her voice tinged with its usual cheerfulness, though a hint of concern shone in her eyes. "Well, mes amis, this has been quite the enlightening visit! Perhaps we should all go for a nice, calming cup of tea? I hear it's excellent for digesting new information!"

Agatha smiled softly at Lorraine's attempt to lighten the mood. "Thanks, Lorraine, but I think Emma and I need some time to process all of this. Rain check?"

Gemma saw them to the door, her expression a mix of relief and lingering suspicion. "I hope this visit was... helpful," she said, her tone measured.

As they walked away from Gemma's house, Emma turned to Agatha. "You're awfully quiet. What are you thinking?"

Agatha took a deep breath, her brow furrowed in concentration. "I'm not sure yet, Emma. But I feel like we're on the verge of something big. We need to review everything we know, connect all the dots."

Emma nodded, sensing the weight of Agatha's words. "Back to the drawing board, then?"

"Exactly," Agatha replied, her voice filled with determination. "Let's head back to the bookstore. We've got a lot of work to do."

Agatha and Emma stepped out of Gemma's house, the

cool afternoon air a stark contrast to the warmth inside. They walked in silence for a moment, both lost in thought.

Finally, Emma spoke up. "What do you think, Agatha? Do you believe Devin?"

Agatha nodded slowly. "I do. Why would he voluntarily give me forged documents if he knew they were fake? It doesn't make sense."

"Unless he hoped you'd never realize they were forgeries," Emma pointed out.

"True," Agatha conceded. Then, a thought struck her. "What if Mr. Collins' documents were the fake ones?"

Emma shook her head. "That would be interesting, but he had bank statements and everything to go along with it. I think his is legit."

"You're probably right," Agatha agreed, frowning. "My gut tells me Devin's innocent, at least of the forgery. But someone's definitely not telling the whole truth here."

They continued walking, their footsteps echoing on the quiet street.

"It's ironic, isn't it?" Emma mused. "The crime happened at Green Acres, and now it seems like that's where we'll find our answers too."

Agatha stopped abruptly, her eyes widening. "Emma, you're right! And I think I know exactly where we need to look next."

Just then, Agatha's phone buzzed with a text. She pulled it out, her face paling as she read the message.

"What is it?" Emma asked, concern etching her features.

Agatha's voice was barely a whisper. "It's from an unknown number. It says, 'Stop digging, or you'll be next."

34

SHADOWS OF THE PAST

Agatha stared at her phone, her brow furrowed with concern. She took a deep breath and looked up at Emma, her voice resolute. "This has to end now. We need to free Aunt Edna and get this murderer behind bars before anyone else gets hurt."

Emma nodded, her eyes wide with worry. "Absolutely. Especially considering that threatening text. The next victim could be you if they meant what they said."

Agatha began pacing, her mind racing. "We need to figure out our next move." She stopped and turned to Emma. "It seems pretty obvious that Green Acres should be our next stop, don't you think?"

"Definitely," Emma agreed. "But who can we talk to that might give us some solid leads?"

Agatha's forehead creased in thought. "Well, we've already concluded that Mr. Collins doesn't know much. Then there's Tilda, but she's new to Green Acres and it seems she's already told us everything she knows. I doubt she'd be much more help."

Emma's eyes lit up with sudden realization. "Speaking

of Tilda, where has she been lately? I can't remember the last time I saw her around town."

"You're right," Agatha mused. "I haven't seen her at the bookstore either. She's probably just busy with her job and life... maybe she's met someone new?"

"Maybe," Emma shrugged. She paused for a moment, then snapped her fingers. "I've got it! We need to go back to the drawing board. Let's start at the beginning and go see Beatrice again. We might have missed something the first time we talked to her. Plus, who knows Harold better than her?"

Agatha's face brightened. "That's a brilliant idea, Emma! It makes perfect sense." She grinned at her friend. "This is why we make such a great team."

Emma waved her hand dismissively. "Oh, come on. You're the real amateur sleuth here. I just tag along."

"No way," Agatha protested. "We've solved all these cases together, haven't we? Your input is invaluable."

Emma chuckled. "Sure, but you're the one with all those Christie books ingrained in your brain. I bet if they did an MRI of your head, they'd see those novels etched right in there."

They both burst into laughter, the tension of the moment briefly dissipating.

As their laughter subsided, Agatha turned to Emma. "So, can you come with me to Green Acres now?"

"Of course," Emma replied. "It's my day off. Let's go."

As they gathered their things, Agatha remembered something. "Oh, speaking of your schedule, when do you start your new job at the Tribune?"

Emma's face fell, her earlier mirth evaporating. She looked down at her hands, twisting them in her lap. "I... I won't be starting there," she said softly, her voice thick with disappointment. "They called me last week. Apparently, due to budget constraints, they're putting that position on hold indefinitely." She sighed heavily, her shoulders slumping.

Agatha reached out and squeezed Emma's hand, her heart aching for her friend. "Oh, Emma, I'm so sorry. I know how much that job meant to you. You've been working towards this for so long."

Emma nodded, blinking back tears. "It feels like all my hard work was for nothing. I really thought this was my big break, you know?"

"Your hard work wasn't for nothing," Agatha insisted, her voice firm but gentle. "This is just a setback, not the end. Your talent and dedication will pay off, I'm sure of it."

Emma forced a small smile, appreciating her friend's support. "Thanks, Agatha. They did say they'd let me know if anything changes, but..." She trailed off, shrugging.

Agatha sat quietly for a moment, her brow furrowed in thought. Suddenly, her eyes lit up. "You know, Emma, maybe this is an opportunity in disguise. Have you ever thought about starting a blog?"

Emma looked puzzled. "A blog? About what?"

"About our mystery-solving adventures!" Agatha exclaimed, her excitement growing. "Think about it. You're a talented writer with a knack for unraveling mysteries. Why not combine those skills?"

Emma's eyes widened as the idea took hold. "That's... actually not a bad idea. It could be a way to showcase my writing and build a portfolio."

Agatha nodded enthusiastically. "Exactly! And who knows? Someone at the Tribune might stumble across it and realize they can't live without your talents."

A spark of hope ignited in Emma's eyes. She reached for

her purse, pulling out a small notebook and pen. "I love it! Now all I need is a catchy name for it."

Agatha smiled, her eyes twinkling with renewed enthusiasm. "We can brainstorm names later. Right now, let's focus on solving this case. It'll make for a fantastic first post."

Emma tucked the notebook back into her purse, her earlier disappointment replaced by a sense of purpose. "You're right. Let's go catch a killer and kick-start my new career!"

As they headed out the door, Agatha's phone buzzed again. She pulled it out, her face paling as she read the new message aloud: "I warned you once. This is your last chance. Back off, or someone else dies tonight."

Agatha, Emma, and Mike set off for Green Acres in Eleanor, Agatha's cherished companion on countless road trips. As they drove, Mike sat contentedly in the back seat, his tail wagging as he watched the familiar Bristol Lake scenery roll by. The vintage car's engine hummed steadily, a comforting sound that had become synonymous with adventure for Agatha over the years.

Agatha's hands tightened on the steering wheel. "You know, something's been bothering me," she said, breaking the comfortable silence.

Emma turned to her, eyebrows raised. "What's that?"

"Devin," Agatha replied, her brow furrowed. "Isn't it odd that he suddenly returned to Bristol?"

Emma considered this for a moment. "Now that you mention it, the timing is a bit suspicious. You think he might be involved somehow?"

Agatha shrugged. "I'm not sure, but something doesn't smell right. It's just... convenient, isn't it?"

"It could be," Emma agreed cautiously.

Agatha nodded, but the seed of doubt had been planted. She gripped the steering wheel a little tighter, her knuckles whitening. As they continued their drive to Green Acres, she couldn't shake the feeling that there was more to Devin's return than met the eye.

After a moment of silence, Emma spoke up again. "You know, if you stop to think about it, there's another angle we haven't considered."

"Oh?" Agatha glanced at Emma curiously.

Emma's voice was hesitant. "Well, who would benefit the most if Harold was gone... and also Beatrice?"

Agatha's eyes widened as realization dawned. "Devin," she breathed. "He is Harold's only living relative."

"Exactly," Emma said, her tone serious. "I'm not saying he did anything, but it's something to consider."

Agatha fell silent, her mind racing with this new perspective. The case suddenly seemed more complex than ever. After a moment, she spoke up again. "But what about Amanda? Why would he take her out?" Agatha asked, her brow furrowed in concentration.

Emma tapped her chin thoughtfully. "Maybe she discovered his plans and threatened to tell someone," She suggested, her voice low as if she were piecing together a puzzle.

Agatha nodded slowly. "That could make sense. If Amanda stumbled onto something, she shouldn't have..."

"It would give Devin a motive to silence her," Emma finished.

They exchanged worried glances, the weight of their speculation hanging heavy in the car.

"We're getting ahead of ourselves," Agatha said finally, shaking her head. "We need more evidence before we can accuse anyone."

"You're right," Emma agreed. "But it's definitely something to keep in mind as we investigate."

Upon arriving at Green Acres, they entered the facility with Mike leading the way on his leash.

Lindsey greeted them with a warm smile.

"Hello ladies, and hello to you too, Mike," she said, bending down to pat the dog's head. "Are you here to volunteer today?"

Agatha shook her head. "Not today, Lindsey. We're here to see Beatrice. Is she in her room?"

Lindsey's smile wavered for a moment. "She's here, but not in her room. I saw her heading to the community room a little while ago."

Agatha nodded her thanks, and she and Emma made their way to the community room, their footsteps echoing in the unnaturally quiet hallway. As they entered, they spotted Beatrice seated at a table, sipping tea and nibbling on toast.

Beatrice looked up as they approached, a smile spreading across her face. "Agatha, Emma, what a pleasant surprise! How are you both?"

"We're doing well, thank you," Agatha replied, trying to keep her voice light. "Do you have a moment to talk?"

"Of course, dear. Have a seat," Beatrice gestured to the chairs across from her, hastily moving some envelopes out of the way. "Pardon the mess. I just picked up my mail on the way to tea."

As they sat down, Agatha took a deep breath. "Beatrice, I know this might seem out of the blue, but we're still looking into Harold's murder. Aunt Edna is still in jail for a crime I'm certain she didn't commit."

Beatrice's expression softened. "Edna and I may have our differences, but I don't believe she's a murderer either."

"Is there any way you could help us?" Emma asked, leaning forward.

Beatrice nodded thoughtfully. "I'll certainly try. What do you need to know?"

Agatha hesitated, choosing her words carefully. "I know the police have probably asked you this already, but can you think of anyone who might have wanted to harm Harold? Or any reason someone would want him dead?"

Beatrice sighed, shaking her head. "I'm afraid I don't know anything I haven't already told the police."

Agatha pressed on. "What about Green Acres itself? Did Harold have any financial interest in this place?"

At this, Beatrice's eyebrows shot up. "Financial interest? My dear, he had a significant financial stake in Green Acres. It's the whole reason he moved here in the first place."

Agatha and Emma exchanged surprised glances. "He did? How so?" Emma asked.

Beatrice leaned in, lowering her voice. "Harold always had a keen financial mind. When Roger Collins reached out to him about a loan, Harold saw an opportunity. He figured he could move to a retirement community like he'd been planning and invest in it at the same time. He even talked about buying the place outright eventually." She paused, a shadow crossing her face. "Unfortunately, he didn't live long enough to see that plan through."

"I'm so sorry, Beatrice," Agatha said softly.

Beatrice's expression hardened unexpectedly. "I was sorry too, at first. But now? Now I think he got exactly what he deserved."

Agatha and Emma exchanged shocked looks. "I'm sorry,

what did you say?" Agatha asked, certain she must have misheard.

"You heard me correctly," Beatrice said, her voice cold. "That dirty old man was cheating on me with a younger woman. At least, that's what Amanda told me."

Agatha's hand flew to her chest. "Are you serious?

"Yes, Amanda told me, though she didn't give me all the details. Unfortunately, she wasn't around long enough to tell me who the other woman was," Beatrice explained, her gaze distant.

As if suddenly remembering the envelopes on the table, Beatrice began rifling through them. "Credit card statement? That's odd. I haven't used a credit card in ages." She tore open the envelope, her eyes widening as she scanned the contents. "Oh my... There are charges here for makeup, clothing, and designer brands. Fourteen thousand dollars in charges? This can't be right!"

She frantically opened the other envelopes, revealing two more credit cards with astronomical balances, all in her name. "Look at this," she said, shoving the statements towards Agatha and Emma. "Jewelry, more designer brands... I think I've been a victim of identity theft!"

Agatha frowned as she examined the statements. "These cards aren't new, Beatrice. Don't you usually check your mail?"

Beatrice waved her hand dismissively. "I don't usually bother with that. Tilda takes care of it for me. She's still sort of my assistant, albeit unofficially."

As Beatrice continued to sift through the pile, she opened another envelope. "Oh, this one's for Marilyn... I didn't notice her name at first." Her eyes widened in shock. "She's in a tremendous amount of debt... Wait, bankrupt?"

"What? You're bankrupt?" Emma asked, confused.

"No, not me. Marilyn," Beatrice clarified. "I opened her mail by mistake."

"Who's Marilyn?" Agatha asked, her detective instincts on high alert.

"Tilda is Marilyn," Beatrice explained. "Well, her name was Matilda, then she changed it to Marilyn. I suppose that's why she goes by Tilda here in Bristol Lake. She must be running from debt collectors."

Agatha and Emma sat in stunned silence, trying to process this information.

"It's the same with Amanda, you know," Beatrice continued, almost casually. "When I first met her in California, her name was Leocadia."

" Agatha and Emma's jaws dropped. Ignoring the bizarre name change for a moment, Agatha leaned in, her voice urgent. "You knew Amanda before you moved here?"

"I didn't know her well, but Marilyn did. They were roommates," Beatrice explained, her voice trailing off as she seemed lost in thought.

Agatha and Emma exchanged glances, their minds racing with this new information. Before they could ask more, Beatrice added nonchalantly, "Yeah, they shared an apartment with Amanda's fiancé." She paused, her eyes distant as if recalling a long-forgotten memory. "Harold's nephew, Devin."

35

THE LAST PAGE TURNS

"Amanda was engaged to Devin?" Agatha exclaimed, exchanging looks with Emma.

"He failed to mention this small detail," Emma said, her eyes conveying to Agatha that Devin was even more deeply involved in the situation than they'd realized.

Suddenly, Agatha's expression changed, as if she had just remembered something important. "Marilyn," she repeated, her brow furrowed in concentration.

"What?" Emma asked, leaning closer.

"I feel like I've seen this name 'Marilyn' before," Agatha muttered, more to herself than to Emma.

Emma chuckled, "Of course you've heard the name Marilyn. That was the name of one of the biggest stars in the world."

Agatha shook her head, "No, somewhere else." Suddenly, her eyes lit up. "That's it, that's it!" she exclaimed, reaching for her purse.

Beatrice and Emma watched in bewilderment as Agatha

frantically rummaged through her bag. She pulled out a folder and began flipping through the papers inside.

"Here!" Agatha triumphantly held up a document. "Marilyn Morrison was a witness in a transaction with Mr. Collins."

The silence that followed was deafening. Agatha felt as if the air had been sucked out of the room. Her mind whirled with the implications of this revelation. Harold's nephew? Amanda's fiancé? How did all of this connect to the murders at Green Acres?

Before Agatha could voice any of the questions swirling in her head, the lights in the community room flickered ominously. She felt a chill run down her spine, a sense of foreboding settling over her. As she opened her mouth to speak, the room was plunged into darkness.

A blood-curdling scream pierced the air, followed by the sound of running footsteps approaching the community room.

"What's happening?" Emma whispered, her voice trembling in the darkness.

Before anyone could answer, emergency lights flickered on, casting an eerie glow across the room. The door burst open, and Lindsey stumbled in, her face ashen and her blouse splattered with what looked horribly like blood.

"Help," she gasped, her eyes wild with fear. "It's Mr. Collins. He's... he's..."

As Lindsey collapsed to the floor, Agatha caught a glimpse of a shadowy figure darting past the doorway, something glinting menacingly in their hand.

"Emma, call Detective Dawson now!" Agatha shouted, already sprinting after the figure.

Emma nodded, pulling out her phone as she rushed to

Mr. Collins' side. To her relief, he was stirring, a nasty bump forming on his head but otherwise seemingly okay.

Dr. Hartman burst into the room, immediately kneeling beside Mr. Collins. "I've got him," he assured Emma. "Go after Agatha!"

Emma didn't need to be told twice. She raced down the hallway, her heart pounding. Suddenly, Mildred appeared, grabbing her arm.

"This way," Mildred urged, leading Emma down a narrow corridor. "It's a shortcut to the back door. That's where they're headed!"

They burst through the back door into the parking lot. Agatha froze, her eyes widening with sudden recognition. The figure she'd been chasing all along stood before her - not a ghost, but Tilda in the flesh. As the realization hit her, Agatha instinctively moved to corner Tilda.

Emma gasped, her gaze fixed on the gun trembling in Tilda's shaking hand.

"It's over, Tilda," Agatha said, her voice steady despite the danger. "We know everything."

Tilda's face contorted with rage and desperation. "You don't know anything!" she spat. "I had it all planned out perfectly."

"Then enlighten us," Agatha said calmly, buying time.

Tilda laughed bitterly. "It was supposed to be simple. I'd been Beatrice's assistant for years, always in the background, never appreciated. But I was good at my job - too good, perhaps."

She began pacing, the gun still trained on Agatha and Emma. "You see, I discovered something interesting while managing Beatrice's affairs. The old fool had made me her sole beneficiary in her will. Can you believe it?"

"Then Harold made her his beneficiary," Emma added, her voice low.

Agatha's eyes widened in surprise. "So with Harold gone..." she trailed off, the implications sinking in.

"I'd get everything once Beatrice was out of the picture too," Tilda finished, a cruel smile playing on her lips. "I just had to be patient."

"But you couldn't wait, could you?" Emma pressed.

Tilda's smile faded. "Harold complicated things. His wealth, his connection to Beatrice - it was too tempting to pass up. So I orchestrated the move to Bristol Lake, making sure Beatrice would follow Harold here. I even convinced Amanda, my old roommate, to take a job at Green Acres."

"Did you have an affair with Harold?" Agatha asked.

Tilda's face twisted in disgust. "A necessary evil. It gave me access, information. I even made sure Beatrice found out, driving a wedge between them. It was all part of the plan to isolate Beatrice, make her more dependent on me."

"But something went wrong," Emma guessed.

"Amanda," Tilda spat the name like a curse. "She fell in love with Devin and grew a conscience. Threatened to expose everything. I couldn't let that happen."

"So you killed her," Agatha said softly.

Tilda shrugged. "She left me no choice. But that's when things really started to unravel. You," she pointed the gun at Agatha, "you just couldn't leave well enough alone."

"What about Aunt Edna?" Agatha asked, her voice hard. "How does she fit into all this?"

"Collateral damage," Tilda said dismissively. Her eyes glinted with a cold satisfaction as she continued, "Amanda stole an experimental drug from her previous job at a pharmaceutical company. It was meant to treat Alzheimer's, but had some... unexpected side effects. I convinced her to slip it to Edna and Beatrice, making them forgetful and easy to manipulate. When Amanda grew a conscience and threatened to back out, I needed a new plan. Edna was the perfect scapegoat - old, confused, with a history of tension with Beatrice."

"You're a monster," Emma whispered.

Tilda laughed coldly. "I'm a survivor. And now, thanks to your meddling, I have to tie up these loose ends. Starting with you two, then Beatrice. It's not too late. I can still fix this. Once you're gone and Beatrice meets with an unfortunate 'accident', I'll have everything I've worked for."

Tilda's cold laughter sent a chill down Agatha's spine. She glanced at Emma, who looked equally unsettled.

"Get in the car," Tilda ordered, gesturing with the gun. "We're going for a little drive."

Agatha's mind raced, searching for a way out. As they inched towards Tilda's car, a familiar bark caught her attention. Mike came bounding around the corner, his tail wagging as if he'd just found a lost toy.

"Shoo, you mangy mutt!" Tilda hissed, momentarily distracted.

In that split second, Mike's playful demeanor vanished. With a growl, he lunged forward, clamping his jaws around Tilda's wrist. She yelped in pain, the gun clattering to the ground.

"Good boy, Mike!" Agatha cheered, quickly kicking the weapon away.

Tilda lunged for the gun, but Emma blocked her path. "I don't think so, missy," Emma said, her voice steely.

Just then, the screech of tires filled the air as Detective Dawson's car pulled up. He leapt out, hand on his holster. "Freeze!" he shouted, taking in the scene.

"Perfect timing, Detective," Agatha said, relief washing over her. "I think we have a confession to add to your case."

As Dawson cuffed a fuming Tilda, Agatha knelt to scratch Mike behind the ears. "Who's the best crime-fighting schnauzer in the world?" she cooed.

Mike's tail wagged furiously, clearly pleased with himself for saving the day.

~

As Detective Dawson began to guide Tilda towards the waiting police car, Agatha suddenly remembered something. Her heart racing, she called out, "Wait!"

Dawson paused, looking back at her with a raised eyebrow. Tilda's lips curled into a smirk, as if she had been waiting for this moment.

Agatha stepped forward, still clutching Mike to her chest. "Tilda," she began, her voice steady despite her inner turmoil, "did you take my book manuscript?"

A flash of triumph gleamed in Tilda's eyes. "Oh, you finally figured that out, did you?" she sneered.

Agatha's grip on Mike tightened unconsciously. The small dog let out a startled "Yip!" and wriggled, his tongue lolling out comically as if he were being squeezed like a furry toothpaste tube.

Ignoring Mike's squirming, Agatha demanded, "Where is it? What did you do with it?"

Tilda's smirk widened into a malicious grin. "Oh, Agatha," she said, her voice dripping with false sweetness, "I knew how much that manuscript meant to you. When I realized you were foolish enough not to make any copies, I saw an opportunity."

She paused, relishing Agatha's growing distress. "I thought I could use it as leverage. You see, your constant meddling was becoming quite the problem. I was willing to give it back if you'd just stop poking your nose where it doesn't belong."

Tilda's eyes narrowed. "But now? Well, let's just say it's... gone. You should have backed off when you had the chance, Agatha. Your precious book was the price of your stubbornness."

Mike, still trapped in Agatha's vice-like grip, let out a muffled "Woof!", as if offering his own canine opinion on the matter.

"What do you mean, gone?" Agatha pressed, taking another step forward. "What did you do with it?"

Tilda just laughed, a cold, mirthless sound that sent shivers down Agatha's spine. "That's for me to know and you to never find out. Consider it my parting gift to you, dear Agatha."

Detective Dawson, sensing the rising tension, started to pull Tilda away. "That's enough," he said firmly. "We'll add theft to the list of charges."

As Tilda was being led to the car, she twisted once more to look at Agatha and Emma. Her eyes, once filled with triumph, now burned with a cold, hard anger. The intensity of her gaze sent a chill down Agatha's spine.

"This isn't over," Tilda hissed, her voice barely audible over the distance. "You have no idea what you've done."

Detective Dawson gave her a firm nudge, urging her towards the car. "That's enough out of you," he grumbled.

As Tilda was forced into the back seat, her eyes remained locked on Agatha and Emma, filled with a promise of vengeance that made both women shudder.

Agatha hugged Mike closer, seeking comfort in his

warm, furry presence. Emma's arm tightened around her shoulders.

"What do you think she meant by that?" Emma whispered, a note of worry in her voice. "And what about your manuscript?"

Agatha shook her head slowly, her eyes still on the police car as it pulled away. "I don't know, Emma. But something tells me our adventures in Bristol Lake are far from over. And my book..." She sighed heavily. "I guess I'll have to start over."

As Agatha paced back towards the building, her shoulders slumped in dejection, Emma walked beside her, offering silent support. Mike trotted at their heels, sensing his owner's distress.

"I can't believe it's gone," Agatha murmured, her voice thick with disappointment. "All that work..."

Before Emma could respond, they spotted Beatrice hurrying towards them, her face alight with curiosity and concern.

"Agatha, dear! Emma!" Beatrice called out. "I heard the commotion. Is it true? Did you catch the real culprit?"

Agatha nodded, managing a small smile. "Yes, we did. Aunt Edna should be cleared and released soon."

Beatrice clapped her hands together in delight. "Oh, that's wonderful news! But why do you look so glum, dear? You should be celebrating!"

Agatha sighed heavily. "It's my manuscript, Beatrice. Tilda stole it, and now she says it's gone for good."

"Manuscript?" Beatrice's brow furrowed in confusion.

"Yes, I've been writing a book," Agatha explained. "A mystery novel, actually. I had just finished the first draft when it disappeared."

As Agatha spoke, a look of dawning realization spread

across Beatrice's face. "Oh, my goodness!" she exclaimed, her eyes widening. "I can't believe I forgot! You did mention finishing a book, didn't you? It must have slipped my mind with all the excitement lately." Without another word, Beatrice turned on her heel and hurried back towards the building, leaving Agatha and Emma exchanging puzzled glances.

"Beatrice?" Emma called after her. "Where are you going?"

But Beatrice was already disappearing through the entrance, her sudden departure adding to the mystery of the moment.

Agatha and Emma followed, their curiosity piqued. They found Beatrice in her room, rummaging through a closet.

"Aha!" Beatrice exclaimed triumphantly, emerging with a large manila envelope in her hands. She thrust it towards Agatha, her eyes twinkling. "Could this be your manuscript, dear?"

With trembling hands, Agatha took the envelope. She carefully opened it, her breath catching in her throat as she peered inside. Her face lit up, joy replacing the sadness that had been etched there moments before.

"This is it!" she cried, pulling out a stack of papers. "Oh, Beatrice, you've found it! But how? Where?"

Beatrice smiled, clearly pleased with herself. "I found it in a box Tilda had stored in my room. She said it was just some old papers she needed to sort through. I hadn't given it much thought until now."

Agatha clutched the manuscript to her chest, tears of relief and happiness welling in her eyes. "Beatrice, I can't thank you enough. You have no idea what this means to me."

Emma beamed, giving Agatha's shoulder a squeeze. "See? Things have a way of working out. Now you can focus on getting that book published!"

Beatrice nodded enthusiastically. "Oh yes, you must! I, for one, can't wait to read it. A real-life mystery writer in our midst – how exciting!"

Agatha smiled as she listened to Emma and Beatrice chattering about the manuscript and the day's excitement. With her book safe, Aunt Edna cleared, and Tilda in custody, she felt a deep sense of satisfaction settle over her.

Mike dozed contentedly at her feet, and as Agatha caught Emma's eye, they shared a look of quiet triumph. Despite the chaos of the past few days, Agatha realized she'd never felt more at home in Bristol Lake.

The following afternoon, the sky over Bristol Lake turned a soft watercolor blue, and a hush settled over the town.

Agatha glanced at the clock and smiled. It was finally a quiet afternoon—no clues to chase, no suspects to interrogate, and no emotional whirlwinds to untangle. Just the perfect time for tea.

The warm clink of china echoed through her kitchen as she moved with deliberate calm, setting out a pale blue teapot, two mismatched cups, and a plate of shortbread biscuits she'd picked up from Eliza's Bakery that morning. Mike flopped at her feet with a soft sigh, already eyeing the biscuit plate with theatrical hope.

"You're not getting one," she said, dropping a crumb anyway.

Just as the kettle began to whistle, the door creaked open.

"Smells like a proper tea party in here," Emma called as she stepped inside, carrying a wool blanket and a small box of lemon tarts.

"I brought reinforcements," she grinned.

Agatha smiled. "If by reinforcements you mean sugar and sarcasm, we're already well-stocked."

They settled in the living room, the curtains drawn open to let in the afternoon light and a view of the quiet street. For a while, they didn't speak. It was the kind of silence only earned after a storm—the comforting kind.

Emma finally broke it with a soft chuckle. "It's strange. After all that happened, this feels... almost too peaceful."

Agatha nodded. "It does. But I'm not complaining."

Emma leaned back in her chair. "Aunt Edna's sounding more like herself again. That sparkle's back in her voice."

"She even asked if she could restart the book club," Agatha said, a smile tugging at her lips. "I think she wants to pick the first book this time."

"Dangerous move."

"Extremely."

They chatted about books, upcoming events at the bookstore, and a customer who tried to return a mystery novel because they "solved it too fast."

Agatha looked at Emma, warmth in her eyes. "Thanks for today. For everything."

Emma lifted her tart. "Any time. As long as there's tea. And no more knitting feuds."

Agatha raised her cup. "Deal. But we're keeping the lemon tarts. Some things are worth the chaos."

EPILOGUE

The cozy interior of One Deadly Chapter Books and Brew buzzed with animated chatter as the mystery book club meeting wound down. Agatha stood at the front, a steaming cup of tea in her hand, addressing the group.

"Before we wrap up, I have some news to share," Agatha announced, a smile playing on her lips. "You'll never believe this, but Aunt Edna and Beatrice have not only made up, they've decided to move back to California together!"

A chorus of surprised gasps and chuckles filled the room.

"Mon Dieu! Those two? Roommates?" Lorraine exclaimed, her eyes wide with disbelief. "Now that's a mystery I'd like to solve!"

As the laughter subsided, Lorraine leaned forward, her expression turning serious. "What about that Devin character? Harold's nephew? Was he involved in all this mess?"

Agatha shook her head. "No, it turns out Devin was just

as much in the dark as the rest of us. He's been cleared of any wrongdoing."

Emma, who had been restocking a nearby shelf, joined the group. "Speaking of mysteries, Agatha, any progress on your book?"

Agatha sighed, running a hand through her hair. "Well, I've got the manuscript back, thanks to Beatrice, but I'm struggling to finish the second draft. After everything that's happened, I feel like I need some fresh inspiration to really bring it home."

"Writer's block, chérie?" Lorraine asked sympathetically. "Perhaps you need a change of scenery to get those creative juices flowing again."

Suddenly, Celeste's eyes widened, and she sat up straighter in her chair. "Oh! I just remembered something," she exclaimed, drawing everyone's attention. "When Lorraine mentioned a change of scenery, it reminded me of an envelope I put behind the counter earlier today."

She quickly stood up and made her way behind the counter, rummaging through a stack of papers. After a moment, she emerged with an envelope in hand. "Here it is! Agatha, it's addressed to you. I remember noticing the word 'safari' on it when it arrived."

Celeste returned to the group and handed the envelope to Agatha. "It seemed important, but with the rush of customers, I forgot all about it until now."

Curious, Agatha opened the envelope and scanned its contents, her eyes widening with each line. "I don't believe it," she murmured.

"What is it?" Emma asked, peering over her shoulder.

"It's an invitation," Agatha explained, her voice filled with excitement. "To a mystery author retreat... in Africa! On a safari, no less!"

The room erupted in excited chatter.

"Africa? How exotic!" Lorraine exclaimed. "Oh, the adventures you'll have!"

Emma's eyes sparkled. "That sounds amazing, Agatha! It might be just what you need to find that inspiration and finish your book."

Agatha nodded, her mind already racing with possibilities. "You're right. A change of scenery could do wonders for my creativity. Maybe I can even weave some of the safari experience into the story!"

Emma's eyes lit up. "Oh, that would be fantastic! Just imagine the exotic locales and wild animals as a backdrop for your next mystery."

Lorraine, who had been quietly perusing the letter, suddenly exclaimed, "Oh là là! Listen to this, mes amies." She cleared her throat dramatically before reading aloud, "'Our lodge prides itself on being pet-friendly, so feel free to bring your furry companions along for the adventure.'"

Agatha's face broke into a wide smile as she glanced down at Mike, who was sprawled at her feet. "Did you hear that, boy? Looks like we're going to Africa.!"

Mike's tail thumped against the floor, his ears perking up at Agatha's excited tone.

"A crime-solving schnauzer on safari," Emma giggled. "Now that's something I'd love to read about!"

"Agatha laughed, excitement bubbling through her. 'Well then, it looks like Mike and I have some packing to do. Africa, here we come!"

"Well, you're not going alone," Emma declared firmly. "I'm coming with you. Someone needs to keep you out of trouble!"

Lorraine stood up, her hand raised dramatically. "And you'll need a translator, non? I volunteer as tribute!" She grinned mischievously. "Besides, who knows what mysteries we might uncover on the savannah?"

Agatha laughed, feeling a surge of affection for her friends. "A safari with my two best friends? How could I possibly say no? Well, ladies," Agatha said, raising her teacup in a toast. "Here's to our next great adventure. Safari, here we come!"

Emma and Lorraine clinked their cups against hers, their faces alight with excitement.

Lorraine suddenly furrowed her brow. "Wait a minute," she said, her voice laced with curiosity. "Agatha, chérie, there's something I don't understand."

Agatha and Emma turned to her, puzzled by the sudden change in her tone.

"What's that, Lorraine?" Agatha asked.

Lorraine's eyes narrowed as she posed her question. "How did they find you? This invitation... it's so specific, so tailored to you. But you've never mentioned entering any contests or applying for a writer's retreat." She paused, her brow furrowing deeper. "It's not like you're a famous author, and you haven't even published your first book yet. So, ma chère, how did these people know where to send this letter? How did they know about you at all?"

The room fell silent as the implications of Lorraine's question sank in. Agatha felt a chill run down her spine as she realized she had no answer. She looked at Emma, whose expression mirrored her own growing unease.

What had seemed like an exciting opportunity now cast a shadow of mystery. As Mike sensed the tension and pressed closer to Agatha's leg, she couldn't shake the feeling that this African adventure might be more than she bargained for.

AUNT EDNA'S FAMOUS LEMON LAVENDER SCONES

Ingredients:

- 2 cups all-purpose flour
- 1/4 cup granulated sugar
- 1 tablespoon baking powder
- 1/2 teaspoon salt
- 1/2 cup cold unsalted butter, cubed
- 1 tablespoon dried culinary lavender
- Zest of 1 lemon
- 2/3 cup heavy cream
- 1 large egg
- 1 teaspoon vanilla extract

Glaze:

- 1 cup powdered sugar
- 2 tablespoons lemon juice

Instructions:

1. Preheat the oven to 400°F (200°C) and line a baking sheet with parchment paper.
2. In a large bowl, whisk together flour, sugar, baking powder, and salt.
3. Add the cold butter and use a pastry cutter or your fingers to work it into the flour mixture until it resembles coarse crumbs.
4. Stir in the lavender and lemon zest.
5. In a small bowl, whisk together heavy cream, egg, and vanilla extract.
6. Pour the wet ingredients into the flour mixture and stir until just combined.
7. Turn the dough onto a lightly floured surface and gently knead it a few times to bring it together.
8. Pat the dough into a circle, about 1 inch thick, and cut into 8 wedges.
9. Place the wedges on the prepared baking sheet and bake for 15-18 minutes, or until golden brown.
10. While the scones are cooling, whisk together the powdered sugar and lemon juice to make the glaze.
11. Drizzle the glaze over the scones and let it set before serving.

GREEN ACRES APPLE CINNAMON BREAD

Ingredients:

- 1 1/2 cups all-purpose flour
- 1 teaspoon baking powder
- 1/2 teaspoon baking soda
- 1/4 teaspoon salt
- 1 teaspoon ground cinnamon
- 1/4 teaspoon ground nutmeg
- 1/2 cup unsalted butter, softened
- 3/4 cup granulated sugar
- 2 large eggs
- 1 teaspoon vanilla extract
- 1/2 cup sour cream
- 1 1/2 cups peeled and diced apples (Granny Smith recommended)

Topping:

- 2 tablespoons granulated sugar
- 1/2 teaspoon ground cinnamon

Instructions:

1. Preheat the oven to 350°F (175°C) and grease a 9x5-inch loaf pan.
2. In a medium bowl, whisk together flour, baking powder, baking soda, salt, cinnamon, and nutmeg.
3. In a large bowl, cream together the butter and sugar until light and fluffy.
4. Beat in the eggs, one at a time, then mix in the vanilla extract.
5. Add the sour cream and mix until well combined.
6. Gradually add the dry ingredients to the wet mixture and mix until just combined.
7. Fold in the diced apples.
8. Pour the batter into the prepared loaf pan and smooth the top.
9. In a small bowl, mix together the sugar and cinnamon for the topping, then sprinkle it over the batter.
10. Bake for 50-60 minutes, or until a toothpick inserted into the center comes out clean.
11. Allow the bread to cool in the pan for 10 minutes, then transfer to a wire rack to cool completely before slicing.